GHOST IMAGES

GHOST IMAGES

Stephen Minot

HARPER & ROW, PUBLISHERS

New York, Hagerstown, San Francisco, London

Special thanks to Ginny for long hours spent on this manuscript.

I am indebted to the National Endowment of the Arts for a fellowship granted in support of this work, 1976–77.

A part of this novel appeared in modified form as "A Passion for History" in the *Sewanee Review* 84 (Spring 1976). Copyright 1976 by the University of the South. Reprinted by permission of the editor.

Other portions appeared in modified form in *The North American Review,* Winter 1975–76, and in *The Virginia Quarterly Review,* Winter 1974, the latter reprinted in *Crossings,* University of Illinois Press, 1975.

FIRST EDITION

Designed by C. Linda Dingler

Library of Congress Cataloging in Publication Data

Minot, Stephen.
  Ghost images.
  I. Title.
PZ4.M665Gh 1979   [PS3563.I475]   813'.5'4
ISBN:0–06–012978–6   78–69509

---

79 80 81 82 83 10 9 8 7 6 5 4 3 2 1

For my parents, with wry affection

GHOST IMAGES

1

Crack! A rifle shot! A second. He sprang upright, edge of his chair, flung from dreams, heart pounding. Again! Ah, the screen door slamming. They were back. Here already?

He stumbled to the window. Yes, there it was: Tammy's International Scout, right down there below him in the tall beach grass, all four doors flung wide open.

Had he been sleeping? At his desk? A hell of a thing. What time was it? What day? Somehow he thought they'd be coming tomorrow. But there they were. Two and a half months of bachelorhood ending with a bang; he was hardly ready for them.

Two and a half unreal months. Uninterrupted work. Almost. Chance of a lifetime. Walled off. His own domain in Nova Scotia. His realm. Oddly dreamlike. Now waking . . .

"Dad! Hey, Dad!" Ric's voice from below. From a different world—Tammy and the three kids living all this time in Connecticut, their lives filled with good teachers, bad teachers, grades, friends, lack of them, all the rest just as

1

if he were there; and she with her clients and causes and deadlines as always. Plus running the house. Incredible Tammy; booming kids. Booming, blooming, boisterous kids, and Tammy humming like a high-tension wire. Too much too fast. He needed a day to adjust. At least an hour. Feign sleep.

"Daddy!" That was Hildy. His youngest at eleven. If only he had caught sight of them coming across the uncut field, making paths in the tall grasses. A home movie's view. He really wanted to see them, but they had snuck up on him. Goths in the palace without warning.

"He must be outside." Weldon's voice. Oldest and deepest. The rationalist of the three. He couldn't imagine a grown man hiding. Well, he'd learn, he'd learn.

"Go out and look for him. Maybe down to the beach." Tammy's voice. Marvelous sound. Unmistakable. That cool tone of authority. Used to handling police chiefs, judges, city councilmen, welfare mothers down on Dixon Street. Not overbearing, no. Deceptive that way. Cheerful, usually. Crisp. A sense of positive sureness.

Pounding of many feet. Slams of the screen door. "Crack! Crack!" Barking. The children and the dog off on the false scent. She without hesitation marched upstairs knowing perfectly well where he was. Astonishing intuition. No, that was a sexist notion. Astonishing . . . Well, just astonishing.

Knock. Turn knob. Sigh. Knock.

"Kraft." Her clear, straightforward tone. Resonant. No nonsense. Then, in her eager-young-student voice: "Hey, mister, we have no hostile intentions." Silence. He considered slipping out the window and heading north for Newfoundland. An old dream. A fresh start. Alone. Almost alone. Maybe a fisherman's shack and some soft-spoken country woman to keep him company. "Look, Kraft, we do appreciate the band, the confetti, and the speeches, but right now all we want is a private meeting. Like face to

2

face?" Silence. "Damn it!" Cool lost, she kicked at the door. It rattled, held. Silence, then two steps toward the stairs, two steps back. A third tone, softer: "Look, Kraft, just say something so I won't picture you lying face down in a pool of blood."

That got to him. A human appeal. He had nothing against her, after all. Nothing against her or the kids. It was only the pace of it, a kind of culture shock. Bends, maybe. In any case, nothing to do with her.

He opened the door. They stared at each other, strangers for just a moment. She was taller than he had remembered, her eyes exactly opposite his. Boots, perhaps; or had she grown? Her shirt was khaki—stylish, not surplus, perfectly cut, opened far enough to be interesting; pants in matching fabric. Trim safari style. Hair still a mass of tight natural curls, a short, sandy-colored Afro. Good-looking without trying. Competent. Even strangers knew at once that she was a lawyer, a mother, and a political activist. She radiated competence.

"No blood, I see," she said.

"Disappointed?"

"Well, there would have been some interesting legal work."

"On?"

"On Canadian laws regarding the shipment of bodies out of the country. Heavy stuff."

"Burial at sea would do."

"You'd only wash up. You always do."

They stood there for a moment. Then held each other—a trembling, cautious tenderness, each steadying a jar of explosives.

⋙⋘

The coffee ritual. Neither of them was in the mood for it—Kraft far too tense; she probably ready for some flurry of physical activity. But something had to be drunk to formalize the occasion. Rum crossed his mind, but no. Keep the image pure. Puritan. Let the work ethic excuse the mess.

"I've been busy."

"Not here, you haven't."

He looked around the kitchen, seeing it through her eyes. True, there were a few dishes in the sink and on the table. And the counters. And on one chair. He'd meant to get to them before she arrived, but somehow he hadn't expected her until later. Time was uncertain. The ferry across from Bar Harbor was probably on the same old schedule, but she drove faster than he did. He usually talked too much on those long trips. Or at least they said he did. And he kept slowing down when the analysis turned complex. He did some of his best thinking on the road, but it didn't keep them on schedule. Tammy drove like a trucker.

A flurry of action: Smelling scorch, she dives for the kettle. Red hot. Grabs a ladle; flips kettle off burner. It slides, spinning, falls to the floor. A curl of smoke. Left hand to burner, off, right hand with ladle to kettle, catches the handle, sweeps it back to the stove top, fast and sure as a basketball pro. He watches, spellbound.

"Hey, mister, try some water."

"It's been on awhile."

"No kidding."

"I was upstairs, working."

Cleaning out a saucepan, she glanced over at him sitting there, her corner-of-the-eye look, her appraising look.

"Speaking of work, is it O.K. if I ask how it went?"

"Why not?"

"Well, progress reports got censored out of your letters. Not a mention. So I just wondered if I was supposed to ask."

"Of course. No secret."

"Well?"

"The work? The manuscript?"

"That's sort of what I had in mind. Of course, if you don't want to . . ."

"Why wouldn't I? It's gone O.K."

"O.K.?"

"O.K."

"Good. I'm glad."

Which she wasn't. It was clear from her tone that she had picked up the truth from *his* tone, had understood in a flash that the entire venture had been a disaster. It must have shocked her, left her too baffled to confront him directly.

She ladled water into the pan, slopping a bit on the floor. Not like her to be careless—a sure sign she was in a rage.

The trouble was that she expected top performance from him all the time. The pattern had been set way back when she was his student. Natural enough then—him and his golden touch. He was an unscathed veteran of the Army Air Corps, in just long enough to make WW II *his* war yet short enough to remain undamaged. With those credentials and an excess of energy, he had begun publishing in *The Nation* and the *New Republic* as an undergraduate, had led a student organization in opposition to the Taft-Hartley Act, had headed the local campaign for Henry Wallace, had organized a demonstration against NATO. All this before graduating. By the time she entered his class, he was already famous as the untenured member of the History Department who had tangled with the McCarthy Committee and come out alive.

She had his energy; she soon adopted his faith. She had never seen him fail—except in details. And as soon as they were working together, she took care of those. In easy, natural stages she became his research assistant, his bedmate, and finally his wife.

Never having seen him lose, she always assumed that his major work would find a publisher. *The American Radical*

Movement, 1918–1940. Never mind that the Progressive Party was long since dead and forgotten. Never mind that the country had not fully recovered from Senator McCarthy. She knew he was a winner.

And eventually he was. But not for a decade and not as expected. The book wasn't finally ready until the mid sixties. It reached its tenth publisher in the late sixties. The nation had finally caught up with him. Watts was recent history; the violence had shifted to cities like Detroit and New York. The antiwar march on the Pentagon had just taken place. And his manuscript finally reached an editor who could bridge the academic and the public audience. He skillfully persuaded Kraft to cut the length from 1,250 pages to 700 and to change the title to *The Radical Failure.* It appeared in 1969, the same month as the largest antiwar protest in U.S. history.

It was never quite a best seller, but it was the best-of-the-heavies for '69. *Newsweek* grudgingly honored him as "opinionated, belligerent, energetic; Mr. Means is a Mencken on the left." *Time* called it "outrageous . . . significant." For the first time Kraft had surplus income. It was not what his parents once had—an excess which was swept away with the Depression and litigation when he was a boy. But he had never approved of the Means heritage, never regretted its loss. What he had now was quite different. It was clean. It would buy him space and time.

Had the royalties materialized in the mid sixties, he would have sunk them all into the antiwar movement, a candidate, or an organization. But by the time the checks started to arrive, Kent State was over and there was a collapse of political activity throughout the country. No more peace candidates, no more major protest organizations, no more demonstrations, no more politics except the musical-chair game, the remaining chairs all clustered dead center.

It was a time for inner development. That's when he struck on the idea of a retreat in Nova Scotia. Not a summer home, certainly not an *estate*, as alleged in the *Times*; it was a simple working retreat, a place for study. And for three years now, it had been exactly that.

As far as he was concerned, it was an asset that the house itself was in such bad repair. A shell, really; abandoned for decades. No running water, no electricity, no outside paint, clapboards turned silver in the salt air.

It was one of those turn-of-the-century houses as wide as it was high, a great cube with four shallow-pitched roofs rising from the sides, meeting at the center in the chimney. Two dormers on the sea side.

It had been placed on a bluff which once must have overlooked pasturage down to the sea. Now the view was almost obscured by a tangle of stunted pines, chokecherries, and bullbrier. But he was determined to leave it all just that way. No "improvements" inside or out.

True, there was more land than he needed, but better him as the owner than some developer. Besides, the sandy beaches, dunes, and woodlands came as a unit—all 953 acres of them. He had no choice.

It was here that he would write his second major work. He'd finished with the radical movement. Wrapped it up. This one was on the liberal tradition. The writing hadn't gone as well.

"I sure am glad," she said, clearing dirty mugs and plates from the kitchen table, transferring them to the pile on the sink board. "Glad things went well. Because I don't cotton to raising a family all by my lonesome."

"Just a couple of spring months."

"Two and a half, to be exact. Since April nineteenth. Isn't that one of your quaint Massachusetts holidays? Evacuation Day?"

"No, Patriots' Day."

"Well, I suppose it was worth it. If you've finished the manuscript."

She still couldn't imagine his failing to meet a deadline.

Couldn't conceive of it. She was doing her best to look unconcerned, tending to dishes, not looking him in the eye; but her voice came through like a prosecutor's, corralling him into a confession just to settle the matter.

"Well, *almost* finished," he said.

"Almost?"

"I ran into some new material."

That caused her to put a stack of used soup plates down on the counter and look at him directly. "New material? In your local library?"

The nearest center was an hour from there over their rock-strewn road. It consisted of one general store and a gas pump with an antique Esso sign.

"Well, new concepts. Different ways of getting at it."

She peered at him from the corner of her eyes to see if he were joking. He was not joking. But he was not being candid either. She'd spotted that from the start.

"Speaking of new concepts," he said quickly, "did you remember to bring the journals, like I asked?"

"Journals?"

"My father's journals. In the carton? In the attic? Remember?"

"Ah, your father's journals. Kraft, I thought you were pushing hard to finish up the manuscript. What's with this journal?"

"That's one of the new concepts. More social history—documents, letters, diaries. You know. I mean, that's quite a source right there."

"Sure. Hey, where's the coffee?"

"So did you bring them? Oh, coffee's over there next the roach powder."

"Of course I brought them. Did you say roach powder? There are no roaches in rural Canada."

"I wish I'd brought them when I came."

"Roaches?"

"The journals, dummy. The journals. It's just that they

8

cover the period I'm into—'26 to '38. Real source material. Right under my nose. Don't know why I didn't think of them before. The roaches, by the way, were here when I came. Or a week after. Coming out of hibernation, maybe."

"You told me once they were too personal to work with. The journals, that is."

"That was years ago. Look, it's been forty years since he died. I was only a kid. By now they're historical. Pure documentation."

She handed him his mug of steaming coffee. "Last I heard," she said in that casual, offhand manner which put him on guard, "your work was on the *liberal* tradition. Liberal like Roosevelt and Hopkins and Frankfurter and that bunch."

"Sharp memory there."

"And your father, I think, was about as liberal as Jay Gould. A kind of would-be robber baron."

"What d'you mean, 'would-be'?"

"Oh, Kraft, cut this out. It's not like you, this stalling around. Adding new material at this stage? It doesn't make sense. What's this guy got to do with your topic?"

" 'This guy' is primary source material. The robber baron in his lair. Besides, I don't need all this advice. I follow my trade and you follow yours, right? Wasn't that the contract?"

"Contract? Is that what we have? That's *my* field, pal."

"*Understanding*, then. It was my *understanding* that I was to stay clear of your career and you were to keep your itchy fingers off my writing and my teaching and the rest of it."

"There's a small clause about raising the children, isn't there? Something about joint responsibility? If you take time off, it had damn well better be . . ."

"Daddy!"

"Hildy! Princess, baby!"

A slam of the screen door, a flurry of running. Hildy

tumbling into the kitchen, arms around her father. Laughter. Kisses. End of debate.

"Did you get T. R.?" T. R. was their aged gelding, boarded for the winter, named for the first Roosevelt by a previous owner.

"T. R.'s waiting for you. You know he won't get in that trailer for anyone but you."

"Today? Can we?"

"Tomorrow."

"Today, *please?*"

"Hey, Dad!" This from Ric, plunging into the room with the dog, the screen door slamming. At thirteen, he didn't run with Hildy's abandon, but he could still kiss his father. The dog, Trotsky, a mix of poodle and terrier with big, peaked ears, a cartoon creature, yapped, pranced, and piddled on the floor. Another slam of the door—Weldon, the oldest, fifteen. A grin, but no run. Control. No kiss. Just a warm arm grip and a slap on the shoulder, man to man.

"Where were you, anyway?" His voice sounded older than Kraft had remembered.

"In the house," Hildy said. "He was in the house all the time. I *told* you he wouldn't be down at the beach."

"Can we hitch up the outboard?" Ric. "Mum and us picked it up. Can we hitch it up?"

"We're going to get T. R., silly."

"Tomorrow. I said tomorrow."

"Well, can we?"

"Can we what?"

"Hitch up the outboard? For fishing."

"You were in the house?" Weldon. "Jesus, didn't you hear us call?"

"He was working." Hildy. "Concentrating."

Kraft looked at her, filled with gratitude. Then surprise: there was something in that girl's adoring face, something in that soothing voice, the absolute trust, which was famil-iar, the echo of some adult—and not her mother, certainly.

Some student, probably. No time to recall. They moved in on him as a gang: "Can we?" "Please?" "You promised."

He stood up, trying to brush them off, and they took this as a joke, surrounding him, pressing him to the corner, laughing, trying to clutch his arm, getting his attention. "Come on, Dad." "You promised." "You promised." The joke expanded, they began mauling him, lovingly, a pack of dogs, he the bear. He raised his arm, defending himself against the world, ready to strike.

"Hey!" Tammy's voice, cutting through, sharp as a whip's snap. "Enough. Give the man some air. Out. All of you. Back at . . . noon. You hear? Big cleanup at noon. Right now, out. Give us a chance to catch up."

They backed off, surprised, knowing only that the joke was over, that a dark cloud hung over them all. "Jeez . . ."

When the door slammed for the third time, he slumped into his seat again, shook his head, rubbed the stubble on his cheek and chin, shook his head again. He felt as if he had been pummeled.

"Hey, mister," she said softly. "Sorry. Look, I didn't realize."

"Realize what?"

"You're in bad shape, you know that?"

2

He sat at the table sipping his coffee, watching her. She had hauled down a two-burner copper cauldron from a high shelf, had filled it from the buckets under the table, and had hoisted it up to the stove.

He hadn't planned on telling her that the writing had gone poorly, but she was bound to find out eventually. He was overdue with the first deadline as it was, and the editor was a friend. She'd hear. Well, at least she understood that it hadn't been all that easy. No picnic, these two months. When the chips were down, she always came in on his side. Like now. She didn't have the whole picture, but she had offered some support and that's all he asked.

He wouldn't tell her that he'd been talking to himself. No need to go into that. It was all very well to grant that privilege to sheepherders and prospectors and nod with understanding, but surely not for the likes of him. Well, no matter. Easy enough to explain.

Explain? There was nothing to explain, really. The only time he saw real people was on trips to the general store up on the road—that only once a week—and occasionally, just occasionally, visits with the McKnights, who lived on an estuary a half mile from there. Old Mr. McKnight was a fund of information on nineteenth-century rural life. He was in his eighties or nineties. And his granddaughter, Thea. The two of them, the last impoverished members of a great and dying clan, selling off the land for survival, now down to the last acre. Sea creatures in a rock pool left by the tide. Good source material, vistas into the last half century. Yes, he'd seen something of them.

"Broken or run down?"

Tammy was shaking the kitchen clock.

"Who?"

"The clock, dreamy. It quit. Broken or run down?"

"I guess run down. Forgot."

She started winding it, shaking her head. "You still on Atlantic Standard or is it daylight saving? Forward or back?"

Kraft shrugged. "One or the other."

She stopped winding. "What does your watch say?"

"It's broken."

"The bedroom clock."

"Say, what is this? I don't have the slightest idea. They have to be wound every day, you know. If you forget once, that's it. The batteries in the portable radio are all corroded. What do you have to know for?"

"I don't believe it."

"Believe what?"

"You've been here without knowing the time *at all*? I mean, this could be midafternoon as far as you're concerned?"

Shrug.

"Didn't you ask the McKnights?"

"I didn't see much of them. He probably doesn't know what time it is either." With a grin, "I'm not sure he knows which century it is."

"But the daughter—Thea? Daughter or granddaughter?"

Shrug. Sipping coffee. Watching vapors. Keeping quiet.

"You mean," she said, "that poor woman doesn't know morning from afternoon either?"

"Tammy, will you lay the hell off? What difference does it make? *Jesus.*"

She shook the clock again, set it by her own time. "Weird," she said.

Actually, it was not weird. Not at all. As a social historian specializing in the nineteenth century, he had lectured on this very subject. Notes appeared before his eyes in longhand and he was tempted as always to share his insights with her, give her some historical perspective. (*The factory whistle brought the first notion of precise time to working men of the Western world—more than a notion, a servitude. Trains brought precise time to the middle class, but laboring men could not travel. You might say, they had no time of their own.*) He rather liked the phrasing, but he kept it to himself. This wasn't just the right moment to offer instruction.

"Tammy," he said suddenly, "you're beautiful and bright and it's wonderful to see you, but will you stop whirling around? The kids will help clean up. Back at noon. New Haven time. They've got watches. Good American kids. Timex trained. Meanwhile, sit down here. Relax. Will you?"

"Oh, hey," she said brightly. "The junk mail."

"What about the junk mail?"

"I brought it."

"Should have thrown it out."

"You paid for it."

"Don't remind me."

She went to the back door, to a pile of duffel bags and boxes the children had dumped. One of the cartons was entirely filled with folders, circulars, special offers, and appeals. Two and a half months of them.

He didn't want to see it. He had some notion of asking her for the box with his father's journals and dragging it off to his study, retreating with it. He'd never done more than browsed and that was back in college. But no, this

14

was no time to be unsociable. He'd have to go through the junk with her. *Then* the journals.

"All yours," she said. She brought it over, dropped it beside him. Also a wastebasket.

"Only in America . . ." He picked up a wad and let them sift back into the box. "Public funding for a private monopoly which serves private commerce." Another bunch; another rain of envelopes. "There's private enterprise for you—mail-order houses subsidized through the postal system, paid for by taxpayers. Commercial leeches."

"Knew you'd be tickled pink."

He pulled out a MOBIL envelope, muttering, slit it open with a dirty kitchen knife. " 'As a valued credit-card holder and member of the MOBIL family . . .' Family, my ass. '. . . you're important to us.' Damn right I am." Wastebasket. Next: " 'Frankly, we're puzzled why you haven't taken advantage of our fantastic offer of custom-deluxe . . .' Custom-deluxe crap, buddy." Next: " 'Thirteen thousand Indians look to *you* for . . .' "

"Indian Relief?" Tammy came alive. "Hey, did I tell you I was representing a bunch of Mohawk . . . ?"

" 'Palestinian refugees . . . What future is there for them?' Appeal financed with petrodollars, no doubt."

"Got the case from the Urban League. They wouldn't touch it, Indians not being black enough, so it's developed into a major action—April-Dawn against the Schmidt Construction Company. Nice ring to it? Breach of contract. Third case this April-Dawn's been in. One sharp cookie. Right now we're up to the Circuit Court of Appeals. He's doing more for that tribe than any . . ."

" 'You can't afford to miss the news the *Times* won't print. . . .' "

"You'd think their union would take the case, right? Wrong. It's a sweetheart contract if I ever saw one. This April-Dawn is up against two adversaries and he knows it. Talk about street savvy. . . ."

" 'Three thousand sharecroppers know what American serfdom is. . . .' So three thousand American liberals perpetuate feudalism by making the serfs content. Sad and silly." Wastebasket.

" . . . not getting support from AIM because the Indian Movement is non-urban. Mohawks don't look Indian to them. So here we are with the construction industry and the unions playing footsie with the courts and I've got a red-hot . . ."

" 'Forty thousand American Resisters want to come home again.' Can't imagine why. 'Show them you care.' O.K., O.K., I do care. But through *ministers?* It's up to Congress, not God." Set aside.

"Up to my neck with the Indian case and Hildy gets measles. . . ."

"Measles? Hildy? Oh, boy, here's one: 'QUICK 'N E-Z DISCOUNT. Appliances *factory to you. No middleman!'* So who the hell is sending the junk mail to five million tax-paying citizens? U.S. Postal Service is your goddamned middleman."

"Found a Yale student to stay with her. Of course, it was rough with the roof men. . . ."

"What roof men?"

"Hey, I didn't fill you in on that? Late-winter snow and then a long spring rain. Came through the attic and then down across the joists over Hildy's room. The whole ceiling gave way at once. Pure chance she was in the bathroom at the time. Would have crushed her. Well, I set her up in the living room. She and Ric. The two of them. And the Yale student over with his girl. The two of them smoking dope when I was out. And me with an abortion case running concurrently. Talk about tight schedules. . . . Oh, hey, did I tell you I'm on the board of Women's Alert? It's a local chapter of . . ."

" 'Save the Condor.' Good God, why? Forty million oppressed and starving people in the world and they feed the goddamned condors!"

"Keeps the ACLU on their toes. Do you know the percentage of males on *their* board?"

" 'Willie Thompson Fund.' Now, there's a maybe. Know the Willie Thompson case?"

"Always defending rapists, aren't you? Right down the line. Well, anyway, the plasterers were in and we got to talking about union organizing and they said that in Fairfield County alone . . ."

" 'Planned Population.' Whatever happened to planned parenthood? That's a maybe, but how come they're always out to plan black and yellow populations first? I don't like the smell of that one. What's this? 'Save the Wild Horses.' " Wastebasket with a flourish. "Now, if they wanted to liberate leashed dogs and harnessed horses, *maybe*. . . ."

"Then why didn't you arrange to have T. R. brought back today? You know how much it means to Hildy."

"Tomorrow. I told her. I'm telling you."

"You could have written the guy who has her and said we were planning to come over. . . ."

"So what kind of preparations are necessary to get a horse out of hock? T. R. has to be informed in advance? Shock to his system? Come on, now, I've been busy. . . ."

"Have you really?" Tone carefully neutral. A quiet little grenade. Tick tick tick. Smother it. . . .

" 'Dear Distinguished Historian . . .' How do you like that? 'Your name has been nominated for inclusion in DISTINGUISHED HISTORIANS OF THE YEAR.' Some directory *that* will be—can't even afford a computer that can print in my name. DEAR DISTINGUISHED HUCKSTER, kindly take your invitation and shove it. . . ."

"Kraft, the stove just went out."

"Went out?"

"Both burners. Out. We've run out of gas. Completely out. Couldn't you have at *least* . . ."

" 'ENVIRONMENTAL ALERT! At this very moment we are depleting ESSENTIAL ENERGY RESOURCES . . . a GLOBAL THREAT!' "

He caught her in midprotest, made her laugh, made her call him a perfect ass, made her confess that she had picked up another tank in Yarmouth, had risked breaking the car springs.

"Because you knew I'd forget?"

"Because I knew you'd be working too hard to remember. How's that?"

Couldn't be nicer. Unilateral truce on her part. And now there was plenty to do together, hauling the damn thing out from the Scout, sliding it onto the old wheelbarrow. Having it topple to one side. Having to slide it back in place. Having to trundle the hundred-pound tank around to the side of the house, her taking half the lifting as he knew she would.

Blessed, he thought, grunting with the weight of his turn, blessed be the tasks we can share. Like the first two summers in this place. Camping out. Windows gone, sun shining through the roof, swallows nesting in the upstairs bedrooms, chilly nights in sleeping bags, exhausting days clearing plaster and broken glass, chopping chokecherries and alders, regaining the view of the sea.

They had used local help for the roof, but the rest they handled as a family. A pioneer family, really. And he was going to keep it that way. Once they removed the plaster from the walls, he rather liked the exposed laths, two sets of horizontal stripping which formed the partitions between the rooms. A good open feeling, airy and simple. Above all, simple.

When they finally had the place tight, the pressure was on to install running water, add electricity, pry rocks from the dirt road. But he held fast. Gas for the stove and refrigerator was a compromise—to his astonishment, no one sold ice. But that would be the only one.

Patiently he explained to the children what all the rest would have led to. He'd lectured on that. *(The summer estate became the American merchant's re-creation of European class status.)*

18

What he didn't tell them or draw on in his lectures was that his father and grandfather—indeed, the Means family for several generations—were prime examples. In any case, he'd save his children from all that.

"There!" he said. It was satisfying just to get the damn tank from the car to the house. Then hooking it up. The two of them working together.

Inside again, he had to bleed the line of air before relighting the burners. "We *could* have got the boys."

"The children, you mean." A slip there. Hildy was not to be excused from heavy work, though already she was turning out to be surprisingly feminine.

"The children, I mean. It would have been easier, but we promised them until noon. Union contract. And they've got watches."

"No problem."

"Not for the two of us."

"Hey, don't I get special credit?"

"For what?"

"Well, I brought the tank. And time."

"Probably the wrong time."

"It was good enough for New Haven. Anyway, wrong time is better than no time. All you have to do is believe in it. Or do you prefer to be timeless?"

He grinned at her across the filthy stove, drawn to her and roused. She could do that just with words. Bouncing them around. He reached for her playfully. Then withdrew his hand. Past her shoulder, out the window, down the path came a figure. Tall, slim, an odd skirt, calf length but a drab, country fabric. It was Thea McKnight. The loose-limbed swing of an athletic woman, but too casual. A one-time sprinter, perhaps, no longer in shape.

"Here," he said to Tammy. "Hold this pilot valve down and I'll try to light it."

He could have done both, but he did his best to make it seem difficult. Held the match in the wrong place, then the wrong angle. Three matches. Would that silly girl come right up there and start chatting with Tammy? Hadn't she seen the car? Did she think in her country ways that Tammy couldn't guess in two seconds flat?

Fourth match. He had to look up, through the hazy glass. The path, the scrub beyond, a corner of open sea. But no Thea. Gone like an apparition.

"Let me," Tammy said, taking the matches. "Your hand's trembling."

3

Midafternoon. Surprisingly warm. Songs of crickets, katydids, song sparrows intense. Afternoon breeze flattened. House now deserted except for the two of them sitting on the front porch.

They were surrounded with lamps—simple kerosene and Aladdin. She cleaning each chimney, handing it to him for final polishing, he replacing each. His mind played back a snippet of a lecture from years ago: *(The sharing of physical tasks in colonial homes served as a social contact between husbands and wives; in the absence of such, couples have resorted to shared drinking or smoking grass.)*

Often lamp cleaning was assigned to the children, but they had already finished their mandatory hour of hard work, a flurry set by kitchen timer to the second. Dishes washed, dried, put away, floor scrubbed, a conquering army bringing new order. Released, they took off with whoops down the path toward the beach, zigging and zagging through the old cemetery, the outcropping of ledges, the juniper, the thickets of chokecherry, heading for Front Beach, *their* beach, the sound fading—shrieks, laughter, barking, all blurring, growing fainter, blending into insect song.

"Instant summer," he said. He was holding a chimney up to the light, squinting at treetops through the glass.

"It's been cold?"

He shrugged. "Don't know about that. Too busy to notice. I meant the sounds. Summer sounds."

"Good or bad?"

"Both. Bad because it will knock hell out of my working schedule. Good because . . . well, it's good to have the season fixed. Do you know what I mean? I've been suspended. Nontime. That's a little unnerving."

She had changed to a blue work shirt and jeans, her Chinese laborer outfit. Blue sweatband around her forehead. More of a propaganda poster than the real thing, but he liked it. His worker wife.

"Same with me," she said. "Good to be here, but . . ."

"But . . ."

"But hard to let go."

"Of what?"

"Everything there. You know, the cases pending. Meetings. Like hanging on to a live wire." He nodded, grinned—his image of her exactly. High voltage. Nodded and let her go on: "But by the time I got to the ferry, I wondered how the hell I stuck it out all that time."

"It can't have been easy, alone like that."

"I do all right." A sudden edge in her voice. Defensive. "In fact, I do it very well."

"Of course."

"Things get done."

"I'm sure."

"On time."

"I believe it."

"Roof repairs. Leaks. Problems with the IRS." Pause. No query from Kraft. Lie low. "Conferences with teachers. My own practice. Hassles with the city council. Trips to New

York. Two to Washington. I mean, it all gets done. . . ."

"But . . ."

"And done probably more efficiently than when you're home."

"But . . . ?"

"I mean, you get a hell of a lot done too, but you're damn erratic, you know. I'm never sure whether you've taken care of something or not, you know?"

"But . . . ?"

"Like unreliable. I mean, remember the summons for public speaking without a permit? On the green? Remember?"

"Six, maybe seven years ago. Some memory you have."

"I just mean I thought you were going to take care of it and then you were off in Washington and we got into one hell of a hassle."

"Maybe eight years ago."

"Seven years ago in June. The eighteenth."

"Seven, eight, ten—for Chrissake, what the hell are you talking about? What's the matter with you, come up here and bring that stuff up? Is that what you wanted to say? Came way up here to tell me I didn't show up in court some ten years ago and got a warrant for myself? Is that it? Chrissake, Tammy, why didn't you send me a telegram? Dear Kraft, you were a sonofabitch eight years ago and got me into a lot of needless litigation and I don't want you to forget it. What's the matter with you, Tammy? Goddammit, you're not up here ten minutes and you're on my goddamned back."

"Ten minutes? I've been here for one and one half blissful hours cleaning up the most in*cred*ible mess, a pigsty, and you have the nerve . . ." End of sentence. End of rage. Softly, "Oh, shit."

They put away the lamps in silence. A familiar silence. Charged.

"Come on," he said, "let's get out of here. A change of scenery."

She nodded. "Which way?" Three to choose from. Straight down was where the children were. To the right was what they called Marsh Path, down from the high land, down to the estuary of a stream, to where the McKnights lived in their little boathouse home, then up the stream to the fording point, the route to the main road.

"Marsh Path?" she said. Sounded like a question, but she was already walking.

"No. Ho Chi Minh Trail." It led eastward, to their left, along the coast, along their property, along the endless beaches. "Come on."

"I want to see the McKnights."

"Later. I'd rather talk. Swim, maybe."

"How are they, anyway?"

"Who?"

"Who? Who else? McKnights. How are they?"

"O.K., I suppose."

"You *suppose?* You don't know? You haven't seen them?" Her trial voice. And his error. She'd ask them, of course. "Sure I've seen them. My only neighbors, for Chrissake."

Sigh. Still standing there, not choosing either way. "I only asked how they were getting along. He must be a hundred and five."

"Eighties. A hard life."

"And the girl. Woman. Is she a daughter or a grand-daughter, anyway?"

"I don't know."

"Hard to tell about her. I think maybe she's retarded."

"Retarded! She's . . ." Watch it. In the pause, a flicker of a scene came to him clear as any photo, clear as they all were during the past in productive weeks, still shots filling still time, slightly unnerving. *Picture:* A tall woman by the bedroom window, her back to him, marshland in the sunlight outside, her dress undone and slid to her waist, the fine sweep of her back, the hushed moment before it slid to the floor.

"Look," he said, recovering. "Never mind going down there. There's a family of skunks just off the Marsh Path."

"Lovely."

"And I want a swim, anyway. Come on."

They turned left. What they called the Ho Chi Minh Trail had been made by wagons a century before, ruts tall with grass but still clear of saplings, natural for two people to walk abreast. They passed through stunted spruces, birch groves, moving parallel with the sea, the glare of it flashing through foliage from time to time.

She started talking again. Safe subjects this time. Was there any winter damage along the beach? He didn't know. Was it going to be a good blueberry year? How was one to tell? Hadn't he looked to see if the blossoms had set? No, he hadn't. And were there any fledglings in the osprey nest? He hadn't been that far down the coast.

A New York City girl by birth, an aggressive student, a natural test-taker, a high scorer, she studied nature as if each season would end with a final exam. Bird books, fern books, insect books, toad books. The bark of trees, the age of rocks, the edibility of mushrooms. Latin names, phylum and class, life cycle, mating habits. The works. Not love, surely, but some kind of genetic compulsion.

"Didn't you step out of the house?" she asked.

"To the outhouse, regularly."

"Thank God for regularity."

"Look, I've been busy." With this, a slight reddening of his neck, a prickling. Busy, all right.

He felt the heat of two infidelities—one to Tammy and the other to his work, his manuscript. Hard to tell which was worse.

"Oh, hey, the first-class mail," she said.

"What about it?"

"You haven't been picking it up."

"From time to time."

"The box was jammed."

"It's as bad as the junk mail. Why did you bring all that stuff, anyway? It's crap."

"The first-class wasn't crap."

"I don't have time to answer mail. Too busy."

"Then they'll come after you."

"Who?"

"The Reclamation people."

He winced. The previous summer they had started writing to him, urging him to sell. They were planning a provincial park. He'd only owned the land three years and already they were trying to take it over. He'd hoped they had given up the idea.

"So what do they want now?"

"Land."

"So what else is new?"

"Look, Kraft, they're generating some heat over this."

"Heat? They've got no legal right. It's political. Purely political. Some town councilman gets press coverage by jumping on American . . ."

"U.S."

"All right, U.S. landholders—nonvoters—and runs with it. A regular little Joe McCarthy with his list. And now a couple of M.P.s have picked up the scent. Purely political, jingoistic, bombastic, antiforeign, reactionary and discriminatory action . . ."

"Hey, mister, I'm on your side."

He stopped, arms outspread, a William Jennings Bryan. On his side? An ally? A partner? Not since her arrival. Not before her arrival. Well, maybe. In a way. Her abrasive way. Yes, sort of.

He grinned. "Some coalition this is." Shook his head. The wonder of it.

They started off again. She hummed—no tune, just notes. A habit of hers. A sign of tension. Annoying, but he was on good behavior. She picked wild flowers. Pulled them up by the roots, identified them by English name or Latin, threw them away, leaving a trail, shoving only the mysteries into her pocket.

The path came to an inlet, a cove lined at the end with what they called Deep Six Rock. A rounded shelf of granite, broad as a whale's back and fully as large. From the edge, a vertical drop into the water. Children not allowed except with parents. Ideal for nude swimming. Memories of naked children, a woman too—tanned thighs, backs, arms. Sometimes, like now, just the two of them without children. Looking at the flesh-colored granite, a giant's buttock, roused him.

"Been in?" she asked.

"Not much."

"Once?"

"No."

"Come on, stinky."

He shrugged. *(The abhorrence of bodily odors is a phobia unheard of previous to the twentieth century.)* She was undoing her blue work shirt. He, his red shirt. "That still gets me," he said.

"What gets you?"

"The Reclamation business. They've no right. . . ."

"Let go."

"It's discriminatory. Just because we're American . . ."

"U.S."

"What do they want us to say, United Statesian?"

She was bare-breasted now; small, firm in spite of children; slightly roused. He more so. But it was not their way to act like common lovers—especially after an absence.

"You need a good lawyer." She undoing his buckle, flipping the zipper.

"Also a typist."

"Oh, hey—Harry's coming up."

"He's not all that's coming up."

"For the weekend." He undoing her buckle now, tugging down on fabric. She continuing. "You don't object?"

"I don't object to anything right now." The two of them

naked, pressed together, each rubbing the other's back, still talking, their old and private game. For all his indiscretions, this nudity, this talk-play seemed brazen and illicit.

"For the weekend," she said, voice faltering.

"To review progress on my manuscript."

"On your manuscript."

"Such as it is. Oh, Jesus, Tammy . . ." Ready to stop playing.

"How's it progressed? How many pages?" She winning the point, but her knees buckling.

"Some distractions. Progressing. In good shape, sort of."

Down in the grass, on her, lips on neck, on throat, on breasts.

"Not finished?" Almost inaudible.

"Just beginning," he said, ending the game, entering her, ending talk, beginning the too-fast build-up. Quick squall. Must hold back. Think of the old man, old McKnight, coming on them there in the tall grass; think of Harry coming on them there, waving the manuscript, furious, refusing it, ridiculing it, scattering it to the winds, sheet by sheet. Image fades; new picture: Tidal rip sweeping up the river, McKnight swept under, Harry gone, he and Tammy riding it, cresting, cresting . . . a thundering release.

Songs of crickets again, katydids, song sparrows again. All returning. Human talk spent, insects and birds reclaiming the world. He off her now and feeling for the first time the tall grass, the weeds, the sticks. Ants? Warm sun on his body. Then a quick shade, a slight chill. Eyes open, he saw her up on her elbows. Flicker of disappointment— too quick a rebound. Thought she'd be laid low for an hour.

"Hey," she said softly, looking down at him, touch of a smile, bits of grass stuck to her side. "That's really something." A *but* hanging there in the superheated air. "But you were in a bit of a rush, weren't you?"

He closed his eyes again. He'd forgotten the qualification.

The ubiquitous *but*—a good speech, *but;* a marvelous lecture, *but;* a first-rate article, *but* . . .

"Haven't seen you for a while," he muttered, but she was already up, already out on the rock, already heading for the water. He opened his eyes, turned his head, saw the remarkable figure, winter white, slim, poised there with arms on hips, posed as if on the high board, all eyes on her, up on her toes, once, twice. All that energy, electrical; he thought he'd grounded it. But no. Not quite.

Third time up on her toes; the muscles ripple upward, calves, thighs. Hands up, a diver's pose: back muscles ripple in response, a complete unity, a physical perfection. He was limp with admiration.

Heels down for an instant, she turned. "Hey, come on." In the instant of the turn, a flurry of diagonals across her back. Astonishing. "Hey, come on."

"I just have."

A kid's grin. Turning back, once again up on toes, hands on hips. Arms up—choreography by book, by practice, by YWCA, grace by act of will. With a slight bend of her knees the rock seems to spring down and up, supple as a board; she lands once, twice, then rises out over the water, turns in a perfect arc, a flash of body and a sweet streak of honey-hued pubic hair, body an arrow, straight into the water, *plok!* a trout's sound. Such perfections were natural to her.

He stood and headed for the edge, feeling hairy, stumbling from hibernation, blinking. A lovely thing he had just seen, but . . .

He waited for her to surface, smiling, knowing that it would be colder than she had expected—she remembering the late-summer water, which was almost tolerable. There would be a burst of profanity. Perhaps even a moment of gasping panic. Perhaps . . .

Perhaps as her head breaks the surface he would hear a strangled cry, unintelligible, would see her face twisted in disbelief, would see her go down again. He would plunge in, feeling not cold but pain. It is like fire but he copes, thrashing, struggling to catch an arm, a leg. He works fast now, knowing that minutes count before his muscles go as limp as hers, only a slight edge for being male, a half minute at best.

Arm around her neck and strike out with other arm, kick hard, drag her body and his own, stroke by stroke. The rock, finally. He barely has strength left for her. Limp body slips back; he clutches, clinging to the crease in the granite, grabs for her hair, pulls her face above the surface. In that instant, face just out, he holds in the grip of his fist her entire life.

"Holy Christ!" Her head broke the water like a porpoise, laughing. He, high and still entirely dry above her, still rooted there on the rock, quite unneeded. "Last one in," she cried, "is a dirty capitalist pig."

4

The view from the top of Kraft's house was impressive. Unnerving because of the height, but impressive.

High enough to see over the old cemetery out front, over the tangle of chokecherry, scrub oak, sumac, juniper; high enough to trace the meandering of the path down to Front Beach, twisting like some narrow channel in a salt marsh, slithering its way to the sea. From the living room, the beach was hidden by all that tangle, but not from here. A band of gold and beyond that, vivid as morning, that greater band of blue. Blue right out there to nothing. To the end of the world. To the beginning of the world.

The peaked dormer on which he sat astride, a Brigham Young surveying his acres, faced directly on all this. *(The Mormons' trek west was as political an act as Mao's long march; only the outcomes differed.)*

To his left he could just make out over the tops of stunted spruce the inlet named for the swimming rock, Deep Six Cove. Beyond that, a golden ribbon, a continuing beach; not a house or a car or even a trace of a country road—

just endless beach lying there as it had before the first McKnight sailed from Scotland.

All of it his. His for three years now. His because the last of the McKnights had given up trying to make it pay, had long since moved away—all but those two left behind. A succession of owners had tried farming or fishing but failed. There was neither soil enough nor harbor enough, this being the south side, the sea side, the poor side of Nova Scotia, exposed to the open Atlantic.

So it was Kraft's frontier. Perfect for a man who . . .

"Hey, Dad, more wire." A voice from ground. Weldon? No, younger, more explosive; must be Ric. Picked up that "hey" from his mother. Both boys in on the project, but Ric as organizer. Supervising from the ground, unseen.

"More wire," Kraft shouted from his perch on the roof to Hildy just inside the window, also unseen. And so the four of them began to work together, each hidden from the others, yet linked by this thin wire. Hildy unrolled from the spool, fed it up to Kraft on the dormer roof, who threaded it through an insulated ring and lowered it down to Ric on the ground, who kept it clear from the underbrush as Weldon marched with the lead end.

All this for a crystal radio, a delicate little mechanism which if constructed correctly would receive some distant voice—one station at best—without the aid of electricity. The wire which Kraft now played out was the aerial which eventually would be fastened to a white porcelain-insulated peg. The set itself was to be placed in the tree house a hundred feet away. The key to crystal radios, Weldon had informed them, was in the length of the aerial and its height from the ground. This one would be long and high.

"O.K., that's all." Hildy's voice from inside.

"O.K., that's all!" Kraft bellowed to the ground.

"O.K., that's it!" Ric's voice to Weldon, who must have been ready for the ascent.

Kraft heard something unintelligible from Weldon, then

clearer from Ric, which he repeated to Hildy. She was to wrap the wire over the peg on the window sill, round and round.

How? she wanted to know. He leaned far forward over the end of the dormer, peering down, seeing only her disembodied hands, the ground far below. "Round and round," he instructed, his voice calm, while a wave of terror passed through him.

Done. A time now to wait while the unseen boys crossed the field and tangle of undergrowth and climbed up to the tree house with the other end of the wire, shaking it free from briers and finally pulling it tight.

Kraft waited, making sure his end would hold. He watched wire draw taut, go slack, tighten again and hum with the tension, then ease off. He thought of mountain climbers on a single line and without reason he felt a surge of concern for them all—for him and for the others along this thin wire, all of them attached with such subtlety that they hardly gave it a thought.

Looking out to the right—opposite from that great stretch of beach—he could just make out the top of the tree house, their outpost. No one up there yet. He tried fixing his attention on that, but his eye was drawn past the trees to the salt marshes beyond.

That was the westerly end of his property. It was bounded by a stream which was sometimes no more than a brook. It came down from the swamps in the north and twisted its way to the sea. Their only route to the highway, to civilization, forded it. They had christened it the Styx.

As it worked its way toward the sea, winding through scrub and tall grass, it opened into a network of channels, an estuary, a tidal marshland. It was there that the McKnights lived. Their place had once been just a boathouse. It was now their home.

Even from his height, he could not see their home, but in his mind's eye he could see Thea. *Picture:* A tall, graceful woman on the front stoop bent over a galvanized washtub, scrubbing clothes on a washboard, humming to herself. Odd, since he had never seen her use a washboard.

"Daddy, can I come up now?"

It would be strange indeed if she were at that very instant using a washboard he had never seen.

"*Daddy,* can you hear? Can I come up now?"

"Just a minute."

Her up there? Absurd risk. Yet a pleasure to share his eagle's view with her. Still, he'd ruled against it. That was how they had got him up there in the first place. He had been in his study working—that is, reading his father's journals. It took enormous concentration, deciphering it word by word. The squared-off handwriting was made almost illegible with an italic pen. Gradually he became conscious of scuffling overhead. Too loud for birds. Squirrels, perhaps? Large squirrels. Enormous. *Children?* On the *roof?*

Yes, they had got Hildy up on the roof. His little Hildy! To thread the wire through the insulator. Exploiting a kid sister. A couple of fascist thugs they were.

So he had volunteered. He took her place. Terrifying at first. And infuriating. They were moving in on his sacred working time. But in two and a half months of bachelorhood he had forgotten how to negotiate with organized youth. He capitulated. And survived. The grand view had its compensations.

"Can I *now?*"

There was no logic to having her wait. The height would not diminish. He invited her.

It was no great task, her climbing out the window and up along the roof to the dormer on which he was still mounted. The angle was not steep, was walkable. But it was not as easy for her as it would have been for a modern girl in shorts or jeans. Bent forward against the pitch, she held her long skirt up before her, a miniature Victorian.

She perched sidesaddle on the ridge he still rode.

"Wow," she said softly. "You can see to the edge of the world."

"That's what they used to think." Did *she?*

"Now they think it's round." Grudging acceptance of rationality.

"They *know* it's round. If you sailed straight out there, you know where you'd get to?"

"France?"

"Nope."

"England?"

"Way off."

"Where?"

"We're looking south with a little east. If you sailed out there straight you'd go down the full length of the Atlantic, just miss the tip of Africa on your left, cross the Indian Ocean, and come up on the south side of Australia."

"Wow. That's the other side of the world."

A moment of silence. Wonder. Not a flicker of doubt. When telling that to adults, he always had to haul out the globe and a steel tape. *Then* they'd believe—a greater spread of open, unbroken sea than across the Pacific. Only the tape would convince them. But with Hildy, no proof was necessary. Just his word. His perfect student.

"How long would it take?" Her voice was hushed as if in a church.

"Sailing? Maybe four months."

"Wow."

"If you didn't get becalmed."

"Without seeing land?"

"Without seeing so much as an island. Probably not even a bird. Just day after day, the same horizons."

"Scary."

Silence, the two of them staring in the direction of Australia, staring into two months of suspended time. He had told all that to plenty of adults, had aroused interest; but this was the first time it reached him, gave him a shiver.

"Oh, you'd keep busy," he said. "Adjusting sail, plotting your position, maintaining course. And repairing stuff on board. You know, ropes chafe, sails need mending. You'd keep busy."

She shook her head and made a sour face. "All that time without seeing anybody? That's like a bad dream."

He hadn't thought of it that way. Months without the sound of a human voice? No land to mark his progress? No sense of time? He'd hallucinate. Start raving. There would be a point of no return. Real terror.

"Never mind all that," he said quickly. "Just a crazy idea. What has to be done now?"

"Now what?"

"Now with the radio."

"It's not a *radio.*" His eyebrows up. "It's a crystal."

"O.K., a crystal radio."

"It's not a radio at all. It doesn't use electricity. Not even batteries."

"I know." His instigation, actually. He hated radios, hated mindless music. Hated it in public places, forbade it up here in Worwich. But a crystal set was something else again. One station, maybe. With earphones. One station and a lot of static. Educational. A good hobby. Not a drug. "I know what it is."

"It has a wire in the air."

"Yes."

"And one deep in the ground."

"So?"

"To hear the dead."

His eyes blinked shut, mouth opened. "Oh, Hildy."

"It's true. They told me if I got up here on the roof and did what they say, they'll let me hear voices from the dead. Honest. There's spirits in the air and they talk with the spirits in the ground, and we can listen in with the crystal and they're going to let me. I'll hear them just like Aunt Min."

"Aunt Min? You've been seeing her?"

"She's visited."

"She has?"

"Twice."

"Twice?"

"And she's coming up here real soon."

"Oh, she is?"

"And I'll show her how we've been talking with spirits."

"Don't do that, Hildy. You know how she takes that sort of stuff seriously."

"But it *is* serious."

"Hildy, it's just jokes. The boys were kidding."

"They weren't kidding and it *is* serious."

She stood up and took a defiant step toward the window, but she was down again in one continual motion, foot caught in her skirt. She rolled and Kraft lunged, caught her ankle.

Saved, she sat there for a dazed moment, then brushed her hands and skirt. "It *is* serious," she said, and exactly as if nothing had happened made her way back through the window. Kraft remained, breathing hard, alone again.

5

Picture: On the grassy bank where marsh joins the sea, a lobsterman's boathouse home, gray-shingled and trim, window boxes with blue and white petunias, morning dew drifting in vapor from the roof, a column of smoke rising from the chimney.

Kraft opened his eyes, erased the picture. He would not indulge himself. What the hell was he doing up here, anyway? Lying next the dormer, back against warm shingles, face warmed by the sun. The children were all off . . . everyone was off. Crystal forgotten, voices from the dead forgotten, they were off with the Scout, off to rent a horse trailer, off to get T. R. That miserable old horse was one more complication in the growing clutter of activities. Tammy had swept them all out of there with her usual enthusiasm, leaving Kraft in the wake, still perched on the roof. He knew he should get inside and get to work, but it was too beautiful here, too unreal, floating above it all. Hell, he'd been working like a serf for two and a half months, had hardly noticed the sun. Now in the warmth of it he breathed a long, contented sigh, relaxed those muscles which were tensed, the lines between his neck and back, head and heart, let the spring air ruffle his hair, let his lids drop again.

Picture: In the tall grass near the lobsterman's home stands a couple. She wears a dress only a country girl would buy. It is too long and has one hundred and two tiny cloth-covered buttons down the back. Tall, long-boned, limber, she has beauty enough to obscure her lack of style.

The man has rumpled white pants and a blue polo shirt, the costume of a city dweller going to seed. He's big, once solid, now gone slightly soft. He is older than she, but they are not father and daughter. They are standing too close. As they look out on the grasslands and the twisting channels, his right hand rests ever so gently on her right buttock.

They are mismatched, these two. It is more than her mail-order dress and his rumpled elegance, though that is a part of it. There is something amiss here. No good will come of it. He wants to warn them, acting like a concerned father, advising his son, but he is not sure how to phrase it. Besides, he is not the man's father. He is the man himself.

It is Kraft himself who is standing there. The woman beside him is Thea. He is conscious now where his right hand is and can, in fact, feel the radiating warmth of her body.

This kind of thing had been happening to Kraft lately. He couldn't be sure whether some microcircuit in his brain was loose, blacking out the present and providing vivid re-creations of the past, clear and haunting as old photo albums, or whether these scenes were reconstructions, altered records, distorted in ways not clear to him. He liked to think that what flashed before him was the natural development of a social historian's imagination, a lifetime of study translated into visual patterns. But should he be present in his own visions?

The couple are not entirely at ease. They are both conscious of the fact that his family will soon be arriving, both of them staying clear of all that. When was all this— a week ago? It seems dated, like a generation ago. Time has been giving him trouble lately. Not good for a historian.

"Brooding?" she asks.

"Me? No. I don't brood. That's an indulgence. Thinking, maybe. Just thinking."

"Perhaps you miss teaching. Miss students and all that."

"No, not in the least. I'm not that kind of teacher, anyway. A course here, a lecture series there. Not regular teaching. Not in my field."

He always underrates his academic work, teaching being a bourgeois profession, history departments generally being elitist and unenlightened. He prefers to work with sociologists, though he finds them unread. No sense of historical perspective. The same with students. As a political organizer in the fifties and sixties he was more relaxed with noncollege people, people with more grievances than theories.

But all that was a decade ago. This is no longer a time for grievances *or* theories. This is a time for his Thea, his lovely Thea who has blessedly read nothing, joined no causes, taken no stands, has gone nowhere, does nothing, and who wondrously has no complaints. She has lived her life right here on this desolate coast of this static little province. History here died two generations earlier and life went on without anyone noticing. Thea reads no newspaper and her grandfather allows no radio—not on principle, just preference. She has never heard of Kraft, of course. He is for her just what he tells her about himself. No less and no more.

"I'd like to learn history," she says. "Like you."

"You're fine as you are."

"No, I really would. All those foreign countries. I'd love it."

"Not the way they teach it, you wouldn't. A lot of dates and kings."

"Kings . . ." She says the word with awe, with wonder. But almost at the same instant she realizes that he doesn't approve. "That's not what you teach about? What do you teach about?"

"People." He has given this lecture many times. "History is people. Working people. How they live. What they're frightened of and what they dream about. How they spend their time. Know how one working man lives, how he spends his working day, and you'll understand a whole people. You don't get this from memorizing public policy and diplomatic scheming. How did we get off on this? I don't want to go into it. Don't want to even think about it."

"Of course," she says, taking half a step back and turning just slightly to the right as if to search the treetops, checking to see if an osprey nest had been built during the night, and incidentally, innocently, pressing ever so gently against the palm of his hand with the curve of her bottom.

They turn and start strolling toward the little Currier and Ives boathouse home. Nothing with Thea is hasty. She moves with deliberation, with grace, with the dignity of her grandfather. Musing on this and on teaching, his mind once again replays a parenthetical lecture fragment: *(The pace of preindustrial society was determined by the fact that their only surplus was not in goods but in time.)* "To hell with all that. I don't want to talk about teaching or history or politics." He also doesn't want to talk about how little he has done on the manuscript, how much time he has spent speculating on recent history, on his place in it, on the dramatic disparities between his values and those of his father, on the total transformation of life style between the past generation and his own. No, he doesn't want to talk about all that. "I don't want to talk about all that."

"Of course," she says again.

"Like an overloaded circuit."

"A what?"

"An overloaded . . . An overloaded horse, a tired old horse."

"You're not old," she says.

As they amble, his hand shifts to her shoulder, then the back of her neck, fingers involved in activity unrelated to the subject of his conversation. Seven of the one hundred and two tiny cloth-covered buttons which run down the full length of her back are undone. Ninety-five to go.

Kraft is not entirely certain that this is right. Somewhere he has a wife, a lively, energetic force in his life, a part of him. She would not approve. Would consider this a serious malady. Worse than the flu. Even corrupt, perhaps, like being a double agent. But all that is in another country.

His thoughts are on the little house before them, on entering it, on undoing buttons—and there in the distance, coming out of the woods and beginning to cross the rocky field, is old Mr. McKnight.

"Oh," Kraft says, holding back a profanity, "your grandfather." The old man is pushing a nineteenth-century barrow, one with a thick wooden wheel. *(Hand-fashioned oak wheels disappeared county by county as mail-order houses were introduced.)* Kraft has seen only two—this and a replica McKnight made for him.

"Oh," Thea says at the same instant, "it's Grandpa."

Kraft likes the old man—his rural dignity, his clean, uncluttered mind. He would have liked to have had a father like that—restrained, nonjudgmental, nonpolitical. Everyone in Kraft's family was steeped in social theory—mostly Tory. Old Mr. McKnight values his hands more than his mind.

Still, the old man always seems to show up when he and Thea are heading for the bed. Uncanny. A Puritan shadow over their affair.

"Never you mind," Thea says, reading his mind. "He'll stay for a while and we'll talk. But then it'll be time for his scavenging. Tide's low at ten."

Every day at low tide the old man scours the beaches

for usable items—timbers, orange crates, even nails which can be pried out and ground smooth on the whetstone. *(Recycling was a permanent part of all societies until the production of surplus goods in our own glutted century.)* Old Mr. McKnight lives contentedly in the previous century.

"I don't mind," Kraft says. Actually, he does and he doesn't mind. Both. But that is too complicated to explain. Even to himself. "I don't mind," he says again. They are on the front stoop—a simple porch with a roof. She sits in the big rocker and he is perched on a nail keg old Mr. McKnight has salvaged from the sea. It would be a time before the old man put the wood in the shed and came around to suggest a cup of coffee. Nothing whatever moves rapidly in rural Nova Scotia. Especially time.

"I don't mind," Kraft says, thinking that the last time he said it to himself in his own head. "It's good talking with him. I was writing about him in my journal this morning. 'I hope I see old Mr. McKnight today,' I said. 'He is a personification of this area, a human representation of the district.' Do you know what I mean?"

"I guess." Silence. Then, "Kraft, are you maybe spending too much time with that journal of yours?"

This is, oddly, just the question his wife asked by letter the week before. He finds this unsettling.

"I've kept that going ever since I was ten. I'm not going to stop now." He is, though, spending too much time writing in his journal and daydreaming and she knows it just as clearly as he does; so it is essential that he defend himself. "It's an act of survival, writing in that journal."

"Survival?"

"Like shipwrecked sailors."

"Like what?"

Somehow he had expected her to know, sea lore in her genes. Occasionally there were gaps. "You know, when they row the lifeboat, they keep an eye on their own wake. Otherwise they turn in big circles."

"How did you know that?"

"That's my job—knowing things."

"You never went lobstering, did you?"

"No, but I learned about it."

"It's a wonder to me."

"What?"

"All that stuff you keep in your head. And all that writing." He notices that she is shelling lima beans. Where did they come from? "I never even kept a diary."

"It's like sheepherders—you know, talking to themselves. Except I write it. I mean, it's spooky living in that great ark of a house by myself."

He has thought of inviting her in, urging her to share the place with him, to abandon that aging grandfather. But she would refuse. He is sure of that. Besides, there is a certain mystique to his house. It wouldn't be right having her there. It was one thing sharing the cottage with her from time to time; but having her come up and sleep on Tammy's side of the bed—there was something immoral about that.

"All that looking back," she says gently. "It'll turn you to salt."

As usual, she has it all wrong. It wasn't just looking back that turned Lot's wife to salt; it was her longing for all that corruption, her nostalgia for privilege. But what the hell, he isn't about to correct her on what is probably the one book she has ever read. "Time to do the dishes," she says, salt forgotten. "He'll be in directly and he'll be wanting a cup of coffee. Come sit with me while I fix up."

Picture in sepia: A woman stands by the soapstone sink, her hand on the pump. She is lit by a shaft of sunlight which enters the room through a single small window. *(The advent of the picture window in the late twenties reflected not only a new affluence but a new trust in the law. In previous centuries, the house was one's primary protection against a hostile environment.)*

A whole lecture there—the advent of the city bank without bars on the windows, homes left unlocked, a complete abandonment of the European walled property; all this changing now, being reversed once again. A walling up again. But this is no time for lectures. With effort he erases the entire topic, concentrates on the setting, the scene, the immediate.

The kitchen walls made of the narrow tongue-in-groove boarding, a poor man's substitute for plaster. Open shelves rather than cupboards—the price of a hinge saved. Kitchen table bare pine, unvarnished, scrubbed with salt—to be replaced in the 1920s with white enamel. Kraft can glance at a photograph of an American kitchen and date it within a decade and can lecture without notes on its impact on the status of women, the institution of marriage, and the hierarchy within the family. Here in Worwich he has found a lost valley. Time has moved on like a great flock of geese, leaving a strange silence and sepia prints.

"He's been cutting wood," Thea says, pumping cold water into the dishpan and adding hot from the aluminum teakettle. *(The shift from heavy cast-iron kettles to aluminum utensils was a more significant development for the great majority of women than was receiving the right to vote.)* "I imagine on your land."

"He's welcome to it. I've got enough problems without clearing my own wood lots. They're a mess. Chaos." He is thinking not of his land but of his study, where he should be right now. He can see it too vividly, papers scattered in piles, his manuscript on the liberal movement dismembered by chapters, some revised and some not, pages mixed with his own journal, loose-leaf sheets often undated and left about, some folded into books as he switched from speculation to research and back again, volumes left open at the point his mind left them—the letters of Harry Hopkins, the decisions of Felix Frankfurter, campaign speeches of Bob La Follette. No end to the clutter within, so if the old man wants to clear the clutter out there, welcome to it.

Simplicity. Order. He looks at Thea there at the sink.

She is both. Her cottage, her life, is harmony, a harmony more often found in the previous century than his own. His own is a shambles. How can a man, he wonders, pick a summer home so far from the complexities of contemporary society, so painstakingly distant, and work so hard to keep the place unimproved, simple, truly unmodernized, and still end up with such a clutter of obligations, a rubbish heap of projects. He has brought his own age with him like a virus.

Thea has finished washing. She rinses the plates and mugs with one more spurt from the pump, dries each item, places each on an open shelf, each in the correct place. He feels a great wave of envy for her life, a passionate and agonized longing which he prefers to think of as healthy sexual desire.

No cause for panic. He is in a good position. He is the sole heir of the McKnights' world, the inheritor of the good and gentle life. Back home, America is madly buying spinning wheels, cobblers' benches, modern saltbox houses. Not him; he's got to the root, acquired the life. Thanks to the McKnights.

They are scattered now, down to two, but there was a regular settlement here at one time, generations of them, come from Scotland, looking for the good life. And now Kraft has come, his turn, up from the States, immigrant family, staking out the land as summer residents but soon to move here for good, the new pioneers looking for the good life.

"Find it?" she asks.

"What?"

"Find it?" For an instant he thinks she has a witch's ability to read minds. *(Accusations leveled by reasonable citizens against witches in the eighteenth century closely resemble fantasies of present-day patients described as paranoid; thus, our diagnosis of mental illness depends entirely on a socially determined view of what is reality.)* She does not hear his footnote. She has simply asked him for a pitcher of milk she has left on the window sill to keep cool. She has not read his mind. He has been living alone too long.

And there, suddenly, is old Mr. McKnight. He is standing at the kitchen door. Gray-bearded but with no mustache—a tintype. No smile but not unfriendly. *(It is a significant comment on the impact of the industrial revolution that from the introduction of the camera in the mid nineteenth century until after the First World War it was not customary to smile when having one's picture taken.)* Old Mr. McKnight gives just the ghost of a nod of recognition and extends his hand in an old-world handshake.

"I couldn't seem to get any work done this morning," Kraft says. He doesn't want to seem like a summer resident. He *isn't* a summer resident. He's been here since April, after all.

"All that work with your head," Mr. McKnight says. "It can't be good."

"Right."

"Come look at this," the old man says. Kraft follows him into the workroom where there is a skeleton of ribs fashioned to a backbone. It is the beginnings of a rowboat upside down, raised on two sawhorses. Mr. McKnight builds one a year, shaping the oak ribs in a crude boiler out back.

"Here," Mr. McKnight says, seizing Kraft's wrist. The old man's fingers are armored, rough plates joined. He takes Kraft's hand as if it were a plane and slides the palm along the oak keel. Kraft winces, expecting splinters from any unpainted surface. But of course it is perfectly sanded.

"Smooth as a filly's ass," the old man says.

"She's beautiful," Kraft says. "Like everything of yours."

"Ha!" Mr. McKnight smiles for the first time, the two of them sharing a moment of fellowship, the younger one uneasily. Has he implied that Thea was an owned object? "Time for coffee," McKnight says just loud enough for the statement to serve as an order for Thea. "Tide's not about to wait for me or you."

Kraft nods, thinking: When the tide's out for you, it will be high for Thea and me. He smiles to himself, but Mr. McKnight casts a quick, questioning look. Does the old man read thoughts too?

Thea has placed three mugs of coffee on the kitchen table and beside each a cloth napkin and a spoon. They sit down. Simple as their life is, it is bolstered on all sides with formalities. Ritual talk, ritual eating, they make twentieth century urban living seem erratic, childish, chaotic—the abrupt phone calls, the sandwiches eaten while standing, while conferring, while sitting on the toilet.

"That skiff," old Mr. McKnight says, "is as fine as you can find here to Boston." *("Boston" became a Nova Scotian term for all of New England by the 1780s.)* "Not one bit of metal in her, you know. No nails. All pegged. Even the cleat is cedar heart. Hard as brass and it won't tarnish." He nods, agreeing with himself. "Gives pleasure twice, it does—once in the building and again in the owning."

"In Halifax," Thea says, "they make them out of plywood."

They all three smile. "Imagine that," the old man says. Kraft does not mention fiberglass. For the McKnights it doesn't exist yet. "Halifax skiffs are nailed, too. Full of nails. Rust out on you sooner or later. Ten, fifteen years, they'll rust out on you. Drown you sooner or later. Like putting a metal wheel on a barrow. Takes me a winter to shape a wooden wheel. Six pieces glued and pegged. It's work, but it'll last a lifetime. Two, with luck. Same for lobster traps. Pegged and laced. You can't find a better trap."

Kraft nods, letting the old man continue, though he knows that in the States they are using a plastic lobster trap which is in every way superior. As ugly and indestructible as the aluminum beer can. "I build the best traps around here," the old man says. "The very best." They all nod, a part of the ritual. A pause. Then, "Did I ever tell you two about old Captain McEldridge's fifth child?" They shake their heads. "You never knew Captain McEldridge, but he had a house two miles from here down the coast. There was five families living along there, all related." For a few minutes he sketches the genealogical connections like those long, tedious sections in the Old Testament. He describes how different the area was then, the shore dotted with colonies of lobstermen and fishermen and even some farmers who had drifted down from Halifax—an Italian family here, a black family there, and a Swede woodchopper named Svenson no one could understand. "Never did learn the king's English."

"Well, the first four children Mrs. McEldridge had were all normal. And maybe you'd say the same of the fifth. There was just one thing different, though. After the first week, he turned dark. And in a month's time he was black as a crow. I don't mean tan. Black as a crow.

"News got around from the womenfolk who helped out. Roused a bit of curiosity, you might say. But no one knew just how to bring the matter up. The ladies visited and said all them nice things. Didn't indicate there was anything a mite different.

"But menfolk are more direct. So when we went to visit, we took old Cooper Lane along with us. He wasn't what you'd call a talker, but he always knew what to say when he did.

"So after a snort of whiskey, we went in to the bedroom there and the Captain picked the baby up from the cradle and held him, real pleased like, that dark little face peering out at us from a costume that was all white.

"We all nodded and said what a good-looking child it was, and then Cooper Lane cleared his throat.

" 'Good-looking feller,' he said. 'But he's a wee mite dark, ain't he?'

"Old Captain McEldridge looked him in the eye and nodded his head. 'Could be,' he said. 'But I've been lobstering this coast for forty years now, and I've learned one thing. What I catches in my trap is mine.' "

They all laugh. Even Kraft. A terrible joke, he tells himself. Racist and chauvinistic at one stroke. Nineteenth-century provincial humor. Inexcusable. And still he laughs.

The sound dies and the old man is gone. Just like that. He was there; now he is gone.

Free from constraint, Kraft feels oddly hesitant. The room seems small, airless. Enclosing. Warily he looks to the window, to the door. He hears again the old man's voice: "I build the best traps."

He looks at her sitting opposite him. For an instant she is in an old snapshot again, posed there, a tall woman, high-cheekboned. She is an image which would startle young readers browsing through an old photo album. "Who was that?"—the patronizing surprise of moderns who cannot imagine passion cloaked in formality. A sepia print. How does such a lovely person stand a colorless life?

"What's wrong?" she asks. "You're having dark thoughts again."

"You're the one who should be having dark thoughts," he says.

"Why?"

"Cooped up here, trapped."

"I'm not trapped."

"With nothing to read."

"I'm not much for reading."

"No profession."

"I keep the place neat. I mend. Grow things."

"But being alone so much . . ."

"I'm not alone now."

"Now." She has no conception of future time. *"Now."* He stands up. He needs motion. "You know, don't you, that Tammy is coming up in ten days. Tammy and the children. And the dog. The whole bit. Did you forget that?"

"That's in a week. Now is now."

She floats in an eternal present. He can't imagine how that would be. He feels anger and envy. For him the present is the peak of a slippery hummock; he is forever sliding down one side or the other—either counting the days to something out there ahead of him or slithering back into the past. "Now is now," she says again.

He stands and moves behind her, his hands on her shoulders. Without thinking, he begins to massage her muscles, but this is the wrong move; it is not a signal she understands. She takes both his hands and draws them down and around to her breasts. There is only the cotton fabric between his palms and the softness of her flesh. He feels her nipples. They are raised. He thinks: I am holding the present in my hands.

"You know," he says softly in her ear, "I'm holding the present . . ."

She shakes her head, turns, places her palm against his mouth. He nods and almost tells her that he understands, that she is right, that she is teaching him to be nonverbal, that he is learning, that it will take time. She keeps her palm against his mouth.

His hands are behind her, undoing buttons, nimble as a couple of birds after seeds, and she is pressing against him. It is a faint surprise, once again, how this country girl knows how to grind her pelvis—not a blatant act but a slight, almost imperceptible motion. Instinctive?

Her dress, loosened, slips down one shoulder. She raises both hands, bends slightly back at the waist, and undoes her hair, letting it all cascade halfway down her back, shaking it out, and all this without releasing that pressure, that slight circular motion, pelvis against pelvis.

He leads her up the stairs and into her unadorned room; walls of vertical boarding, varnished dark. The familiar iron bed, a rocking chair, a bureau with a wavy mirror attached, a commode on which stands a kerosene lamp and a wash basin. Two books—two books? He hadn't noticed them before. One a Bible, of course. The other? He lets go of her hand for just a minute and picks it up. *Pilgrim's Progress.* Too perfect! Those companion pieces of nineteenth-century rural Protestant life. Her choice or mere inheritance?

"This one—did you buy it or . . ."

She smiles at him, shaking her head—not in answer to his question but objecting to conversation. Finger to her lip. Then a slight drawing together of her shoulders, a slip of the dress over one shoulder, the material falls to the floor with a slight rustle, as easy and graceful as was the loosening of her hair.

She stands there in a half slip, white, gathered at the waist. Then, once again, there is that extraordinary act— she on her knees, loosening his belt, his zipper, sliding down pants. He has told her that she should not do that, should not perform like that—or perhaps has *meant* to say that. This is no time for instruction.

They are on the bed. Wordless, they are wrapped in each other and then he is in her, building the slow rhythm, feeling her rise and fall under him. The covers fall away. The roof above them rises, lifting like a great lid; he feels the warmth of sun on his back. The walls fold back, the floor sinks below them, the bed floats, suspended in open space. They float above the earth, above clouds, above time and place.

Explosions. Dismemberment. And they drift slowly earthward, light as leaves.

As he touches down, he has a quick vision of this house with historical perspective. *Picture:* The remains of this boat-house, chimney smokeless, cracked and leaning; the roof rotted through, beams exposed, skeletal. Residents gone. Dead and gone.

Erasing the image, he clings to her, burying his face in the moist curve of her neck.

6

Up early. The only way. Up at dawn and down to work a half hour later, the place as quiet as it had been before the invasion.

It was clear what he should be doing. It was always clear, every morning. He should be completing the manuscript. The research was done, the grub work finished; it was only a matter now of translating notes into paragraphs. Publication guaranteed. A good editor. And the subject itself should whip him into some kind of enthusiasm. Shifting from the radical movement to the liberals was like escaping from a little back eddy—fast but circular—and moving into the mainstream. Like it or not (and he did not), these were the men who really ran the show in both parties. Particularly from '32. This was solid stuff. The power source. He should be swept up with it.

But he wasn't.

Each morning started off like this, a pep talk from himself as coach; responses from himself as team: Right on, let's go. Then back to his silent maze of reflections.

Something in him had come unwound. He had never

faced this—nothing faintly like this. Always there had been more activities than hours in the day. In the Army Air Corps he spent his furlough time organizing for AYD— American Youth for Democracy. When the Red Cross arranged four days to attend his mother's funeral, he spent two of them in sincere mourning and the other two at a Federalist convention in Chicago. There was still hope that the victorious nations would form a genuine world government. From Air Corps to college—from Federalists to Progressive Party and Henry Wallace; then the protest against Taft-Hartley at home and NATO abroad. In the Korean War there were the rights of resisters, then the Eisenhower-Stevenson campaign—Kraft organizing for Hallinan, the Progressive. Next came the onslaught of Joe McCarthy— the struggle against the blacklist, the loyalty oath, and, eventually, his own fight to remain in graduate school. Oh, and the Rosenbergs. For years the Rosenbergs. And then, dreamlike, no Rosenbergs.

The protest against the first H-bomb (when "Bikini" was a political term) came the year before his doctorate. Also the year of his marriage. And Little Rock.

There was never a lull—from there to the Woolworth sit-ins, which had their counterparts back in New Haven. His move from Brown to Yale merely turned the volume up, increased the voltage. He was in Washington along with 250,000 others for the civil rights rally of '63, protested the Gulf of Tonkin resolution in '64, marched against the bombings of Vietnam in 1965, believing that they could not possibly be continued in the face of such opposition. The following year his time and energies were spent working for a congressional peace candidate, and how on earth was one supposed to meet classes during that? He helped storm the Pentagon in '67 and the raw burn of gas was still with him. Year after year, the war against the war continued and more quietly there was the underground railroad to Canada. Would it ever end?

It did. The end came May 4, 1970, at Kent State University, though no one knew it at the time. An explosion of protests, a kind of convulsion, and then a collapse of political activity.

He hadn't believed it had really died until the mid seventies, though there was every indication. The horrors continued, but the resistance was over. The war wound down through exhaustion. Charles Manson took over the headlines. The public bought *The Radical Failure* and Kraft selected Nova Scotia as a forgotten corner of the world in which to collect his thoughts.

And now at the end of the decade he had bought his land, paid for it in royalties, created his retreat, found peace, found time—and was utterly adrift.

So began another morning, same as the others, the lost navigator's only recourse: a review of all previous fixed points. Step by step, all calculations checked and rechecked. Yet here he was beyond landfall, in the center of empty horizons. For all he knew, he was taking the long route to Australia. Where was the wind?

This was getting him nowhere. He raised his eyes, escaping the inner seascape, and stared outside. The real world. Sun just up; dew still glistening on the grass and the bullbrier. And old McKnight scything. . . .

Old McKnight scything? What the hell was he doing that for? In among the tombstones, tall grass and weeds falling before him. The old man like an apparition—dark pants, dark jacket, old black cap.

Kraft plunged downstairs, footsteps booming, shaking the house. The screen door slammed behind him. Strode out through the tall grass, boots turning dark with the wet of the dew.

Old Mr. McKnight kept working, the blade just missing the rocks and headstones, never even ticking. Kraft stopped, had to wait for the old man to recognize his presence, had to wait for the end of the row. *(The prerogatives of age, another casualty of the 1920s.)* He stood there trembling with impatience. To break in on Mr. McKnight when he was scything, sanding, hammering, whatever, would have been like interrupting a man at prayer.

"Morning," he said at the end of the row, wiping his blade with his thumb, not even looking up, knowing without even looking that Kraft had been standing there.

"Morning," Kraft said. He groped for casual topics, for traditional fillers. It was not correct here in this province, in this delayed age, to move directly in on anything; but he was in an urban mood and could not wait. "There's been a misunderstanding," he said.

"That so?"

"My wife, I suppose, asked you to do this?" The old man nodded—perhaps an eighth of an inch. "Well, I usually do this myself. Just haven't got around to it."

"Of course."

"I guess she didn't understand." An understatement. She didn't understand that he would never have anyone working on the place, would never be an employer, would never take the first step to making this place into a summer home with staff and all. Least of all the McKnights—at his age?

"Shall I put the scythe away?" the old man asked.

"No, leave it." Each nodded to the other. Awkward at best—a wife hiring people without consultation. An embarrassment for the two men. "I'm sorry about this," Kraft said.

"No never mind," the old man said, nodding again, and left. If there were hard feelings, they were encased in formality. Thank God for that.

Kraft watched the man moving off through the tall grass, heading back to the riverbank, back to his cottage. Tammy's fault. Her blunt kind of signal, using the old man to pressure Kraft.

He was too angry to get back to work. He waited until Mr. McKnight was well out of sight and then started to scythe. He had taught himself, learning how to keep the blade parallel with the ground, learning how to slice into grass like cutting bread, not meeting it at a right angle, learning to cut when it was still damp, passing all this on to his boys, picking up techniques lost for two generations. He was excellent compared with his students, but he could not take so much as a first sweep with Mr. McKnight on the scene.

He worked slowly and without pleasure. Twenty minutes, a half hour. He wished he had brought his watch. He had forgotten how many tombstones there were here, most of them knocked over, some half buried, working their way down to join the deceased, corpse-gray marble with blotches of orange fungus.

Of those right side up, many were too weathered to be read. Erased. A terrible thing, Kraft thought, to have one's stone rubbed blank by time. Who was to remember? Family Bible sold at auction, county records destroyed by fire, letters and journals carted to the dump, unread, memories fading, flickering out. History—real history—sweeping out to sea, out to nothing.

His blade caught for the fifty-fourth time, clank against someone's headstone, loud enough to wake the dead. Well, it was getting hot, anyway. Whom had he nicked?

"Thaddeus McKnight," it read, letters faint like the voice of a dying man. "1872–1922. He drew life from the sea and the sea drew him from us."

It was insidious the way these McKnights moved in on him. Unfair.

Unsettling. He was standing on the exact spot where old Thaddeus' sons stood the morning of the burial more than half a century before, the preacher doubtless talking about dust turning to dust and meeting on judgment day and all that cant, the sons not listening, their minds filled with a jumble of love and hatred and relief and despair. Maybe envy too. Right on this very spot.

Kraft stared at Thaddeus' dates, hoping somehow that the old man had lived to 102. 1872–1922. No, that was no century. 1872 to 1900 was 28 and then to '22 was 22 more. 28 and 22—*50* sprang up in the green, squared-off numerals of his mental calculator. Thaddeus was only 50. Kraft's father had died at 55, leaving an only son, 11. His grandfather had been only 55 too. Kraft himself was presently 49. And 49 leaves only 6 years before reaching 55 and only 1 to 50. In the spring of 1921 Thaddeus, mindlessly scything this same field, had 1 year to go. Just 1, and here it was 8:15 A.M. on 6/30 with the family about to spring forth and with 0 done, houseguests due on 7/3, the end of all privacy, the termination of 2.5 strange months of solitude, 9 dreamweeks, 53 acts of adultery, 0 work done.

He headed for the barn. He had scythed enough. Too much, perhaps. Sun getting to him. He would oil the blade, hang it in its proper place, return to his study and do his proper work. He was thinking too much, indulging his imagination. As he walked slightly bent with exhaustion, carrying that great scythe, he saw himself as a cartoon, that absurd figure which newspapers print without failure on 12/31.

The barn was dark. It smelled of horse. T. R. was in residence—that poor, swayback old gelding. Kraft stumbled about until he found an oily rag and began rubbing the wet blade with new energy. Action was what he needed, physical action. *(Until well into our own century, the best method of preventing rust was to create a gunmetal surface through daily oilings and repeated exposure to the elements. The introduction of stainless steel marks not only an advance in technology but a corresponding decline in the painstaking maintenance characteristic of societies in which goods are scarce.)*

When they moved in year-round, they would have the time to care for what they had. They would be freed from the habits of a high-consumption society. They would learn the value of things.

58

The sharpening stone lay right there on the bench. He should get back to work, but he should also take those nicks out. No good workman puts a tool away in that condition. He began grinding the edge with a circular motion. Except for the tip and the base, the blade had been ground down to half its original width. At least one and perhaps two generations of McKnights had stood in this very barn, chilled in the early-morning air just as he was, grinding this same piece of steel with this same well-worn stone. Right here. On this spot. Yet almost all of them were gone now, a lost tribe, their life, their whole era, receding with the speed of light. No way of stopping the process, sweeping out into the blackness of outer space like those galaxies already 350 million light-years away which are at this very moment racing from us at the absurd speed of 5,000 miles per second. How to catch them? How?

As a reward for making this or that quota, he would occasionally proclaim a day of exploration. They would all go out, manic, a Swiss Family Robinson without all that bourgeois praying. Together they discovered and named the far reaches of their domain—Vanzetti Beach, Rosenberg Cove, Gompers Pond. For the children it was a game, but for Kraft it generated an endless variety of possibilities, practical ways to transform this wilderness into productivity.

The sea, for instance: Salt. Colonists built salt-water evaporation tanks. *(Sea-water salt with its beneficial charge of iodine continued to be used well into the nineteenth century.)*

Picture: Wide, flat evaporation tanks along the shore. Water pumped up by windmills. Barefoot children raking out the gray granules and spreading them to bleach white in the sun; then, singing, they gather finished salt and pack it in small wooden boxes. Richer in minerals that the mined stuff, it is sold across the nation. Also specialty woods. He and his sons cut ash, cedar, apple, and trim it to planks with a saw driven by tidal currents. *(During the eighteenth century more than fifty mills were powered by tidal waters, of which not one has been kept in operation.)* In an age of plastic, they find a national craving for the genuine.

The same for foods. An unlimited market. A great longing for new sources. The horseshoe crab, for example. Not even Indians were able to extract the meat. Yet the creatures are abundant. Surely an intelligent man using scientific methods could. . . . Kraft discovers a new process, teaches it to his family. On the shore, great vats of boiling crabs, the meat extracted by clever hands, packed in jars, sent to gourmet shops around the world. No, not gourmet shops: Dehydrated and sent to developing nations, providing much-needed protein. And the shells: The shells ground to a rich brown powder, a new, entirely natural fertilizer sold only to Nova Scotians in gratitude for their welcome. Kraft and his family, the recent immigrants, serving their new land.

"Hey, what are you doing out here?" Tammy's voice. He jumped, almost cut himself. She stood in the door, a silhouette against the glare of sunlight.

"Give a little warning."

"What are you doing? Where's McKnight?"

"One at a time. I'm sharpening the blade. And *Mr.* McKnight has gone home. He got the impression that you hired him."

"I did."

"Well, I unhired him."

"Are you serious? After I talked him into it?"

"I'm not going to have servants around this place."

"Oh, fuck that." Ah, the honeymoon was over. "This place looks like a rural slum. No kidding, Kraft, you haven't done a damn thing to it. It's spooky." Then softer, a different tack. "You've got enough to do."

"Just leave it to me."

"I have, and look at the damn place." Tough again. "This

place is a bad dream. You haven't done a thing, have you? Not one damn thing."

He held out the scythe. "Guess what this is."

"I'm serious, Kraft. Except for ten minutes this morning, you've done absolutely nothing to keep the place up or even keep order. Right?"

There was no answering her when she used her prosecuting attorney voice. He put the scythe up on its peg, laid the stone down in its place, and marched out, headed for the house. There were times when they talked too much, he and Tammy. Too much verbalization. He'd learned that here.

Up the path to the back door, he was heading straight for his study, straight for his own work. No argument.

There on the back stoop was his Thea.

He stopped short, his face prickling. She saw him, but not a flicker of a muscle suggested that she knew him. She had a gray bandanna around her head, a faded denim apron around her waist. She hung a small rug on the clothesline and began beating it with a broom.

"What's this?" he asked, speaking to Tammy beside him, voice too low for Thea to hear.

"The McKnight girl."

"I know that."

"Helping."

"Hired?"

"Well, not working for nothing, Kraft. I mean, that's not legal, you know."

"Tell her to go home."

"Screw you, baby."

Involuntarily he turned to see whether *she* had heard. There was just a pause in the beating. Just long enough. He thought he saw a smile—not humor but something harder, tougher. Something tinged with bitterness. Not at all his Thea. He had a sick flash of a fear that he and his wife had brought their city corruptions with them—their vulgarities, their harshness, the shards of competitive living—and had contaminated his Thea.

"Watch your language," he said, whispering.

"Why?" Their eyes met and the question became charged. He was about to send Thea back too, get her back to her little boathouse home, to her grandfather, to her gardening, her mending, her own world; but now he saw that he couldn't. Warning lights were already flashing in Tammy's skull; no more talk about Thea.

He shrugged. A retreat. Then headed for the house. He would have to give Thea a nod. An employer's nod. But as he passed, she was busy pounding dirt out of a rug, her back toward him, raising clouds of dust. She could have been any hired girl called in for spring cleaning.

7

The journals: The first volume lay in the center of his desk, open and seductive. It was here— 1926—that he had begun to interpret the italic script, begun to master his father's language.

The carton Tammy had brought was perched on the right side of the table, obscuring his manuscript and notes. The box was old and stained with mouse urine, but he could just make out the label, NAPOLEON COGNAC, and the faded silhouette of the emperor. It contained the rest of the volumes, each year through to his father's death in 1938.

There were, of course, rational reasons for turning to them at this point. Tammy didn't understand, but then Tammy was a lawyer, not a historian. Any set of documents running chronologically through more than a decade would be of value, and to have them reflect business attitudes during the Roosevelt years was invaluable. The only surprise was that he hadn't turned to them earlier.

Perhaps it was listening to old Mr. McKnight that had turned his mind in that direction. The anecdotes the old man told were glimpses into recent history, unrecorded details about the life of rural people, their values, their frustrations and pleasures. And when he died, they would be lost, would drift away like smoke.

Not so with the life of the elder Means. It was recorded— at least the final decade. All there for history. Extraordinary that Kraft had not thought of using them.

Extraordinary, yet understandable too. He had tried to read them years ago and found difficulties. He was a student at Brown then and feeling as if he had been thrust abruptly into adulthood. He had survived boarding school, the Army Air Corps, and his mother's death without trauma, and now at twenty-one had just been published in the *New Republic* ("A Veteran Looks to the Left"). He'd been launched. He was ready for anything.

The journals had once been private, of course, but his father had been buried ten years. They were no longer personal property. They were history. Social history.

He examined them with cool objectivity. He was already majoring in history, concentrating on the impact of Hegel and Marx on the American labor movement. In 1948 that was still a viable notion.

He also had adopted a special interest in the quality of life, the daily activities of nonhistorical individuals through letters, receipts, sales figures, newspaper advertisements, whatever he could get his hands on. It was not yet called New History or Social History. It was not called anything. It was just his interest. So what could be more appropriate than a set of diaries? The fact that this particular author bore his own name was entirely incidental.

Kraft's image of his father was hazy, like blurred, faded snapshots taken when he was ten and eleven. Exploring these entries at twenty-one, Kraft found himself reconstructing, reconceiving the man who had once conceived him.

Picture: A tall crane of a figure on a tennis court, white ducks, white canvas hat, a New England King Gustaf. A tight-lipped, tense player, a demanding partner and a brutal opponent. He usually won.

An economic royalist by faith, he was a real estate investor. He took pleasure in his work, was demanding as an associate, harsh as an employer, and brutal as an opponent. Here, too, he usually won.

He had been a strikebreaker (the Boston police strike), a blockbuster (slum property in America's finest cities), a Yankee imperialist (Brazil, Argentina, Guatemala), a chauvinist and an anti-Semite; he was also charming, gregarious (off the court), and an accomplished violin player. Good primary-source material.

Young Kraft, historical and objective, sampled entries with complete confidence, sure that his major problem would be the handwriting. Guilt he never expected.

It crept up behind him so close that he could feel its breath against his neck, making the little hairs rise. He was only a few scattered entries in, but already it was clear that he was a spy in this man's bedroom. He read spasmodically, in hot flashes. Finally he swore off, slamming the books back in the old liquor carton, closing the flaps. It was worthless as source material.

So he thought then. Now, almost a lifetime later, he was older, more mature, more in control. His father, too, had ripened. In Kraft's ten weeks of solitude, weeks in which to ponder on what was wrong with his work, he became steadily more convinced that he needed a firsthand look at the period. He needed a personal touch. The diaries were essential.

Yet he would not risk the mails. There were no copies. No, he would have to wait for Tammy's arrival and she could not leave until the children were out of school. He felt an impatience, though he wasn't sure whether it was for Tammy or his father.

That was all behind him. Right now he was in his study, sitting at his desk, which he had built right into the dormer window, with time to read the journals at last.

Back to February 1926. Now that he had mastered the handwriting, more or less, he returned to the start of it all. It began with a death.

It was the month his father's first wife died. Weakened by a difficult pregnancy, the first Mrs. Means gave in to scarlet fever. Even the very rich died of scarlet fever in 1926.

In fifteen years she had failed to give him a child and heir. Not that she hadn't tried. She had done her duty. At the moment when it must have seemed that duty was indeed rewarded, it killed her instead. An infant was buried *in utero*. They would have, Kraft thought, made an interesting archaeological find, child in parent—assuming one maintained perfect historical objectivity.

The little books were visually more like diaries than journals. The one with which he started was faded blue. It was once locked with a clasp. He had broken that in the first foray. By now, the book fell open naturally to February 26, 1926. This may have been because a newspaper ad had been pasted there. It was from the *Boston Herald.* It had begun to yellow, but it was entirely legible. It read as follows:

HELP WANTED—FEMALE

Housekeeper of extraordinary qualifications wanted by widower to manage house and staff; should be between 25 and 35; must be completely at ease in any society and competent to run a town house and a summer home each with permanent staff; must be able to buy supplies, order repairs, etc. Must be in vigorous health and have disposition that is invariably sunny, responsive, and spontaneous; must be nominally a Protestant but not obtrusively religious; must be logical and preferably intellectual; must be serious in outlook yet also good-humored. This is an exceptional opportunity for an exceptional individual.

Kraft had read that in the first foray, so long ago now that it had become myth. Here it was again. It prickled his scalp. With his eyes closed he could see cosmic dust out there in deep space, spiraling inward, a faint nebula, the very first sign that something—some body—was about to take shape, particles being drawn together through the gravitational force of the *Boston Herald.*

Meanwhile, there were the dead to bury. The first Mrs. Means and her nameless child *in utero.* Dutifully as a member of the family, Kraft helped vicariously with the burial and the mourning, entry by entry.

> Feb. 21, Sun., 1926. Day of mourning before the funeral. Had to remain home in spite of inclination to go off by myself. Would have preferred to be in Croftham alone— no friends and no staff. Instead, I had to remain on the scene, responding to banal phrases of sympathy.
>
> The sense of loss is terrible. Was in no way prepared for it. The obligation to "keep a good front" is a solace. Keeps me from feeling sorry for self.
>
> Feb. 22, Mon., 1926. Funeral at noon at King's Chapel. The place is not as important to me as it was for my father. I still pay for family pew but of course have not attended except for mandatory funerals and weddings. Associate the place with heavy smell of flowers. Service was conducted by Dr. Sears who married us. Same setting, same voice. Bitter ironies.

The real irony was that he should be drawn back to that church at all. He was an evangelistic atheist. He considered religious faith an insult to the rational mind and excused those who attended church with the same patronizing shrug with which he excused alcoholics.

He maintained membership as if it were a club he no longer used. Unitarians were used to that. He also maintained the pew merely from a sense of familiarity—the way the church itself kept the discredited baptismal font, an inheritance from the days before the war, when King's Chapel was still Church of England.

67

The building was divided into square pew boxes, seats on three sides of each. The Means pew was down front on the right, the family name engraved on a small plaque.

Not the first name, however. *Kraft* was not introduced until 1804. It was the maiden name of a German wife, an infusion of new wealth into the family. Perhaps in gratitude, they had used *Kraft* for the first-born male for four generations.

Except for her, the family roots were English. They had come to the Bay Colony in the second wave—1630. Kraft had heard about the unused family pew when he was an undergraduate. It had struck him as comic, an absurd footnote in history. He took the time to track down the church, and the pew. The plaque was silver but discreet, hidden on the inside.

He stood there on a rainy Wednesday afternoon, stood on the exact spot where his father had during the funeral, where his grandfather had stood regularly, and his great-grandfather. An odd sensation. A clutter of emotions. He tried to sort them out and was not successful.

> Feb. 23, Tue., 1926. Went by train to Croftham for a prolonged weekend. Took the cook and Henly. Met there by Christina and Howard at my invitation. It is a time for a sister's solace and I can always put up with Howard if the shooting is good.
>
> February thaw. Light easterlies. Bay a pale blue. Most beautiful spot in the world. Went hunting with Howard. Poor pickings. Not a pheasant in sight. Entertained ourselves by bagging two woodchucks, three crows, two jays, four starlings, and an old tomcat.

Kraft shuddered. One of the few direct memories he had with his father was murderous: holding a shotgun, firing it at a target shaped like a cow—perhaps a deer—being thrown back by the kick of it, feeling sick at the noise and the smell, cleaning the damn thing. Yes, and another one, the .30-30. Different target. Silhouette of a man. G-man style. Aim for the heart. Shoulder aching, ears ringing, stomach rising and falling.

> Spent evening around the fire with Howard and Christina, their children packed away. Christina expecting and happily knitting things. Howard and I drank too much port, sang old-time songs in harmony for her. Recalled good old days. Shameful sentimentality! How Leona would have loved that evening!

Kraft paused, stared out at the sea before him and the salt marshes off to the right. He would have to stop this browsing. He should either quit altogether or go at it like a scholar, reading the set right through to the end. The end? A bleak phrase.

Odd to feel the old ambivalences. After all these years. The journal was still the private property of another man. But the man had been buried forty years—almost half a century. There was nothing left to him. Not even a body. Surely the deceased give up all rights once they have decayed. Surely he was history at last, public property at last.

There was every reason to invade this territory, take possession. It was a part of Kraft's professional work. And he really should have a second source to verify what he had learned from his mother. As a poor girl joining the clan with some awe, she had accepted the patriarchy as holy, had memorized the genealogy as she once had the tribes of the Bible. Only a woman born in poverty could have presented that family history with such a blend of reverence and periodic disdain.

The incorporation—the creation—was in 1832. The founder, the one whose mother came from Nuremberg and lent her name to all succeeding generations, became known for simplicity's sake as *the Founder*. Rather than buying land, he bought commercial properties scattered in different states. A trust, he called it. More than a century later it would be called a conglomerate. He was not interested in terminology. He just kept adding blocks—warehouses in Philadelphia, docks and dwellings in Boston, a shipyard in Savannah. Unit by unit. Like Monopoly.

Means and Means, he called it, including his infant son by assumption. The firm got its start just as the country's economy did; the two progressed in tandem.

The son took over as expected in midcentury, the firm now twenty years old. He made a good thing of the war. While his fellow Bostonian were calling for abolition and, later, going off to fight, this Means, *the Victorian*, Kraft II, dumped his southern properties just in time and paid $851 for a draft replacement. Then he added a meat-packing plant in Chicago and two railroads. The call for abolition would need both.

He survived the postwar slump nicely, buying back his southern buildings at bargain rates—Kentucky coal, Georgia turpentine, Mississippi shipping—and received from President Johnson a double citation for his patriotic contribution to the Union cause and now to the task of binding up his country's wounds.

It was an expansive age, the 1880s and '90s, and this grandfather of Kraft's, *the Victorian*, was an expansive spirit. He gave up the family summer place in Marblehead—already crowded—and bought a spread of coastline just south of Cape Cod. It was two hours from Boston by express train and almost wholly untouched.

For ten years he, his brother Frederick, and a younger friend of the family set about to redesign nature. They had a harbor dredged, converted marshland into solid land, forced back the Atlantic with sea walls, created channels for their boats and held them against time with jetties. And they built their summer homes—large, sprawling affairs, shingled, set off with lawns and gardens.

Kraft found this period the most reprehensible, the most socially inexcusable, the most fascinating. It drew him like a great obscenity. In a world desperate for reform, for redistribution of the good life, the Meanses were reclaiming Eden for themselves. They had cleared themselves of original sin by buying a pardon and were refurbishing the Garden, complete with plumbing and higher walls. They weren't in the mood to share it.

Steam was their slave force and everywhere black pistons worked for them. The dredge: a barge on which sat a great black boiler, smokestack spuming smoke, engine turning an iron wheel thirty feet high, wheel turning a chain to which were attached scoops, chain and buckets whining and wheezing, descending into the water and rising up the other side filled with mud. The pounding of the pistons and the shrieking of a hundred iron hods being dragged around that wheel could be heard two miles off.

Kraft could hear it, could feel its vibrations, could see the whole scene as if it had been his own childhood, as if the sounds and the photographic record had been implanted in his genes, a racial memory.

Each detail generated more. Back in the woods there was another machine ripping logs to timbers, timbers to boarding, boarding to shakes, enough to shingle a hundred gabled roofs.

Yes, and one more—the largest machine of them all—on the beach. Tall as a locomotive tipped on end, the stack towering above that, guyed with chains, the great flywheel turning a rock crusher, smashing beach stone to gravel for roads, creating sand for concrete. Rock being broken by steel sounds like a herd of cattle at slaughter.

Unlike men. They were silent. Midst all this barking, wheezing, screaming machinery were the laborers, dark-faced men, Cape Verdeans mostly, referred to without rancor as "portagees." Not for half a century would whites discover that their term was the northern version of *"nigger."* Unprotesting, the Cape Verdeans were hard workers, used to long hours weeding in the cranberry bogs. They were willing to dig with pick and shovel for a dollar a day, filling two-wheeled carts drawn by mules, changing the contour of the land, expressionless as Egyptians. If they spoke, no one knew it, the air filled with the cries of steam.

Above them—far above—were the Italian stonecutters, marking boulders, blasting them free, cutting them into slabs, fitting them together for the jetties, breakwaters, and piers.

Still higher were the Yankee carpenters, most of them trained in shipyards, craftsmen who built homes the way they built ships.

Everything on a large scale. Coal for the machines and later for off-season heating was shipped in by barge. In the houses, iceboxes were walk-in vaults, tall enough to hang a stag. Ice was cut in hundred-pound slabs from a man-made pond. Drinking water was pumped to the houses by a windmill copied exactly from Holland's largest. Kraft could remember the insides, dark and shadowy, great iron rods, greased flywheels, enormous cogs. Floor after floor, until at the top, peering out the trap door, you could see across the tops of trees, the tops of houses, right out to a faint line on the horizon which must have been France.

The designer of all this, Kraft's grandfather, was a big, merry man, tall but heavier-set than either his son or his grandson. Kraft had never met him, knew only his beaming smile from a portrait, knew also that he had a special talent for managing slum property.

He died in 1890 of gunshot wounds—some unrecorded dispute with tenants—leaving his motherless seven-year-old son, Kraft's father, in the care of his bachelor brother. All the buildings had been completed and so had the tennis courts, stables, boathouses, the windmill, and a nine-hole golf course. The steam engines had been silenced, dismantled, and shipped off by barge. The portagees had all been fired, the Italians shipped back across the Atlantic, and the Yankee carpenters returned, not to shipyards—the day of wooden hulls was over—but to rural poverty.

The family, winners, entered the twentieth century with a money machine which fueled itself, close to perpetual motion. All it required was minor adjustments, an occasional polish, and protection against the meddling of reformers.

Dull work, that. Bland. Kraft's father, known to his son as the Old Man, inherited Means and Means Inc. intact; also his father's energy. Like the old steam engines, he needed firing, needed pressure. The war kept him busy. As a builder of wooden sub-chasers in Savannah, supplier of Chicago ham, owner of Navy warehouses in South Boston, he was much too important to draft. He did his part— and was paid for it.

With the war over, he became, in addition, manager for the Boston branch of Conti and Co. This brash, energetic New York firm was doing on an international level what the Means family had made such a good thing of doing within the country. Expanding, developing, making inroads on South America, eyeing Europe; it was surely the kind of opportunity the victors deserved after a war like that. "A glorious vision," Kraft's father wrote. "Grand as Marco Polo's."

Now, reading those journals in the quiet of Worwich, Nova Scotia, separated from his parents by almost half a century, by geography, by conviction, by basic philosophy, Kraft IV found himself exerting all his energies to maintain a cool, historical objectivity.

> March 28, Sun., 1926. Am tired of the continuing condolences and empty offers "to help." Am taking another trip to Croftham, this one by myself. Am much in need of a week of solitude and physical exercise.
>
> Took no staff. Met at depot by Mr. Higgs, who drove me in his flivver to the shore and left me. None of the houses open yet, though of course Higgs had the Cottage cleaned and stocked with food and Madeira on short notice.

First day was raw. Wind easterly with a little sleet. Managed to clear winter damage in the pine grove. Uncovered rosebushes partially and removed burlap windguards from rhododendrons.

Kraft could remember making those enormous plants into fortresses, playing in the cool, mossy shadow under thirty feet of green, hiding not from Eden but from the old man.

March 29, Mon., 1926. Wind shifted to the south. Light. Much warmer. Forsythia starting out. All kinds of birds in profusion. But the beauty of it depresses me too. Can't help thinking of how Leona would have loved it. I combat such thoughts with intense activity—mulching rose beds, clearing deadwood, pruning apple trees and grapevines.

The Cottage is a reminder but also a solace. It is perhaps my most treasured inheritance, filled with childhood memories, simple pleasures.

Kraft shook his head in disbelief. Did his father really mean *simple?* Was that possible?

Picture in sepia: A rambling, elegant spread of a house, shingled, fringed with porches and terraces—the "Cottage." Lawns with tree roses (here and in Alice's Wonderland, surely nowhere else); two marble statues (Neptune and Athena), and a copper birdbath shined daily to catch the sun's rays.

Inside, up the stairs, down the hall—the nursery. Still called that, though it became Kraft's room for as long as the house survived, he being the only child. The nursery: large, with a bear rug, a fireplace, a bust of Marcus Aurelius on the mantle. On the sea side, two large built-in bureaus, between which was a dormer window with cushioned bench about the size of a child's bunk, a kind of nest from which a fledgling could watch the sea. The green glow of the lawns and the flow of the waves, which he studied from there by the hour, washed into his dreams, would not wash out.

They washed back now as he stared out over his Nova Scotian marshland.

> March 30, Tue., 1926. Old Higgs by in the morning to see how I was. He will move into barn chambers next week when grounds staff move back. Today he simply worked along with me almost without a word. Typical.
>
> After he left, I burned some brush on the beach. Found a dead seal. Terrible smell. Tried to burn carcass, with little success. Terrible how one loses what one wants and can't get rid of what one tries to discard.
>
> Had odd experience. Was standing there at twilight, poking the fire and the smoldering corpse, utterly alone. Bay and beach deserted, dead calm, not a breath. Had the distinctly morbid impression that I too had died. Felt like some displaced spirit. Was struck by a crushing depression, almost despair. A shocking self-indulgence.

"Suicidal," Kraft said aloud.

"No, only a dark despair," his father said.

"Suicidal. And no thought of me."

"Of course no thought of you. Not even a conception of your existence."

"So you would have taken me along with you."

"If I had in fact done away with myself, of course I would have done away with you."

"Like that? Not a thought?"

"Of *course* not a thought. You weren't a conception, I tell you. I hadn't even met your mother. You were nothing. A cipher."

"Not now. You've got things backward. Right now, *you're* the cipher. Zero. You understand? Nothing."

8

Kraft jumped up, started to leave the room. Conversations like that weren't healthy. Nothing new. They had been going on. But not healthy.

He was about to go downstairs, make himself some coffee, perhaps do more scything, go for a walk. But the sound of women's voices stopped him at the door.

Tammy and Thea. The two of them right here in his house. Not good. Keep clear of them. When the house was officially cleaned, perhaps he could get rid of Thea. No telling what might slip. A simple phrase would do it, would blow everything up. Dangerous as fire. But he would have to chance it. Just stay clear of them.

He stepped back from the door, a prisoner in his own study. Bound to his work. Well, not a bad servitude, really. He should get back to it. To hell with the journals. His manuscript. It was right there.

He knew exactly where he was, where he had to take it up again, where he should move on from. He was up to the early Roosevelt years, had completed the campaign of 1932, had proved conclusively that Roosevelt had no conception of a New Deal during that period, had no notion what to offer but that radiant smile of confidence, did not even recognize the value of the slogan *"New Deal"* when he used it almost parenthetically in his inauguration speech, and from there on moved as he always moved, not as a radical or even a dedicated liberal but a pragmatist, an over-rated pragmatist at that. His reputation, like that of most heroes, had been simplified, exaggerated, distorted.

Kraft would set the record straight. His notes were all there, almost down to the paragraph. All that remained was for him to render his logic and convictions into a flow of cohesive language.

He sat down at his desk with a burst of energy and determination. And picked up his father's journal.

> . . . a crushing depression, almost despair. A shocking self-indulgence. Was tempted to return to Boston early. Worked out of it with long run along beach and then a hot rum in front of fire. Will stay to end of week. Reassuring to know that staff and household affairs at Boston are now in good hands. Miss Winslow has taken over as new house-keeper. She is young but astonishingly efficient.

"Ah!" from Kraft. For there she was, Miss Hilda Winslow, housekeeper, winner of the twenty-five applicants. He had read that particular entry years before, but her entrance was still a dramatic moment—like a famous actress stepping on stage: "Oh, this is my new housekeeper," and the audience breaks into applause which has nothing to do with the action of the play, has everything to do with who the player is. Kraft was greeting his mother.

Hilda Winslow, country girl. Raised in a small town on the Bay side of Cape Cod. A tall, lanky girl. At fourteen she was driving the school barge—a long, open two-horse wagon—and having to discipline the cutups and wiseacres. Had trouble until her father taught her to use a fifteen-foot bullwhip accurately enough to flip off buttons. No trouble after that.

She was a good Baptist girl. She had never danced, played

cards, sipped wine, or touched a boy. Cape Cod was not yet contaminated by tourists. It was very rural. She had been taught that the seeds of a tomato would kill you and she knew from experience how many hours it took picking them out with tweezers. She knew that the devil existed in visible form, crouching in the wood closet or under the bed, ready to touch your thigh with his long, scaly finger.

She had been baptized in the sea, townspeople on the beach singing, some wailing. It was a ceremony which, if repeated on the same Cape Cod beach today, would bring indignant protests.

She took off for the city as soon as she could. So did four out of five in that family. The only one left was insane. In Boston, she went to nursing school. Flu epidemic made a farce out of training program. Everyone too busy taking care of the dead. Bodies lined up in the hallways. Main problem was to keep the rats from gnawing them before someone took them off to wherever they went. Hilda Winslow's training consisted of guarding corpses in the corridors, midnight to ten in the morning. They armed her with a poker. To hell with nursing.

Then a job as "companion" to an elderly block of a woman named Mrs. Jamieson. The old Bostonian was tough and active, but she needed help to fight off what she imagined to be creeping senility. Insisted that her companion study for and receive a chauffeur's license—this including the skills of changing a tire (pry casing off rim with a wrecking bar; patch puncture; work tube and casing back on; pump up to pressure; allow one hour working time), also changing oil, greasing, removing and cleaning plugs, etc. Drove Mrs. Jamieson out West in 1921. Was the first driver to make it up to the top of Pikes Peak that spring. May have been the first woman driver to do same in any season. Took great pleasure in driving. Detested Mrs. Jamieson.

Somewhere Kraft had seen a photo of Hilda Winslow at the wheel. Tall, straight-backed, long hands, long fingers curled around the wheel, a Roman nose, large and dark eyes. She could have been a Vogue model in period costume.

She hadn't discovered her beauty yet. The nurses didn't notice. The corpses didn't speak. And Mrs. Jamieson kept it a secret. Companions are hard to find. So Hilda still thought she was an awkward, too-tall country girl. But beneath those layers of Baptist repression there were needs which startled her.

"When I first worked for your father," she told Kraft years later, "I was a very lonely young girl. I can remember going down to Filene's bargain basement just to brush against people."

When she told him this, she was dying of cancer. She had been a widow for six years. The nursing home was filled with much older people. Again she was lonely. Wistfully, she told him that there were only two experiences she would like to have once more: eating lobster thermidor and having sexual intercourse. Neither was likely.

Everything was running out for her then. But that was much later. Back in 1926, the tide for her was on the flood. She had never slept with a man or tasted lobster thermidor. All that was sweeping toward her. Kraft marched on into April.

April 17, Sat., 1926. Completed train trip tour of Detroit, Chicago, and Cincinnati offices. Thirteen meetings and conferences in two days. Returned via New York. Midnight conference with Conti in his apt. re. Argentine holdings. Limitless possibilities. Limitless.

April 18, Sun., 1926. Took day off. Slept three hours and then drove Miss Winslow to Arnold Arboretum, which except for Croftham is my favorite spot. Great profusion of budding and blossoming apple, dogwood, pear trees. Miss Winslow shows remarkable talent for retaining Latin names which I give her.

Took her to dinner rather than face the tedium of another

meal at home. Also managed to obtain two tickets to Gillette's *Sherlock Holmes.* Astonished to discover that Miss Winslow has never seen a play of any sort. Hard to imagine such wide-eyed joy in an adult.

Joy? In an adult? How long had it been since he had felt an emotion like that? A few whiffs, perhaps, during that first summer at Worwich. And from time to time in Hildy's eyes. But what would it be like to know an adult— a woman—who was still capable of wide-eyed joy?

April 30, Fri., 1926. A harried morning at the Means office. Situation in England has shocked investors here. King George's proclamation of a national emergency is entirely justified. Baldwin has to add that they are on the edge of civil war. Damn fool should keep his mouth shut. A general strike will ruin them. May well be the end of stable govt. in England. Reaction on State St. is anxious uncertainty. Major investment decisions being postponed.

After a full morning at Means office, spent most of afternoon at Conti regional planning session. Managed to sneak out early enough for a motor tour with Miss W. Went by ferry to East Boston and around through Charlestown to inspect tenements of Dwelling House Associates. Have been buying and selling in units of three or more to save legal fees. Negro tenants still paying 10% to 15% higher rent to move into mixed neighborhoods which don't stay mixed for long. Block must be sold just before tip point. Timing is everything. A fascinating chess game with considerable profit.

In evening played Vivaldi sections on violin with Miss W. as appreciative audience.

Kraft stopped reading. Only with difficulty did he recover his historical objectivity. As an evasive tactic he concentrated on that violin. It was still vivid in his memory and noncontroversial. It was a rich golden brown, almost a living thing. The case was a dark blue. It was about the same shade and degree of wear as the cover of the volume he was then reading. After being played, the violin went back in the case and the two latches were snapped shut, *clak . . . clak.* He could recall that sound better than the playing.

The catches were brass and pitted—like the clasps which once locked each volume of the journals until he wrenched them open with a screwdriver in that first raid more than two decades earlier. Raid? The term made him a fellow traveler with Goths and Vandals.

He studied the cover of the 1926 volume again, fingering its dead-dry, faded blue surface, letting it nudge his memory. It was like the blue tie-print kerchief which his father kept in the violin case and placed under his chin when he played.

Picture: A lean, tower of a man, violin firmly under his chin, body swaying slightly, not keeping time but as if bent by the music, his expression unchanging, intense concentration, angular jaw set, slightly blue with stubble which even a straight razor could not clear, beads of sweat seeping into that handkerchief.

The image was sharp, detailed, because Kraft at eight and nine had been compelled to endure weekly musicales as if somehow they would improve his moral fiber: his father and three or four friends playing—the men in tuxedos and the women in long dresses—and perhaps four others as "audience," sipping cordials. Nothing for a boy to do in the aging company but study the lean, towering figure with the angular jaw slightly blue with stubble, and the beads of sweat seeping into that kerchief. Nothing to do but study it carefully, memorize it, record it like a camera. And cultivate his hatred.

> May 1, Şat., 1926. Another heavy day divided between the two offices. No time for lunch. Strong tea brought to desk. Work is a blessing. Without it, I would get despondent.

In the evening, Miss W. is a great comfort. She has meals with me, which dispels the boredom of being served alone. Also a safeguard against self-pity. When there is time, I practice the violin and she listens with fascination and wonder. After each piece she asks questions. What key was it in? Which movement was it? Would I repeat the dominant theme? She has never heard music before, much less studied it. My Miranda!

We are also working on Brazilian history & economics (re. Rio holdings). I read chapters aloud. Miss W. has an extraordinarily retentive mind.

May 2, Sun., 1926. News from England is dark. Trades Union Council has voted to call a general strike. A shockingly immoral decision. Country is heading for anarchy.

Played squash at noon today. Was doing well until I broke a tendon. Had to hop to taxi and home to bed. Great pain. Fury.

May 3, Mon., 1926. In bed all day. Considerable pain. In a foul mood because of work pending at both offices. Will have to postpone inspection of Chicago meat-packing plant. Suddenly realized there is no one at Means office whose judgment I trust. Shrewd men are in terribly short supply.

Only consolation in present mess is that Miss W. not only manages to run house staff flawlessly but is a talented nurse as well. She is patient, thoughtful, sweet, entertaining. Has been reading aloud to me.

Being in bed where Leona died adds to my daily heartaches and sorrow. Cannot help reviewing her last days and moments.

Spent afternoon on telephone. Had to forgo pain-killers to keep head clear. Stopped phoning at 6.00 p.m. and had Miss W. refuse all calls. Took rum and something Dr. Manning provided—probably codeine. Floating sensation. Beats liquor. Miss W. turns out to be a remarkable masseuse.

May 4, Tue., 1926. Still in bed. Day of big parade of 26th Division. Normally I watch it from Gen. Edwards' house on Commonwealth Ave. He has fine stock of port. He also knows military tactics the way more refined men know chess. A great pleasure to hear him. But had to forego all that because of bum foot.

Miss W. watched from the street. Reported that it was bitter cold. Unseasonable. Snow flurries with gale winds. Several seaplanes flying around. One crashed in the bay. Damn fool.

May 5, Wed., 1926. England in economic convulsions. Like watching a drowning man. Big question on State Street is whether we'll be dragged under too.

Called cab and managed to get into office. Hobbled about on crutches. Felt like a damn cripple. In a terrible temper most of the day. Secretary in tears. Fired her without notice. Chaos in both offices, of course.

Home after 7.00. Pain worse due to activity. Miss W. apparently watched me prepare a hot rum grog sometime last week and had a perfect one waiting for me on my arrival. She has an extraordinary sensitivity to other people's needs, is completely unself-conscious, and absolutely even and sweet in disposition. Has a tremendous amount of character and ability. Flawless!

"Flawless!" Kraft put the volume down, his face prickling with envy. Was it really possible to believe in perfection then? When they spoke of love, did they say it straight without putting it in quotes by gesture, without laying on enough sarcasm to protect themselves? What had happened in the decades since then to make even the word absurd?

He sighed, breathed deeply, a diver about to descend again. Mid-May, 1926, and his father was about to take an extended business trip to New York. There were apparent references to Conti Associates, but they were in code. A simple precaution.

May 17, Mon., 1926. Took 8.30 a.m. train to N.Y.C. Had lengthy and rewarding conference with jIEMB re. Conti Assoc. (BGFL) for lunch and afterward in hotel. Celebrated with claret cup at Henri's. Leisurely five-course dinner at Delmonico's. Excellent cognac and good cheer. Then to Mrs. Fiske in "Miss Nell of N'Orleans" in evening. Arrived late, but no problem since we had box seats. After theatre we went to Hotel Claridge basement for drinks. A most unusual and rewarding sort of evening.

Kraft had used this as anecdote years ago. "Typically American," he would say. "An honest and open journal except for his business affairs. Those he put in code."

It was an easy, offhand judgment, an entertaining irony; but now that he was taking his time with the entries, he found this section puzzling. Why the claret cups at Henri's and the theater engagement when normally he would not allow himself time off for lunch? What would make that man of tight scheduling arrive at the theater late and not even worry about it?

It was the "conference with jIEMB re. Conti Assoc. (BGFL)" which didn't quite ring true. There were no figures here to hide and no contracts signed. An underworld character? Claret cups at Henri's with the Mafia?

He decided then to break the code. Chances were that it was simple. Kraft wrote out the alphabet on two sheets so that he could line them up and then slide them first up and then down. He tried various alternatives. None produced words. But by moving each letter back one, B to A, C to B, "jIEMB" became "IHDLA." Vaguely familiar. Ah! Reverse each pair of letters: "HILDA."

So Kraft III was off to New York with his beautiful housekeeper, Hilda. Flawless indeed! And following the same code, Kraft IV learned that the next phrase, "re. Conti Assoc.," was "Fake."

"A trick. Set for me? Did you know I would go prying? How could you guess? I was only eleven when you quit on me. You hardly knew me."

Or was it only to guard against servants? Always worried

about domestics spying, always tearing up letters, locking journals. Codes. Ciphers. Just a touch of paranoia.

"Got to watch that talking out loud," Kraft muttered. It came from living alone too much. A bad sign. A symptom. Like the storekeeper up on the main road who had been locked up the previous January, committed, packed off to a Halifax asylum, talking a mile a minute. Old Mr. McKnight blamed it on the Nova Scotia climate and that seemed reasonable.

Plunging back into the journal, Kraft struggled once again to maintain his cool, historical detachment. It shouldn't be difficult. After all, he was forty-nine and his subject was only forty-three. That should give him the upper hand. It was crazy to be calling his subject "the Old Man." He wasn't even old yet. More of a kid brother. A muddleheaded kid brother.

Kraft didn't approve of this adventure. After all, what did these two have in common? What would come of it all?

He tried to concentrate on the Old Man's financial activities instead. They were charged with hard work, courage, and an inborn instinct for exploitation. There was something solid and familiar in all that. It was a pattern with which he as a historian could deal. Here was the avarice which opened the West and industrialized the North. It was a part of his country's heritage.

June 9, Wed., 1926. Busy day in N.Y.C. Negotiations in a.m. with three U.S. firms and a Brazilian holding company. Spent afternoon in four-hour planning session at Conti office. Dinner and late-evening session with Samuel Conti himself in his apartment. Place slightly ostentatious. Discussed new steamship line to Cuba. Once launched, we can move in on S.A. trade routes. Conti has boundless energy. Six hours of conversation w. no drinks! Endless plans. Future looks good indeed.

June 10, Thur., 1926. Up after four hrs. sleep. Spent day at Conti office. Successfully launched our participation with Blake Bros. in Conn. Mills. 7% Pfd. Tax Free in Mass. @ 98½. Big Rio Issue launched. Twice oversubscribed. $10,000,000 serial 6½% basis. Great success and awakened lively interest. Put in fifteen-hour day & returned to Boston on the midnight train.

June 11, Fri., 1926. Met at South Station in early morning by jIEMB. Headed for Croftham secretly. Parked on country road in drizzle somewhere between Milton & Stoughton. Hot kidney pie served in chafing dish on jump seat in back of car. A cozy feast—like cruising. Then continued to Croftham. Built roaring fire. Had place to self w/out servants, and no one else has moved down yet. Much tender conversation, but both of us influenced by constraints.

June 12, Sat., 1926. Woke to sound of song sparrow. Beats hell out of any English nightingale.

Early morning fog burned off by 8.00. Sea utterly calm with traces of mist. The air still. Sun and sea brilliant. Breakfast in kitchen. Saw doe and buck feeding near rose garden as trusting as if this were Paradise.

Toured property for rest of morning. Assistant took notes on clipboard, all very formal in a comic sort of way. Front lawn gutted in places by winter storms; sea wall needs masonry repair again; beach needs rock removal; bathhouses need trim paint, rhododendrons slightly wind-damaged and need pruning and heavy feeding. Path to Howard and Christina's needs clearing, tennis courts will require complete new surface this season. Usual details. Pleasure to have secretarial assistant.

Haze gone by noon. Had picnic of chicken and a new Alsatian white which has more novelty than quality. Price somewhat inflated by bootleggers, but worth it. Ate in lee of greenhouses for warmth. Watched hummingbirds and a family of chipmunks.

After short snooze we went for four-mile walk. Found

old trail through Uncle Frederick's woodlands and came out on meadow at head of Marsh Harbor. Red-wing blackbirds in profusion. Two mallards and a great blue heron feeding in tidal pond. Sun more like August.

Rested in the fall grass. Explored new aspects of the relationship. A leisurely unfolding. Eventually and splendidly the PDtONVBNJUOP was made PDQNfMFU and FQgSDFU—re. Conti Assoc. stock option (BGFL).

And so in salt hay the "CONSUMMATION" was made "COMPLETE and PERFECT," and as usual the reference to Conti Associates was "FAKE."

Marsh Harbor. So that was where it happened. Kraft remembered the very spot, but from the other side. He used to enter a narrow opening from the sea in his kayak, used to spend hours exploring the channels. Those winding inlets working up into the marshland were a primal realm.

He remembered it first as fact. Yes, he had been there. He had seen that very pond, that bank, that field. Now he saw the boy he once was, paddling a homemade kayak. It was red. The paddler turned first one way and then the other, mobile as a tiny, wriggling fish, working his way upstream, the dank saline smell heavy about him, past tall grasses and peaty banks.

The boy beckons. Startled, Kraft realizes that this child of eight, this explorer with his own name, is reaching out to him. It is a seductive invitation and he gives in, allows recollection to slide into fantasy.

Kraft is the boy in the kayak now, reeds high on either side. He sees them part before him, whispering against the canvas sides. He is startled by the splash of an otter, a vibrato of wings. Then silence so perfect he can hear crabs scuttling.

There are only inches of water under him. He hears the bottom scrape on the sea moss and eelgrass. He begins to use his paddle as a pole.

The headwaters: That is what he is seeking. Like the Nile. No, more mysterious than the Nile. No historian has written up this search because no explorer has come here before him. Virgin territory, a white, unprinted section on the map. He alone would find the headwaters.

Surprisingly, the channel grows deeper now. Wider too. He begins paddling again. Could this be the source at last? Possible, yet he has the distinct impression that he had never really reached it. Something is happening; this is no longer pure memory.

He forces his prow through a thicket of cattails and catches his breath as he finds himself in a salt pond. In the center he sees two herons standing motionless, one upright and one inverted in the mirror of the sky, the two joined, one real and the other illusory, identical.

Noiselessly they part, moving in opposite directions. Will they ever meet again?

He paddles across this dream pond to the other side. The land is solid there, a field of salt hay dotted with wild plum. Startled, he sees a couple in the tall grass, half hidden. Gently he takes silent strokes in their direction, left and right, stalking, cautious. He is oddly aware that this cannot be memory. He is witness to a scene previous to his own birth, a scene intimately connected with his own birth. He moves as if a single splash of his paddle will dissolve the illusion, cause it to lift like morning haze.

They are clothed, entwined. Two more strokes. They kneel, facing each other, and begin removing clothes. Water drips from his paddle; sweat trickles across his forehead. Their bodies appear to be naked now. He can hardly believe it until he sees the dark patch of the man's groin.

They are prone now, deep in salt hay. He watches the forms—an arm, a leg, the curve of a buttock—writhing in what he takes to be joy, not a struggle. The greens of the marshland and the flashes of rosy skin sing harmony to him, though there is also an ache in his stomach.

Play turns to rhythm, regular. A loon's cry; and then they are still. The boy breathes deeply, backs off, wanting to give them privacy yet not willing to turn his back.

Left paddle, right paddle, blades dripping. The couple grows smaller. They stand and dress. Left paddle, right paddle. The couple begins to walk away from him, hands clasped, as he glides back from them. Noiselessly he and they part from each other, moving in opposite directions. The space between them widens. Will he ever be rejoined?

9

July 2. This is the third day with the family here. I still see them strangely. It's as if they were on film. I watch their images flicker and listen to their talk. I am fascinated but removed. I am still not a part of this.

It's worse than that. It's as if I hardly knew them. Like old home movies. Figuring out who is who. My own family. Don't put *that* in your journal.

I am fond of them, but I have been so involved with my work I can hardly reach them.

My work? That's the myth. Recorded right there in a personal, private journal. Am I obliged to admit that I've been daydreaming my time away here? And Thea? Should I put her in code? I write what I can't say out loud, but I think what I can't write. And is there thinking I can't admit to myself, can't locate? Boxes within boxes.

Tammy is so brisk and competent. I suppose more so for having run things in my absence. A real organizer.

A real pain. How marvelously responsive she was as a student!

> And Weldon—so self-contained for a boy of fifteen. A quiet, stubborn independence.

Crazy, his insisting on using his middle name. Weldon is no name for a boy. It was only intended to fill the space in applications. Some hidden hostility, no doubt, to the non-New England sound of it. But hell, he doesn't even know what New England is. No real sense of regional identity.

Kraft lifted his eyes from his journal and said softly: "It isn't easy, you know, having a family and a professional commitment like mine. A lot of fancy footwork. Diplomacy. Not easy." He half expected Thea to say, "I know, I know"; but she wasn't there.

"Hey, Dad." Ric's voice. Full of energy. Enthusiastic. Demanding. His mother's genes? "You coming or not?"

"I'm working, goddamn it."

"But you promised. . . ." He stopped, cut off by Tammy's voice telling him to shut up, reminding him in tones which drifted up the stairs clearly, intentionally, that his father had a lot of work to do, that he had a manuscript that just *had* to be finished.

"O.K.," Kraft shouted. "Right after lunch. If the weather holds." He didn't need Tammy's subtle suggestions.

He turned back to his own journal.

> If Weldon is aloof, then Ric makes up for it. Thirteen is two years less sophisticated. But it's more than age. There will always be show biz in him. I'm an audience for him.

Audience. Kraft paused on that one. Who was *his* audience in his own journals? Someone he trusted. Children at some future date, perhaps. After his death? Children grown adult and understanding. How long will that take?

It was quite possible that most of what he had said aloud

to Tammy since her arrival had been oblique, slightly off the truth. Or downright dishonest. Yes, completely so. Sparring. Well, at least his journals were honest. Mostly. Or at least partly. Errors by omission. Deletion. To protect the guilty. Perhaps worse than no journal at all, since it was a false story. No, not false; just amended. Given a certain wholeness. Ragged edges snipped off. Surely this was a better gift than no message at all, than utter silence. Surely half truths were better than blank pages.

"Hildy is the most unspoiled," he wrote. "The most honest. It is more than being only eleven. She will always be true."

He paused, read over the paragraph, making sure that he had mentioned all three in equal terms. Like balancing Christmas presents.

That was enough for July 2. This was the third. It always seemed vaguely dishonest to write about a previous day as if one was in the middle of it. Occasionally he would slip a week behind—even a month during busy times— and still maintain the as-if-now voice. Even if his memory altered history a bit, the dishonesty could be paid for in verisimilitude. Couldn't it?

> July 3. This afternoon I went fishing with Ric. He wore me down with arguments. All his challenges: Did I want to be one of those absentee parents? Was I trying to escape my own children? My role as the head of the family? Was I so goal-oriented as to exclude my own family? "Goal-oriented"! Jargon at 13! All this delivered with a grin—a featherweight boxer throwing quick jabs. Unlimited energy. I'm not up to it. Driven to the ropes.
>
> Hate fishing. Murderous sport. Hate being trapped in a boat with no cabin, no escape from the sun. Nightmare of being adrift in a lifeboat. Hoped all morning for rain or wind. Weather remained obstinately clear. Sun brilliant. Air still. Seas glassy. Beach actually hot under foot for the first

time this season. All elements plot against me. My son included.

Still, I went through with it. Played the good bourgeois father. And it really wasn't so bad. The sea was flat as a parking lot, the air cool, the hum of the motor soothing. We caught no fish, which was fine with me, and I did an enormous amount of valuable reading in. . . .

Stop! You can't say that. It hasn't happened yet.

Absurd, this habit of finishing the day's entry before the day was half over. Absurd and risky. How much easier, though, than having to live it out hour by hour.

Directly after lunch, Kraft—true to promise and prophecy—was at sea. He was sitting sideways on the center seat, stiff and frowning in his discontent, hand clutching a slim volume in which he had expected and predicted that he would do "an enormous amount of valuable reading." It was a penetrating analysis of the legal decisions of Felix Frankfurter. The print was very small.

His eyes froze, snow-blind, on a blur of gray lines against a field of white glare. He was acutely conscious of the fact that Ric was running that miserable motor at its top speed— absurdly uneconomic—and that in spite of its winter overhaul by native craftsmen whose own lives depended on motors like this one, it missed at irregular moments. He was also conscious of the fact that Ric was going a hell of a long way out. There was nothing in Felix Frankfurter's career that could outweigh that.

He had misjudged the sea too. Glassy it was, without a ripple; but what he had not seen from the shore was that it rose and fell in long undulations. The boat climbed and descended as if crossing dunes. Kraft hated the motion as much as the sound.

When the roar finally did drop to a mild throb, trolling

speed, they were nowhere. The coast had shrunk to a smudgy line. And even that disappeared in each descent. The rest of the uncertain horizon was unbroken, blue against blue. Entirely unpeopled. Unnerving.

Ric moved fast, as if there were fish all about them just under the surface. Kraft watched, peering over the top of his book, his bulwark. He missed nothing. The energy. The sureness. The self-taught skill.

Like his mother, Ric assumed that everyone shared his unlimited energy, his perpetual involvement, his continual motion. Normality puzzled him; daydreaming alarmed him. Like that morning. He had forgotten that there was no acoustical privacy in that house, had said to his mother, voice drifting upward to Kraft's study, "What's wrong with Dad?" The question cut through Kraft's concentration on his father's journal. "Like sometimes he just stares into space."

"He's very wrapped up in his work." Tammy, covering. But it couldn't have satisfied either of them. Staring at space was incomprehensible for them. You could stare at a book, stare at the *Times* for the length of a sightless Sunday, even stare at public television, but stare at space and you're ready for electroshock.

Electroshock? Headache! How long had he had that? He had *claimed* one at lunch, had used it as a final excuse to avoid the agony of fishing. He was told earnestly by his son that he should ignore it, that it was just psychosomatic.

"Where on earth did you learn that?" Kraft asked. "In Life Science or Sex Education?"

"Oh, come on; it's right out of *Mad.*"

"You might as well go," Tammy said. He wasn't sure whether she meant "mad" or "fishing." Small difference. In any case, she had switched her position from pushing work to supporting recreation. No real shift, though; she supported anything as long as it was active.

Right then she was working to open a stuck window, deftly tapping a chisel along the crack, spreading the swollen frame, talking to him over her shoulder. She had a blue work shirt on and a red bandanna around her head—the uniform of the barricades.

"Might as well what?"

"Go."

"Fishing?"

"Anything. I mean, it's not exactly healthy sitting up there all day."

"Never mind about my health."

"*Some*one has to. You need sun and air. You're musty."

"Oh, come on," Ric said. "He shouldn't go fishing because it's *healthy*. Jesus!"

"Lay off the profanity," Tammy said, pounding up on the window.

"Why? It's not *my* religion."

"It is if you have to dump on it, pal. Hey, give me a hand." The two of them shoved up on the window frame, grunting. It slid up. "There," she said. "We could do with some fresh air in here."

Fresh air? Kraft had ended up in the boat in the middle of nowhere not because of any respect for fresh air but simply because, he decided, of his son. The boy wanted company. He wanted his father's company. Now, that was something.

Belief in fresh air as a folk curative was one of Tammy's few irrational convictions. He blamed it on her New York upbringing. Having known from childhood that city air was poisonous, she believed by extension that rural air was miraculous. Whenever someone was sick in their Worwich place, she opened the sickroom windows as if rural oxygen had the powers of rebirth.

Well, here he was in the middle of the unpolluted Atlantic, rising and falling on a glassy, undulating sea, baking healthily in direct sunlight, and moving through what was doubtless as pure a sample of air as any since before the industrial revolution, and he felt like throwing up.

The boy's line was over the side and played out in moments. He trolled in silence, drawing the line toward him from time to time as if to imitate the erratic pace of some small fish. The motor continued to cough; the sea rose and fell, rose and fell.

"I got it," he said suddenly. "I got it. I knew this was the spot." He was pulling in the line hand over hand, not bothering to coil it on the board. Kraft wondered how on earth his son had marked this section of the ocean.

"Hey!" The line had come taut, went slack, snapped tight again. With no rod, there was no way to play the fish except by letting tangled line out. "Bastard!" Ric pulled back in and almost at once let ten feet run out.

"You could help," he said without looking up, concentrating on the activity of the line. "All that tangle—could you get it coiled? This mother's giving me a hard time."

"Lay off that expression."

"Mother?"

"You know what it's short for."

"Motherfucker."

"Not very pretty, right?"

"Jeez, it's just a fish." He grinned without looking up. "Fish don't have the same taboos."

"Just lay off."

Shrug. Silence. Ric continued. Occasionally the fish would seem to be coming straight for the boat and Ric would dump great hanks of line beside him; without warning it would streak out. Knotted tangles of line went overboard.

"Aren't you going to help?"

"It's your show."

The boy looked back over his shoulder at his father. Kraft tapped his book in explanation. Ric turned back to his work.

No matter how clear Kraft had made it that he was along

only for the ride, Ric would expect him to join the action. He had never learned how one might conceivably want to do something alone. He was forever inviting his father or his older brother to fish or hunt crows with his .22 or play chess or badminton or throw a baseball back and forth in endless tedium.

It was not just with sports; he couldn't even *read* without looking up every five minutes and delivering passages aloud to anyone who would not throw a pillow at him. Naturally, he preferred works which lent themselves to oral rendition—Buchwald over Max Lerner, Brautigan over Vance Packard, Vonnegut over Marx. Performance over substance.

Kraft spied on his son, peering over the top of his book, noticed that the boy had placed another line and silver spinner with wire leader on the seat next to his father as a lure, assuming that no one could resist sharing the sport. Ric had no notion of how compelling one's inner life might be.

Since for him outer life was everything, he had become a sportsman. The only one in the family. A throwback. Kraft never dared to tell the boy about his grandfather's shotgun and .30–30 rifle which lay interred in shrouds of oily sheeting in a locked seachest back at the house. They had been unused since the old man's death—almost forty years now. Moved from house to house, they had ended here for dead storage. Secretly. At the very mention of such treasures to Ric, an electric spark would arc across half a century, linking two generations which had never met. And Kraft himself would be the conductor. Some jolt!

His father had more, of course; a collection of hunting pieces as well as a revolver. All sold but two—these saved because Kraft himself had been taught to fire them, could remember handling them, recalled them with fascination and revulsion.

Sportsman? The old man was more of a born killer. He caught fish, speared eels, shot quail, ducks, geese, deer, woodchucks, pheasants, stray dogs. As one of the many articles of faith which ordered his world, he believed that you could not plant a grapevine without throwing a dead cat in the hole for nutriment.

It unnerved Kraft to see his son with a gun or line. Bad blood coming to the surface. Not that he was a pacifist. No, guns had their place. So did pacifists. He had a secret admiration for the Quakers, their pigheaded refusal to bear arms; and he read with grudging respect the nonviolent set—Thoreau, Gandhi, King. But he could never quite forgive them for bowing before fascism. When it came to wars of liberation, his support was automatic, a position which was repeated in almost every article he wrote. *(The litmus paper which differentiated liberals from radicals during the Korean and Vietnamese wars was always a matter of determining first priorities: peace or liberation.)*

Blood sports were another thing. A leisure-class activity, a needless destruction of natural resources, an arrogance of the rich in ignoring the need of the poor. Only here— living as a family commune, eating what they killed—could he justify hunting and fishing in political terms. But that didn't mean he had to enjoy it.

He sat there, hands gripping the book before him, his eyes on Ric, whose performance was both absurd and admirable.

The fish was suddenly at the side of the boat. Ric reached over the gunwale and just as suddenly pulled back. "Holy shit!" He gave a great tug on the line and flipped the thing into the bottom of the boat. "Dogfish," he shouted. "Watch out!"

Corpse-white, two feet long, it was a lean, agile shark. It flipped over and over, tangling itself in fish line, the tackle box, the pail. Ric picked up an oar and tried to hit it. He had lost his cool, striking wildly, leaping forward and jumping back, rocking the boat. "The knife," he was shouting. "Get the knife."

Kraft dropped his book, found a knife in the clutter of equipment spilled in the bottom of the boat; he also grabbed a rusty wrench. Stumbling back to Ric, he saw that the boy's leg was bleeding. The dogfish, belly up for a moment, bared rows of teeth more murderous than a Doberman's.

Ric stunned the fish momentarily with the oar, grabbed the knife from his father, tried to drive it through the gills. The fish gave a lunge and Kraft tried to hold it down, one hand on its dorsal fin, knife-sharp; with the other he kept beating with the bloody wrench.

Picture: A city street; two policemen beating a prone form; a billy club rises and falls, blood on the pavement; legs and arms convulse, the form twisting, writhing; the truncheon rises and falls, rises and falls.

It occurred to them finally that they were striking a dead fish. Ric's knife had worked its way clean through, had opened both gills. Kraft's weapon had crushed the entire head to a mass of blood and cartilage. There was no way of knowing how long they had continued in needless fear and unspent fury. Their hands, the bottom of the boat, the seats were covered with blood. Kraft wondered how much was theirs.

"Holy cow!" Ric grinned, sat back against the gunwale, wiped his brow, streaking it with blood.

Kraft smiled, a fellow victor, the good guy at the end of the war film. He also felt tricked, trapped. Somehow he had been maneuvered into laughing at a bad joke. A flicker of a memory. Then they were both leaning over the side of the boat, washing the blood from their hands in the sea.

Ric broke into his Indian chief routine: "Paleface do O.K. on initiation. Secret bond. Him now blood brother."

"Paleface grateful, but him no like bloody business. Him go back to book now."

He wiped his hands on his pants, helped pick up the boat in a half-hearted way, and then went back to Felix

Frankfurter. Ric broke out a new line and started trolling. Kraft squinted, concentrating on the text. The lines of print blurred against the glare, unintelligible. His hands, holding the book before him, trembled.

10

In an hour's time, Ric caught three reasonable, edible fish. Kraft had no idea what kind they were. They flopped in the bucket piteously, slowly dying of sunlight and healthy fresh air.

After that there were no bites. Not even nibbles. Sweat trickled down Kraft's neck; his shirt was soaked. He kept thinking about the fish in the bucket. That was a hell of a way to go. He wished they would lie down and die.

"How much more of this are you planning to do?"

"We don't have to do any." Ric shrugged. "I thought maybe you were getting to like it."

Like it? Sitting in this stinking boat? Listening to those fish dying? "Well, it's not exactly my thing, you know. It's hard for me to get much work done. And that motor's beginning to sound like a dentist's drill. Doesn't it ever get to you?"

"The motor? The *sound* of it?"

"Unrelenting." A fish flopped again in the bucket and Kraft had a sudden urge to throw them over, get rid of them.

"O.K., let's take a break," Ric said. Another shrug. "No sweat." He killed the motor. Silence. "Jeez, you could have asked before, you know. Why didn't you? Look, have your ale and a cigar or something and we'll just drift."

"O.K." His voice neutral, not a hint of his overwhelming relief. Why *hadn't* he said something?

He looked about him, hoping to see a sailboat or a lobsterman. Even a gull or a jet stream would do. But this was not the Bay of Fundy. This was the unspoiled coast. Almost no summer people. Lobstering forbidden that season to protect the species. The ocean remained trackless, featureless.

Ric was being his most gracious self. He opened the tackle box and unwrapped the one cigar Kraft allowed himself each day since giving up cigarettes. The boy had even remembered to bring matches. And a bottle of Labatt ale. And an opener for the pre-twist-off cap.

"You don't really like it, do you?" Ric said.

"Like what?"

"This fishing bit."

"Well, I don't *object.*"

"But you still don't *like* it."

"I guess not. Is that important?"

"I guess not."

There was a silence which suggested that it *was* important, but neither of them pursued it. The boy, mercifully, busied himself with polishing spinners, granting Kraft the luxury of silence. Utter silence.

But what was the point of silence if he could do no work? What was the point of this expedition, anyway? His cigar smelled of fish and the glassy undulations of the sea spoiled the ale. It rose and fell in his stomach. Ric even at his kindest, his most considerate, was determined to impose himself on his father's time. It was true of them all. Each of them wanted a piece of him.

It's not that I resent the family. Not just them. It's the whole of society—the complexity of it, the clutter, all bits and pieces. Too many moving parts. You understand? I mean, that's why I came up here. You understand?

I know, I know, Thea said, suddenly appearing at his side, real as a dream, tanned and striking in the navy turtleneck he had just given her.

With children it's the bickering, the hurt feelings, the demands for your time. And adults are no better. Hell, every organization and every committee wants eight hours of your day. You can't divide yourself that way.

Of course you can't. There'd be nothing left of you.

There'd be nothing left of me. Maybe I was born to be a bachelor. Maybe I just stumbled into the business of parenthood. Like my father. How did he ever produce me? And why?

Maybe he thought you'd be Ric.

"You should have known my father," Kraft said suddenly. "He was big on fishing."

"Sounds like a great guy."

"Not really. Hyperactive. Tall, lean, all action. You know, zipping about on the tennis court like the king of Sweden or playing golf or slaughtering deer. The personality of a Teddy Roosevelt, but tall. Republican to boot."

"But he liked fishing."

"He did like fishing. Yes."

"Did he go camping?"

"Oh, sure; that too."

"I'd like him."

"O.K., so I'm not the camping type. But you'd have a hard time putting up with all that nineteenth-century discipline. He'd be bossing you around all the time. A damn fascist. Ran the house like a general, us the troops. You'd have to call him 'Sir.' "

"And hunting?"

"Sure. Big on killing. That was high on the list."

"What list?"

"It's an expression: 'high on the list.' But he also had a

real list. I came across it years ago in his journal. It was all the things his son should be expert in."

"Like what?"

"Oh, lots of things. Like 'the three essential competitive sports'—golf, tennis, and sailing."

"Sailing's competitive?"

"Racing is. And then there were skills like swimming, diving, canoeing, hunting."

"He taught you all those things?"

"In a kind of joyless way. Gruff. He was getting old. And as it turned out, he didn't have much time for me. He died when I was eleven."

"Zowie." Pause. "You were two years younger than me." Pause. "How did he die?"

"Unhappily."

"Come on, I'm being serious."

"So am I. He couldn't get anyone to play golf with him because it was April and cold. Also raining. So he played eighteen holes by himself. Caught pneumonia. That's the official story. He also had liver trouble. You get that from drinking too much. Anyway, between the pneumonia and the liver trouble—that's what got him. He was only fifty-five."

"Are you fifty-five?"

"Not quite yet. Give me a few years."

Pause. A fish gave a final flop in the bucket.

"Hey, what was it like—his dying and all?"

What was it like? Morbid kid. Persistent too. Unthinking. Jumps right in. Still, what the hell? What *was* it like?

"What's the matter? I'm not supposed to ask?"

"Why not? I was just trying to remember. I guess it wasn't so bad. I mean, because he was getting old and all. Crotchety. Opinionated. Impatient with children. I never got to know him. Which was a blessing, really. It meant his death never really hit me. I can hardly remember it. He just sort of dropped out of sight."

104

Kraft reached over the side of the boat, cooling his wrist in the water and filling his empty ale bottle with water. When it was full, he released it, let it sink slowly into the blackness. So much for immortality.

"Don't you even remember the funeral? Your own father?"

Did he? It must have been in Boston, being April. It would have been King's Chapel. Was he remembering himself as a boy standing there in that box pew or was that years later? He could picture himself in knickers, cap in hand, or was that a reconstruction? Leaving—yes, he could remember leaving. Crowds on both sides. And photographers. He hadn't realized until then that his father was so well known. Yes, that moment stuck. Being stared at. Not unpleasant. Sidewalk crowds held back by ropes strung across the sidewalk, solemn faces staring, wordless. The occasion made terrible and grand.

"Did you? Hey, what's the matter? Don't you feel good?"

"*Well?* Of course I feel well. You ask too many questions."

"O.K., never mind, then. Jeez. I was just wondering. . . ."

"Whether I could remember about his dying? No, not much. Almost nothing. But then a lot of other things happened that year. It was 1938. Everything got upstaged by the hurricane."

"What hurricane?"

"*The* hurricane. The first one." He recalled old men saying that about the First World War, historically egocentric. Still, this was the first. . . .

"Aw, come on. The *first?* In the history of the world?"

"In anyone's mind. In memory." Since when? Mid nineteenth century? He'd never asked. "They'd never come that far north."

Until that fall. The fall after his father's death. Somehow it was all lumped together in his mind. Erasing—one way or another.

"The fall of l938."

"What was it like?" Hadn't he just asked that? The pictures were clear enough, but what's an album to someone who hadn't gone through it? "Hey, Dad!" Ric was clicking his fingers like a hypnotist.

"What was it like? Well, it started out like a regular gale. Just blew hard all day. They used to call them line storms."

He could see his mother, still in mourning, staring out the kitchen window, shaking her head; he could hear her say to his aunt, "It's the worst line storm I've ever seen." For him, exhilaration. The wonder of impending disaster. The energy of it. He and his two cousins dashed out into it, ran along the beach, zigzagging, arms raised like wings, the three of them veering and banking like terns. And then racing to the house to get their kite, tearing back to the beach, shrieking like the birds they had become, trying the kite and having it rip loose, free, winging higher and higher into the hurtling clouds, a dot, and then gone. Cries of delight. They had given it life, given it freedom.

Then running out to the end of the breakwater their grandfather had built, spray whipping their faces, holding hands, bending low into the wind, screams halfway between delight and terror. Never had spray washed over that line of granite which extended like a great fist into the sea. None of them had thought it would be possible. Incredible as death. As exciting.

"That's all? Just a storm? That's no hurricane."

"I said that's how it *started*. Don't rush me. Things picked up by midafternoon. Began to get scary. Little things, like the way the wind broke off the tops of waves. Just ripped them off. And the sky. A weird yellow."

Sulfur yellow, it was. That would mean nothing to Ric, sulfur yellow, but that's what it was. Unreal and demonic. That's when they noticed that when it should have been low tide the water was already at the highest point. The tides reversed. He had never seen that. The whole of nature was being disrupted. Even then Kraft knew that something was going on larger than a storm, that after this nothing would be the same.

"Then what? Hey? Then what?"

"I guess it was about four o'clock when it started to get twilight—about four hours early. A yellow twilight." Dreamlike. More like a nightmare. "The sea had covered all of the beach even though it was low tide. It was up against the bathhouses. You know, pounding at them. But there was nothing we could do."

They hadn't known that at the time. They had run back to his house to tell his mother. He could see her by the back door, holding it open for them, holding a black sweater together at her throat, tall, cool, in perfect control. "There's nothing we can do," she said. "Nothing whatever." Her words made the storm more terrible, more marvelous.

Back again to watch the rollers—irresistible now—knock over the bathhouses one by one. Watched the water break them apart. Watched the contents being sucked out with each receding wave, bits of their lives rushing down a stream—beach balls, bath towels, terry cloth robes, badminton rackets, wooden beach chairs, beach pails, water wings, and Kraft's own set of five model boats—all jumbled with boarding and window frames and steps, all rushing out into the dark.

Too much. Too terrible now. Back to the protection of the house. They stood there in the living room, looking out, dripping, he and his Clarendon cousins, all of them pressed against the rope line his mother had strung across the room to keep them well back from the window. "Keep back," she kept murmuring, but they leaned against the line, watching the storm without words, awed now. Scared.

Between the lawn and the sea was their grandfather's sea wall, the absolute guardian and protector except in his dreams. Now, dreamlike, it was being battered, spray peeling off and hurtling toward the house. Unlike the dream waves, these were not clean and blue. They were brown and cluttered with boards, branches, and tree roots. The wind came in gusts, made the house shudder. The place darkened, electricity long since off. They stood there in silence, licking the salt from their lips.

"All right," his mother said, cool as if it were a school morning, "pack your things. If the water passes the sea wall, we'll all go to Uncle Howard's. Put your things in your pillowcases. Warm things first. Don't forget your toothbrushes."

"There was nothing we could do."

"You said that."

"Yes, well, it was a strange feeling. You can't imagine what it was to see the surf pull those granite blocks right out of the sea wall. Pulled them into the sea. Quite a show."

Show? More nightmare than memory; but how could you say that? Each ugly roller now broke on the lawn, leaving a line of rubble just a bit higher than the previous one.

His mother herded them together at the rear door, Kraft and his two cousins, the maids—were there two?—and the cook. They were told to watch out for falling branches and to stay together. Then they were out in it, sand and spray stinging their faces. They scurried, half running, half walking, crouching low to keep from being knocked over.

The path to the Clarendons' could not have been more than a hundred yards, but it became a journey. Aunt Christina held the back door for them, greeting her own two children and the others with a nod, silent as at a funeral. Her husband, Uncle Howard, was still in the city. Although they didn't know it then, the rail line had been washed out already and so had the roads. They were cut off completely. The strangeness of it all was made stranger still by the lack of men.

On slightly higher land now, but no real comfort in that. This was the last refuge. The peninsula must surely have become an island by now, the water inundating woods and road between them and the village, between them and the rest of the country. No way of knowing for sure, telephone lines long since down and no portable radio. Probably the entire country was being lashed by this storm. Perhaps it was the end of America. Fear; also a heady excitement. It was every desert island, every treasure island, every adventure story turned real and vivid.

In the last bit of light they clustered by the side window, watching the breakers attack the home which he and his mother now shared. The water had crossed that side of the point entirely. Rollers swept by the house and down into the cove on the other side.

For a while it stood, entirely surrounded by water, an island fortress. Then the porch went, exploding into a jumble of boards. He had a sudden and terrible vision of what it must be like inside—churning water, chest high, in that living room where only the day before he had been reading *The Wind in the Willows.* Carelessly, he had left it open on the back of the couch.

"My book, my book," he shouted, seeing it in his mind's eye swept by dark waters out of sight forever. He would never see it again. Never. All loss became centered in this one object, something he never knew he treasured. The sense of adventure vanished; fear turned to terror. What he had taken for granted had been wrenched from him and swept out, destroyed, drowned in that black water. He wept—more than he had at his father's death, more than he would later for his mother. A chasm of loss too deep for words.

"The next morning, the house was gone."

"Gone? Nothing?"

"Nothing. The cellar was just an indentation in the sand. The sea had washed over the entire point. It looked like a moonscape."

Rock and sand. Even the trees were gone. All but one

huge oak. Stripped of leaves, sandblasted, salt-encrusted but still standing, it was a weathered gray skeleton. In its upper branches, an Oriental rug was draped like a shroud.

"We couldn't even find the gardens. Couldn't figure out where they had been." But how could he explain it? He recalled walking slowly in a daze, no one talking; here and there they would find a chair, a sink, an iron bedstead half-buried.

Timbers, roof sections, doors, windows—the great bulk of the house and barn and boathouse had been broken into sections and scraped into the cove behind. As the tide receded, some of that tangle was revealed. In the middle, just showing above the surface, at an insane angle, was a clearly indentifiable section: a panel of roof and a dormer, the dormer of his own room.

"I've never been back," he said. "It's stupid to go back to places like that."

"Couldn't they build it again?"

"Oh, you could build something. I guess they've put up a lot of little places there since then. That's what I've heard. But you can't recreate a place that's planted and all." Planted? That wasn't really it. Rooted was more like it. "Well, you wouldn't want to build a place like that. I mean, hell, it was the kind of place that had to be staffed, you know. You had to live off the backs of others to build a place like that, to make it work. A rotten system. Besides, the money's gone. He was in bad financial shape when he died. He'd taken risks. Chances. He never really survived the Depression. It's all gone. Good riddance."

A great wave of melancholy and hatred rose up under him; he could feel the thrust of it in his stomach. Gone? Dead and gone? All of it?

It passed and in its wake came a sudden fear, a panic, sharp and hard like spray: What on earth was he doing drinking ale miles out in this desolate sea? Water cold enough to paralyze a good swimmer. That smudge on the horizon—it could be a fog bank building or maybe a line storm sweeping in from the open Atlantic. There they were with no compass.

"Ric," he said. "Ric!"

"Jesus, Dad . . ."

"Let's get back."

"What for? What's the matter?"

"We're too damn far out. Come on, let's get back!"

11

⊷❦⊶

Meeting them at the ferry was no simple matter.

He knew it wouldn't be. He had predicted it out loud while driving his Jeep to Yarmouth. "Something will go wrong," he said, speaking over the whine of the engine. "I'll have spent an entire morning getting there and something will go wrong."

Never you mind, a gentle country voice said from the vacant seat beside him. Maybe you can work this evening.

"Oh, sure. Work with three kids and Tammy and two houseguests. Sure."

Well, then, take time off. You deserve it.

He shrugged with a modest smile. No, he didn't really deserve it, but it was nice of her to say so. And it was good to be driving the Jeep again. He nodded, affectionately pounded the steering wheel, increased his speed for no reason. Yes, there was something right about this hunk of utilitarian metal. Not at all like Tammy's chrome-covered Scout. This thing—muddy-green and dented—was in the spirit of Worwich.

He looked at his watch. Tammy had wound it, discovered

it was not broken, had set it from the radio in her Scout, had set all the clocks. But why? "No point," he said aloud. "I was doing all right without watching the time every minute. I was getting things done." More or less. "I was just getting into the manuscript. Another month of uninterrupted solitude and I would have cracked its back. Maybe I'm just a bit behind schedule, but I'm on the right track. *Was* on the right track. But family. Kids. Guests. *Guests!* What a crazy idea! Two more bodies cluttering up that ark of a house. That's Tammy's way. Invite them in pairs, and mismatched pairs at that. Nothing in common. Instant hatred. Guaranteed. Beautiful week in store."

Well, of the two of them, Harry wouldn't be much trouble. Harry was his editor. He had traveled a lot. Unflappable. At home in foreign parts, spoke four languages, could tell bilingual jokes, had friends in all major cities. Never a tourist, never on vacation, he made an avocation of his profession. Everything for Harry was tax deductible. He'd get along.

Still, he'd never been to Nova Scotia. "Until you started going there, I wasn't sure whether it really existed or not. I mean, was *Evangeline* fiction or new journalism?" But he finally got to doing some research. "I know all there is to know about the place now—really more than I want to know."

Factual research was one of Harry's specialties. He liked being on top of everything. But he couldn't possibly know what it was really like at Worwich—how they lived and all.

How could he know? Always traveling first class. Insulated. Walled off from real living.

There was no way of predicting how he would react to Kraft's great shell of a house, to the lack of plaster on the bare-lath walls, the lack of plumbing, the lack of electricity and phone, the lack of the *New York Times.*

The worst part of his impending visit was the dishonesty.

Posing as a friend, Harry was coming as a one-man tax-deductible fact-finding committee. He and Tammy were in on it together.

He would stay three days, talking about everything *but* the book, and on the last day he would raise the matter in an offhand way. "Oh, by the way, about that manuscript . . ." Kraft could hear the practiced informality. Once Harry had his worst suspicions confirmed, he would shake his head, shrug his shoulders, raise his hands in Gallic resignation, and make Kraft feel like hell.

Kraft *was* badly behind—behind the contract date, behind their unwritten understanding. Breach of friendship. A wayward son.

Which was crazy. Why should he go limp before Harry Toll?

"A man's not a working machine. You can't just turn this stuff on. You must know that."

It was unlikely that he would say any of that to Harry. Strange. Normally Kraft took a pugilistic pleasure in combating criticism of all sorts from all quarters, pummeling academic and political enemies before they had time to attack, before they knew they were enemies. Keep them off balance. It was the only way to survive in a world of reactionary elitists. But to Harry he gave special treatment. It wasn't his age, since he was only slightly older, and it wasn't his position of power. That never quelled Kraft. Still, he treated Harry with the respect of a younger brother, forgave him all kinds of political outrages.

How could any rational man defend such absurdities as the profit motive and private wealth and still publish the works of a radical historian? With regal disdain worthy of Louis XIV, Harry excused himself from logical consistency.

The day was inexcusably warm for Nova Scotia. When Kraft arrived in town the ferry was docking, passengers crowding along the rail, some waving. The bay was without a ripple.

He found a parking space with difficulty, sliding into a spot too small for most cars, pleased that he had taken the Jeep and not the Scout, as Tammy had suggested.

Harry was easy to spot. There he was, a full head taller than the others, dressed in his white suit and white Panama hat, a Degas gentleman in the park on a Sunday afternoon. An anachronism. A flagrant, almost militant anachronism. Kraft felt a great wave of affection.

"Harry!" Kraft took his suitcase, a deference he gave to no one else, including his wife. "Sorry, but we have to pick up someone else."

"Someone else? Another guest?"

"Crazy Min."

"You're running a rest home?"

"Might as well."

"You didn't warn me."

"Warn you! Harry, I didn't even invite you. You've got to take your chances."

"How crazy, this Crazy Min?"

"You've never met her. Believe me, she's absolutely psycho."

They were interrupted by the jostle of the crowd streaming off the ferry—tourists from the States dressed for some Caribbean cruise, returning Canadians. Shouts of greetings. Embracing. After two months of solitude, Kraft found all this unnerving. He preferred the lean, quiet hostelers with their ten-speed machines. The province, he decided, should restrict tourist travel to bicycle and horse.

Then the parade of cars, trucks, buses, campers, trailers. Kraft and Harry were pressed against the fence to make room. "The bastards are taking over the province," Kraft said.

"There ought to be a law."

"There is, and they're trying to use it against *me*. But never mind that. Keep your eye out for this wretched girl. I hope they had the sense to tie a tag on her shirt front."

"A *child?* I should be looking for a *child?"*

"Yes. Aged thirty-four. Widowed young. Addled brain."

"A relative?"

"Not a Means, thank God, but too damn close for comfort. She's Tammy's younger sister."

The crowd dwindled and the last of the cars came off the ramp. There was no sign of Min. "It would be like her to change her mind at the last moment," Kraft said. "Wrong stars will put her off. Ugly tea leaves. The flight of pigeons."

"Tammy's sister? You can't be serious." They were still shouting at each other though the cars were gone.

"I am and she is."

"Maybe *I* should have put it off."

"Hell no. Min's the one who should be put off. Except you can't. She never gives much warning. I received notification yesterday. A kind of annunciation from Tammy: 'Oh, by the way, Min is coming on tomorrow's ferry. Always room for one more.'"

Harry, he wanted to say, Harry, I'm not ready for all this. I'm not up to it.

"Tammy never mentioned having a sister."

"They have nothing whatever in common."

"Well, she's not here." Lowering his voice for the first time: "You sure this isn't some delusion of yours?"

Kraft gave him a quick look. Had Tammy been complaining?

"Well, if she does show up, you can judge for yourself."

"If?"

"If. In no way predictable. Look, don't expect the slightest echo of Tammy. They spent their childhood figuring out ways to be different from each other."

"Min? Is that a real name? Like the mouse?"

"The mouse was Minnie. Minnie Mouse. No relation. This one's really Minerva. Smaller ears."

They paused, suddenly aware that the cars were gone. So were the passengers. They were standing there alone.

"I've never known a Minerva. Sounds archaic."

"My wife's parents' fault. New York intellectuals. Over educated Fabians. Big on labor law and mythology. It warped her for life. I don't know how Tammy survived with a clear head. Anyway, Min's whole name is Minerva T'sali. T-apostrophe-s-a-l-i. Married T'sali for his name. Figured that if there was anything weirder than Minerva it would be Minerva T'sali."

"Tibetan?"

"Close. Indian. Indian Indian, that is. The fag end of an old merchant family in Jamaica. He came to New York to find God and settled for Minerva."

Harry allowed himself a fleeting smile—the first since he had arrived. It was a game they played, the straight-face game. Forcing a smile from the other was like taking the knight. Somehow that bridged their political differences.

"We'll have to search the ferry," Harry said, as if this were a routine a summer host should accept without complaint. Kraft felt a jab of disappointment. He had been ready to leave, to assume that Min was lost. Still, Harry was right. If she had actually been on the passenger list, there would be a hell of a row.

"Find someone with an officer's cap," Harry said. "Might as well start at the top."

But Kraft hardly heard, imagining a farewell note tied to her tarot deck: "The sea has called me to her forgiving arms." Reporters. An inquest. A great clutter of awkward questions. Did he really search the ship? Did he perhaps *wish* to have her lost? Didn't this raise the question of criminal responsibility? Snide innuendos in the columns of *Time:* "The rose-hued Mr. Means tersely denied all responsibility, though his eyes were significantly dry at the funeral. No mourner he!" The bastards. One inch short of libel, as always.

Harry had found an officer and was exercising his editor's authority, the resonances of which recalled for Kraft the voice of doom in newsreels from a former age.

"One of your passengers has not left the ship." Subtly the responsibility was swung in the direction of the officer. The man stiffened. "She may be in serious trouble. A somewhat unstable woman. We'll help you search the ship."

The officer agreed, grateful for the cooperation.

Searching the ship was no simple task. More than a ferry, it was a small liner complete with casinos and state rooms.

"The bar, perhaps," the officer said coolly.

"Not the type," Kraft said. "Not at all. More likely she's gone over the edge." Both men looked at him. "People do that," he said. "All the time."

They entered the ship and circled the first deck, silently, rapidly. The next deck had the lifeboats and Kraft could visualize her inert body curled up in one. But he didn't suggest that they search them. Some sailor would make the discovery in a year or so, a skeleton in fetal repose, finger bones still grasping her *I Ching* coins, waiting for the final throw.

It was on the top deck that he spotted her. Alive. Disappointment grappled with relief. Then rage swept through him. She was in a secluded corner, hidden among the air vents, lying in a deck chair like a long-limbed ghost of Cleopatra touring the Nile. Smooth black hair parted in the middle curved down both sides of her face, ending with two points, chin-level; hoop earrings in the form of self-consuming snakes; enormous and soulful eyes. She was not to be believed.

"Look at that," she said in her husky voice, which Kraft once thought was sexy.

"Min, for God's sake . . ."

"Ma'm, the ship has docked. . . ."

"Just look at that," she said. "Stare at it a moment."

They looked up as instructed, following the line of her raised hand and lengthy finger.

"That," Harry said with cool patience, "is radar."

"Only on the most superficial level," she said to him. "I've been staring at it since sunrise this morning. It has transported me to places you will never see." Then she stood up and abandoned her Delphic Oracle voice, turning matter-of-fact. "Kraft, you look like death. You can't have slept for a week. You're badly out of balance."

"Min," he said in a tone of exaggerated calm and reasonableness, which he used only when enraged almost beyond reason. "No woman who stares at revolving radar scopes for the length of a morning and has to be sought like a wayward child can claim to be an expert on balance." Then, while he still had her attention, he introduced Harry.

The two-hour drive from the town of Yarmouth eastward along the south shore to his place was made in almost complete silence. If Kraft had been alone with Harry, the two of them would have sat beside each other and chatted amiably about the approaching end of civilization and other topics of passing interest, would have had a good time of it. Their political differences were so deep, so well charted, so clearly labeled ("Warning: hopeless gulf ahead"), that they were easily skirted.

And if Min had been the only passenger, there would have been a conversation of sorts. Over the years they had developed a kind of private language, each of them treating the other as a benign defective. There were times when they almost enjoyed each other on that basis. Crazy, yes; but she did have a kind of languid sexual energy.

By having the two of them together, Kraft became the child of two estranged and hostile parents. It was a sad contrast with the trip down to meet them that morning, when, alone, he had felt free to talk almost continually.

With effort he managed to drive them out of his mind.

He had no need for either of them. After all, he was doing just fine before any of them came up to break into his life.

They were driving by miles of stunted firs and hemlocks, miserable trees which were too short for lumbering. Bad soil and heavy winds kept them from developing. Kraft could imagine Harry's unspoken reaction to this desolation, this emptiness.

Well, *I* like it, he said silently in defense.

Why?

It's desolate. Unsocial.

Why won't those trees grow?

Poor soil, I guess. The real farmland is on the other side, on the Bay of Fundy. Here it's the rugged look.

As in rugged individualist?

Rugged as in unspoiled. No one selling moccasins. Sand dunes too. Miles of dunes and deserted beaches. Not all bought up by motels.

Bought up by people like you.

It came as a package.

Some package. A thousand acres?

Just short of a thousand. Besides, if I hadn't acted when I did, the goddamned huckster developers would have raped the area.

Maybe they think of you as the developer.

I'm developing nothing.

Or a speculator.

I'll never subdivide.

Then you're a reactionary landholder. An American land baron. Isn't that what you said your father was?

Listen, the day United Fruit and Exxon turn over their holdings to the people, I'll give my acreage to the province.

"Here," Min said suddenly. "Turn here." She made him jump, breaking in like that. Her damn regal air. What was worse, she was right. They were at Eldridge's store already, a little gray-shingled building with a single gas pump which

120

seemed to serve nothing but a wilderness of grown-over farmland. Kraft had been on the road almost two hours and would have driven right by the turn if Min hadn't spoken. He wrenched the wheel as if it were her throat.

"He's in terrible shape," she said, turning to Harry, who was sitting in the back seat, leaning forward, his arms resting on the back of the front seat. He agreed with her all too readily.

"Sleepy at the wheel," Harry said.

"Dreamy and forgetful," she said, her voice vibrating on the dirt road. "Would have gone right by it."

"It's not always a good idea to go off like this. Off alone, I mean. Everyone wants to get off alone. You dream about it in the city. But it's not always such a good idea."

"Particularly up here. It's too close to the magnetic pole."

"And too far from a decent restaurant," Harry said. "Bad for the gastric psyche."

Min nodded emphatically, a new bond forming. From that moment, they had something to discuss—Kraft. They analyzed his gastric and magnetic psyche as if he were absent. He tried to concentrate on the driving, weaving around potholes and protruding rocks in low gear, frowning.

"It's one thing if you're in balance," she said. "I lived in a lighthouse one summer. Beautiful. Just me and those gulls and the wind. But I was in balance. Kraft isn't in balance. You can tell by looking at him. I could tell the moment I set eyes on him. Negative aura. He's in very serious shape. You can't live off here if you're not in balance. All this land, but no inner balance."

"This is his? All this?"

"All this. From the store down to the sea. A thousand acres."

"It is *not* a thousand acres," Kraft said savagely.

"Almost a thousand acres. Who's to count? In any case, that's some estate."

"It's not an estate," Kraft said. "Estates have lawns. No

lawns here. Just acreage. Wait until you see the house, Harry." He smiled in anticipation. "Call it a farm. I prefer the word 'farm.'"

"You've taken up pigs and cattle?" Harry asked.

"Well, you could say my product is social research."

"That," Min said, "is a stifling concern. Here you are with trees and sand and the sea—your anima speaking to you—and you spend your time pecking at a typewriter, fiddling with all those sterile concepts. It's no wonder you look like a corpse."

"Harry, do I look like a corpse?"

"Of course not. No mortician would display you as you are."

Betrayal! "Is this how you encourage your little stable of writers?"

"From what I've heard, you haven't been doing much writing."

Min nodded fiercely. "Tammy says you're in bad shape. It's clear from one look at you. What *have* you been doing with all this free time and solitude?"

The full horror of the coming weekend broke on him like a cold wave. Instead of having to deal with two hopelessly dissimilar guests, he was about to face a conspiracy. He slammed on the brakes. The Jeep skidded to a stop in the middle of absolute wasteland—scrubland, stunted trees gray with dust from the road.

"Look," he said. "Hands off my psyche. Either that or you both walk back to Yarmouth from here. Got it?"

His passengers nodded, solemn. "Hey," Harry said, "sorry. Easy does it." Kraft started up again with a jerk. In the ensuing silence, he began to feel better. Back in control.

You see, dear Thea, it's just a matter of tone. If you let people know you really mean it, they respond. They do what you tell them. Did you see that? Did you see how they shut up?

Marvelous, she said.

"Marvelous," he said, nodding.

"What?" Min said.

"I didn't say anything."

Silence. Then softly, not addressing anyone specifically, face forward, Min said, "That's just what I mean. A dangerous disharmony. Psychic bifurcation. Spiritual disjunction. Not good. Not good at all."

12

❧❧❧

Picture: A large Victorian dining table, legs thick as an elephant's, carved with palm leaves and bunches of grapes; about it, two dozen members of an extended family, dressed elegantly, faces lit with candlelight. The host serves, carving a suckling pig, heaping the pewter plates. Red wine in heavy goblets. Sounds: Violinists in the background; at the table, the sparkle of wit, the ripple of laughter, the rumble of argument.

"You," the host says, pointing to one of his sons, "recite for us—something from Cato the Censor." The boy stands and begins without a moment's hesitation; the father throws a slab of meat to the five wolfhounds, who fight for it, snarling, ripping each other, challenging the boy's concentration. "Louder," the father says. "Speak from the diaphragm." The boy performs marvelously.

"When? When was the last time?" Min's voice, strident.

"When what?"

" 'When what?' Where have you been?"

"Off." He took a sip of rum on the rocks, his second—perhaps third—since the cocktail hour.

"We were talking about Tammy's glorious dip in the sea—the first of the season—and I just wondered when you had been in last." Turning to Harry, "Here he is, exposed to the great anima archetype, the most beautiful cleansing agent for the spirit—and body—and"—back to Kraft—"my guess is you haven't even *looked* at it."

"You can't avoid looking at it around here—even if you were blind. Min, if water is so holy-beautiful to you, how do you stand being trapped in lower Manhattan?"

"It's not easy. I make do with a Swedish steam bath—actually, they're Danish—every Wednesday."

"Where?" from Harry, and they were off and running with famous steam baths and health spas they had known. Kraft was off the hook.

Odd, but in the scramble for chairs he had ended up on the back side of the hollow-door table, wedged between it and the homemade shelf which served as side table. He had been used for half the meal as a would-you boy: Would you pass the salt on the shelf there? Oh, would you pass the pepper too? Say, is there some A.1 sauce there on the shelf? Sorry, but did I leave my cigarettes there behind you? Matches? Anything there I could use for an ashtray?

Harry had taken over the head of the table and Min the other end. They lobbed their conversation over everyone else as if they were the only adults present.

But what the hell? The scene was a wonder, a mirage. After two and a half months of solitude, of sordid, utilitarian life, it was difficult to believe the place could become this civilized. He held his jelly-jar glass against his brow and beheld the picture before him through the amber hues of light Jamaica rum: Harry in his white pants, white shirt, blue-and-gold ascot. Panning left, faces blurring, rum sloshing pleasantly against his brow, there was Min in a black full-length skirt, black blouse, and a great jangling clutter of beads, golden bracelets, rings, all aglitter. A gypsy queen! And Tammy—his wife in some other world?—in evening pants and striped shirt, blue-and-white cool, her hair more tightly curled than ever thanks to the sea air. Right now she, a fluid image through his rum, was his student again, efficient, humming with energy, just barely within reach.

The children were also strangers—the two boys right out of Dickens with their untamed hair, and Hildy a Victorian portrait in one of her many long dresses. Such femininity! How had she ever sprung from that mother?

The whole scene was slightly aged, a color photo turning to sepia, yellowed in the amber of the rum and the glow from the Aladdin lamp hanging above.

"When you're through cooling your brow with that drink," Tammy said, "you might try eating. You could do with some food."

He turned his optical device downward and noticed a cascade of rum fall decorously down to a heaping plate of paella, spray rebounding from the clam shells and sinking into the hunks of lobster, fish, and sausage.

"Kraft!" from Min, but she turned back to the others, rippling on about biofeedback. Guiltily he put his glass down and attacked the food. There had been times in his solitude when he had taken perhaps one or two more drinks than he had really needed for survival; he wasn't going to do anything here that would be an echo of that. He listened to the conversation the way one watches waves, smiling, nodding.

Harry and Min, it turned out, were compatriots not only of the same city but of the same six-block neighborhood off Sheridan Square. They had spent a great deal of their time eating in the same foreign restaurants and evaluating them. How had they not met until now? Min saw cosmic forces at work.

They each put up nominations for the best Assyrian menu, settled on a winner, and then ranked three runners-up. Then on to Japanese. More wondrous still, both of them were off-and-on vegetarians. This gave them another, stranger, set of places to discuss, some "dazzling" and others "abysmal." They even shared adjectives.

Kraft remained passive, watching as if he were at the movies. Of course, it would have been pleasant to have been taken in, to have been included in the image. But he didn't feel ready for that. Not yet. It was going to take a while before he could accept them as real people, before he could join them.

Meanwhile, it was enjoyable entertainment. Effectively done as a scene. The lighting, the composition, even the dialogue—superficial but convincing. Stylized, yet true to period. He had high standards for historical drama in film, but if well done it could give a genuine sense of life style. And this one was certainly convincing. Almost real.

"Well, is there?" Tammy was asking.

"Is there? Sorry . . ."

"Are you with us?"

"Sort of."

"About those journals. Your father's. What's the deal? You must have reminded me to bring them in three different letters."

"I did?"

"Are they really connected with your book? You're going to *use* them?"

"Of course. They're prime source material."

"My impression was," Harry said, "that your book had something to do with *liberals.*"

"Brilliant insight." To the others, "Remarkable what a good editor can deduce from a title, an outline, four conferences, and five completed chapters." To Harry again, "Yes, *liberals.* Put your finger right on it. But where do you think liberals came from? Certainly not from factories. Liberals, dear Harry, are mill owners who feel guilty. Liberals talk at length about the downtrodden and the unrepresented, but what they're really scared of is radicals. They know that if adjustments are not made, the fat's in the fire and it's the radicals' turn to take over."

"By *radical,*" Tammy said, translating for the others, "he means activist."

"And by *activist,* I mean *threat.* The activist disrupts, the liberal struggles to restore balance. The New Deal—remember this, Harry—salvaged the class system."

"And where," Min asked, "is your father in all this?"

"It's men like him—inflexible, willful, unbending—who would have destroyed it. You know how a drowning man fights the lifeguard? Tries to drag him under? That's how my father was with F. D. R. That's how all those economic royalists were. The great irony of the period."

There it was, the heart of his book, the thesis, the core. It sounded right. He felt marvelous.

"That means," Harry said gently, "that you and your father are on the same team after all."

Laughter. Kraft grinned, but it was a cheap shot.

"Just like you and me," he said. "Actually, I shouldn't get involved with them at this point. Distracting. I probably should just give them to some library. Take a big Nixonian tax deduction. Or just throw them out."

"Oh, no," Min said. "You can't do that. Absolutely not."

"I didn't know you had such reverence for history, Min."

"History? They've got nothing to do with history. They're *important.* They're messages you've got to use, a language you've got to translate. They're your bridge with your tribal memories."

"Oh for God's sake Min, lay off that crap."

"This has nothing to do with gods *or* crap," she said in her high-priestess voice. And to her sister, "They're his death trip, of course. He's got to work it through."

There was a pause with that one. Tammy filled it as quickly as she could. "Well, how does the place look," she said to Kraft, "all picked up and repopulated?"

128

"I'm sure he had it populated," Min said.

"What?" Kraft said.

"Geminis are notorious for that—filling empty space with people, spirits."

"What kind of spirits?" Hildy asked, bright-eyed. She knew perfectly well. The poor girl had swallowed her Aunt Min's entire mythology and could quote from it as if from scriptures. She was only acting as a wily shill.

"The unburied and the unborn." Kraft had the distinct impression that she had said this from the bottom of a well.

"Unburied?" Weldon said. "You have to bury dead people. It's a law."

"The body, yes, but not the spirit. There are ways of laying a spirit to rest, but sometimes we don't do it right."

"There aren't any spirits," Weldon said.

"There *are,*" Hildy said.

"The unborn," Tammy said. "I hadn't heard that one. Spirits of the unborn? Where did you pick up *that?*"

"You don't *pick up* truth like a virus, Tammy. One *learns.* The unborn are the unrealized. They wander about until given bodies to house them."

"There wouldn't be *room,*" Weldon said. "All those spirits around. Where are they, Aunt Min? All around us?"

"All around us," Hildy said. "I've seen them."

"Have not."

"Have too."

"Show us one."

"You've got to believe."

"That's stupid. Stupid and nuts."

"Weldon!" Tammy sliced into the conversation like a knife. "Time to check the lamps. You take the responsibility tonight, will you? Every half hour. Remember?"

Her tone was cool, pleasant; but there was no refusing. Clocks ticked in her head and she did her best to give her sons the same jeweled mechanisms.

Weldon started on his rounds and she, banishing the spirits, explained to Harry how they had to adjust the Aladdin lamps every half hour. "The only alternative is using those gasoline ones. They'll burn all night on one pumping, but they glare. And Kraft doesn't like the smell."

"Like a garage."

"So it's Aladdin around here. Kraft won't budge on that one. Talk about your inflexible and willful types. . . . Me, I wouldn't mind putting in an electric line. It means paying for poles in from the highway—a year's royalties, I suppose." A flash of a smile to Kraft. "I don't have his passion for the nineteenth century."

"Passion? Me? I don't have passions any more. Just values. And revulsions. You can't have values without a strong set of revulsions. And one of mine is the goddamned power company. I mean, what is there about bourgeois existence that calls out for electric knives and electric can openers? We have no muscles left? How come they're still pushing electric stoves on us when they can't even produce enough juice for lights? Can you imagine brushing your teeth with something that hums? And sleep under wires rather than three blankets? It's the great General Electric hoax. Sell the product—never mind whether you can deliver the wattage. Electric doorbells instead of knockers; electric swizzle sticks; electric back scratchers. Pencil sharpeners! Can you imagine that? Men who can run billion-dollar corporations and control the lives of a hundred thousand workers can't revolve the tiny handle on a pencil sharpener. There's the capitalist for you!

"Jesus, there was a day when a member of the ruling class could boast about his status with a new suit of clothes; now he has to install an all-electric, push-button toilet flusher and paper dispenser that plays 'America the Beautiful.' "

A round of applause. He felt suddenly in possession of a former self—like finding an old uniform in the closet.

"Don't start asking for some high-tension line in here. Can you imagine this place aglow with lighting panels, electric radiators, color television in the walls and ceiling?" He gestured with his wineglass, Chablis wafting in air, children set to giggling. "Push-button window controls, heated water beds, electric dishwashers . . ."

"Well, *maybe* . . ." from Tammy.

"No maybes for alcoholics. No first sip. One dishwasher and before you know it we have a clothes washer and then a drier, and how about a dehumidifier? An electric fireplace, then all-electric central heat and air conditioning. Oh, and a high-voltage line down to the beach for the outdoor lighting, the electric grill and rotisserie, the antibug grids, and the all-weather, five-hundred-watt quadraphonic sound system. For God's sake, Tammy, don't take that first sip."

"O.K., O.K. I take the pledge." Tammy raised her right hand, face alight. "Right on. Give 'em hell."

It was a good speech. Convincing. It convinced *him* as well. There had been times there, drifting through those rooms by himself, when he felt that somehow things weren't entirely right, that his values were askew. But there now with the fresh voltage of his own oratory he was certain that he was on solid ground, that he had every right to defend the place just as it was. Simplicity. Honesty. Frontier values.

"It's the *new* new left." he announced. "Rejection of bourgeois values in a fresh way. We've finally come full cycle in this incredible country—two hundred years it took us to find the populist values with which we started."

He'd never put it that way, never really thought about it in those terms. But it sounded right. And Tammy was smiling; she understood it. Not Harry, of course. And not Min. They were products of urban living. Frozen in the 1950s. But Tammy—still his student in some ways. In the important ways.

"You're unreal," she said, shaking her head.

"Look," Min said suddenly, gesturing. "Spirits!"

What she saw was Weldon's shape moving about in the living room, his image flickering in horizontal bars through the unplastered laths. The division between the rooms was never absolute, especially at night. Between the slats one caught the glimmer of lamps and the shadow of human forms translated into horizontal bars like radiophotographs from the thirties. Kraft enjoyed the effect.

For a moment Weldon appeared in full bodily form as he passed the open doorway to the hall; then a radiophoto again, a hundred little horizontal lines in the kitchen.

"Don't forget the hanging one," Tammy said, not having to shout since sound as well as visual images passed through the laths. In years past, everyone knew when one of the children was having a nightmare. As for sex, Kraft and Tammy had to do it with stealth, late at night and muffled. It added to the intensity.

"The same principle," Kraft said, "as Japanese paper walls."

"There's nothing Oriental about it," Harry said. "It's more like a stack of lobster traps."

"That's all right with me," Kraft said. "That makes me king of the lobsters."

"In a trap?"

"Coffee time," Tammy said. And there was a general bustle, cooperative clearing with Tammy directing. As usual, Min couldn't be content with standard fare. Hers had to be tea. Special arrangements. "It's not love of tea," Kraft said to Harry, the two of them still sitting while women and children ebbed and flowed past them. "It's her craving for special attention."

"You make it difficult."

"What difficult?"

"I was just about to ask for tea too."

"Oh, for God's sake. Of course."

Min turned to Harry, smiling like a cat.

"Guess what? *Major* Grey."

"*Major* Grey?" Kraft said, looking around uneasily. "Where?"

"The tea, dear," Min said, not even looking at him—the offhand way one deals with stupid questions from children. And to Harry, "Do you know Ling tea?"

"Of course. But I've had trouble getting it."

"There's this little hole-in-the-wall place on Christopher Street. . . ."

They were off again on a grand tour of lower Manhattan, ignoring everyone else. For Kraft, this was going too far. Except for politics, Harry was a rational man, a good friend, and absolutely stable. He was above fads and trendy manias. There was some kind of betrayal in his sudden interest in this most unlikely woman.

As for Min, she was getting out of hand too. True, she and Kraft had always played enemies, but there was a kernel of affection in that game. It wasn't right, her playing up to Harry this way. They hardly knew each other.

"Tomorrow," Min was saying to Harry, "I'll show you something spectacular—rose hip tea made fresh from the bush."

"My God," Kraft said.

"What's wrong with vitamin C?" Harry asked.

"Perfect for bee stings," Min said. "Snakebites."

"How about cancer?" Tammy asked.

"You don't believe it. I can always tell when you don't believe me." She turned to Harry. "She was the overachiever all through school. Grade-hungry. Not her fault, really; she was just trying to be a son substitute. Couldn't have been easy. Anyhow, what *she* said was taken as educated truth. They never quite knew what to do with what *I* said. I mean, I saw truth in the form of visions even as a kid. That was just the way it came to me. Not logic. Visions. I was like Hildy here. . . ."

"But I *do* believe you," Tammy said, cutting in. "I believe you except in the really far-out . . . Well, you know. But about the tea and all—I believe you, Min. Really I do. Tell us about rose hip tea."

"Well, you make it up very strong as an herbal cure." She turned to Kraft. "You didn't know that? With all your degrees? Here you are right in the heart of nature and you don't know about herbal teas? That's crazy. Why, there are about fifty kinds of teas you could make from things right around you."

"Like what?" from Weldon.

"Oh, acorn tea. For warts. And sassafras tea."

"What's that for?" Hildy asked.

"Stomachache. Also warts."

"I wish," Kraft said, "I had just one wart to test you."

"I could cure you of anything," Min said sweetly, "if you'd just have faith."

"In what?"

"In the cure, Kraft, the cure. In the tea or the herbal incense or the leeches. . . ."

"Leeches!" from Tammy. "They're medieval."

"What are leeches?" from Ric.

"*Where* do you get your leeches," from Harry.

It was scarcely to be believed. Two members of the educated elite of the most advanced city in the world enthusiastically endorsing a medical practice which was in disrepute by the middle of the nineteenth century. All cults struck Kraft as antirational, regressive, potentially dangerous. Surely this was worse. Blood-sucking leeches were the stuff of nightmares.

Picture: A small, unmarked doorway next to the fruit market in Sheridan Square. A slender woman in a long black skirt pauses, looks up and down the street, and descends a flight of stone steps. She is joined by a tall, distinguished gentleman, a Swedish count, perhaps. He raps a signal on the oak door and they are ushered in.

There in the twilight they select dark, slimy creatures

from a case. Reverently, ritualistically, they place leeches on the face and arms of the other, uttering suppressed gasps of sensual delight.

"But *you*, of course, wouldn't approve." Min's voice. It had been directed at him. There was a pause.

"Wouldn't approve?"

"Diagnostic spiritualism. Kraft, aren't you listening?"

"Listening? Of course I'm listening, Min. I always listen to you. And I recall every word. A very font of inspiration. You are my guide to the land of spiritual fulfillment." He raised his glass of Chablis in her direction as one might dangle a cross before a demon. "One thing you can learn from your Aunt Min," he said to the children, "is that there are more forces at work in this world than are known to the simple historian. Or to any rational mind. Ah, yes, Jung's great seething ocean, the Hindu notion of *dharam*— right, Min? The life force reincarnation, the regenerative power of blood-sucking leeches . . ."

"Hey, easy does it," from Tammy.

"Not so, dear Tammy. Not easy at all. It is our life work, our continuing struggle to reach down into our souls. Right, Min? Min knows. The soul—as Min has told me in confidence—which resides in the right side of man's brain, in the liver of fishes, and in the intestines of reptiles . . ."

"I never . . ."

"And the tail of salamanders—never, *never* pull the tail off a salamander, children—and in the pollen of flowers. The soul . . . Ah, it struggles endlessly for recognition, for release. A captive Ariel. Through it we recall our other lives, but only on rare occasions such as in sleep or when exhausted or taken by surprise or bedazzled by a revolving radar antenna—right, Min? Yes, lives upon lives, all of us like double and triple exposures, an album without labels. Who is that? Me? No, that's my father. Or my brother. Perhaps my son; no, it must be my grandfather.

"The human mind, you see, is an unsteady sea—right,

Min? The great anima archetype. A limitless ocean filled with bits and pieces—flotsam and jetsam from a hundred wrecks. You drift about like a shipwrecked mariner, grasping at a beam here, a mast there, a shattered gunwale. Sometimes you build a raft. Sometimes it breaks up under you, making you start all over again. There's enough junk out there to build a whole ship and set out for where one wants—right, Min? But too often the storms are too great. You feel like drowning. But, children, you must learn to navigate on that great sea of the collective unconscious, the *dharma;* ah, the drama of it all. Learn to navigate. Learn to live in harmony, drawing from that sea, from the great anima, learn to suck up nutriment from that limitless source, drink like a leech on the butt of the universe. Right, Min? Have I got it right, O Delphic Oracle?"

Her chair was empty. To his surprise, no one laughed.

13

"O.K.," Tammy said, giving a single clap with her hands. "Time to get the dishes done."

Abruptly she outlined the system—not just for this meal, but for all of them. It was, Kraft thought, Tammy at her worst. Tammy as recreational counselor, Tammy as CO in a liberated army. Tammy of pep and pepper.

"Breakfasts and lunches we keep simple. Everyone cleans up his own. On supper detail we can use two adults and one child. Those off duty have to go in the living room. No room in that thing we call a kitchen. And"—she turned to Harry as the only one who was not familiar with her house rules—"we draw lots for the first shift. Min, Harry, the kids, even me. Equal justice under the law." There was no escaping.

It seemed unlikely that Harry had ever been asked to dry, much less to wash a dish. It was not his style and he carried his style with him wherever he was. He kept it intact under a life-size plexiglass bubble. He had walked through the student riots in Paris, paving stones ricocheting off the invisible shield; he had toured lower Calcutta during the religious uprisings, oblivious to rocks, clubs, mud, dog feces all thrown in his direction, none reaching the immaculate perfection of his linen suit. It was a case of cosmic favoritism.

And now the bubble walled him off from the task of washing. The lottery went to Kraft and to Min, who had just wandered back in without a word of explanation. Hildy was the put-awayer.

Kraft began with an extravagant flourish, pouring scalding water from the kettle held high over the pan and then adding a slosh of cold from the bucket. It was important to demonstrate his complete sobriety. Besides, it was always necessary for him to provide a heightened enthusiasm for the more primitive aspects of the place, Napoleon enthusing over the splendors of a Russian winter.

Kraft had the feeling that his troops were never far from outright rebellion. They were forever hinting at the worst sort of so-called improvements. It was bad enough to have given in on the bottled gas—the stove and the little Canadian-made gas refrigerator. But there he drew the line. No more. Not another step.

Just the previous summer they had subtly left on his desk a page torn from the Montgomery Ward catalogue, an ad for a hand pump which would pull water from the well and force it up to a tank over the sink, from which it would flow down through a spigot into a sink just as it did in suburban America. He told Min how he had blocked the scheme, how he would not give in, but she was in one of her sullen moods for some reason and told him she had heard it all before.

He refused to be dragged down by her mood. He rolled up his sleeves, a gesture of enthusiasm, took another sip of rum, and gave her a dishtowel with a flourish. "Good, honest, proletarian labor," he said. "It'll do wonders for you. Helps clean out all that musty spiritualism."

"What does it clean out of *you*, Kraft?"

"My bourgeois roots. Simple as that."

He heard Harry's laugh and looked over his shoulder to the flickering image of the living room as seen through the laths. A form on the couch—that would be Tammy—and one now bending over the liquor cabinet: that would be Harry reaching for his cognac and offering one to Tammy, her head nodding, and his voice, low and almost seductive, "Not a bad life, really, as long as you can keep the staff happy."

Kraft let out a yelp of pain. The water had been scalding. "Goddammit," he said, and slopped in more cold. In his rage, he misjudged: the pan was now lukewarm. There was no more hot in the kettle.

"Just right," he said.

"That was quick," she said, brightening.

"What was quick?"

"Cosmic retribution."

"Cosmic *what?*"

"The response of the cosmos to your hostility. Don't you feel in balance now? I knew it would come."

"Predicted it?"

"Of course. Like I knew we'd be on the same shift. If you've been released from your hostile period, I'll tell you why we ended up on the same shift."

"O.K., tell me why. I'll stay in balance like a good boy." He didn't want to know, didn't want to hear any more of her cant, but he didn't want to overhear Harry and Tammy either. "Why?"

"We're both Gemini."

He let a stack of dishes slide into the water, shaking his head. "I thought you'd do better than that. That star stuff . . . Tell me, Min, aside from the fact that we both breathe air, what have we in common? Name one thing."

"Very strong crosscurrents."

"Schizophrenia? You're the one who's schizophrenic."

"What's schizo-what's it?" Hildy said.

"Schizo-phrenic," Min said, enunciating. "It's when the mind works in a different dimension." She had pulled over a high stool and was sitting there, drying dishes in a desultory manner, dripping water on her long black skirt and on the floor. She was, Kraft decided, a *National Geographic* version of the loony at Delphi. "Sometimes a higher dimension than we can imagine."

"She means crazy," Kraft said.

"It can't be both those things," Hildy said.

"Oh, it can," Min said, bending down toward Hildy, nodding wisely. "Those who fear it give it a bad name."

"Have you ever been schizo-what's it?"

"Phrenic. Schizo-phrenic. Try it."

"Min! For God's sake."

"Try *say*ing it," she said to Hildy. And to Kraft, a reptilian smile on her face, "Afraid of words?"

"Schizo-phrenic. Schizo-phrenic," Hildy chanted, delighted with the sound of it. "Schizo-phrenic."

From the next room, Tammy's voice, disembodied: "What's that all about?"

"Your sister's catechism."

"Schizo-phrenic. Schizo-phrenic. Schizo-phrenic."

"Cut that out," Kraft said, "Just shut up."

He washed in a fury. Out of the corner of his eye he caught Min performing a pantomime of a petulant child as if saying, "Just . . . shut . . . up," bobbing her head with each unspoken word. He thought he heard them giggle.

The silence he had ordered settled on them all like an evening fog. Kraft could hear Tammy saying something to Harry in that low, ironic voice of hers and the two of them laughed. Kraft felt a quick flash of uncertain jealousy. She should be bored by such conventions, by such concern for brandy-by-the-fire rituals. She should be making polite conversation, waiting for Kraft to return. It was hardly right for the two of them in there to be enjoying each other that much. After all, Harry was old enough to be Tammy's father.

He struggled to fill the silence in the kitchen. Even cult talk would be better than silence, better than "dead air." She beat him to it.

"Moss," she said suddenly, breathlessly.

"What?"

"Moss."

"That's what I thought you said."

"From the trees."

"That's where it usually is. Yes."

"Purple moss."

"Right, Min. Coming down from trees." He had stopped washing and was staring at her. Was she at last, finally, coming apart? Unhinged? Right here? In front of the children? "Do you really see moss?" he asked. He had lowered his voice as if asking her whether she was having menstrual cramps.

"Where?" she said.

"Where? *I* don't know where."

"Oh, I thought perhaps you were hallucinating. I hoped you had, in fact. It would be a good sign."

"Hallucinating. Min, for Christ sake, *you* started off talking about moss, right out of a blue sky."

"No, on trees. I saw it hanging on trees coming in here this afternoon. Not now, Kraft. Earlier. Don't confuse now with earlier. Keep them separate. Anyway, I saw moss and I thought: No, I can't be seeing moss because it only grows in the South."

"So then you thought *you* were hallucinating. . . ."

"What's hallucinating?" Hildy asked.

"Vision," Min said.

"Everyone has *that*. Like seeing?"

"This is when you see something no one else does."

"Like seeing something from another life?"

141

"Like being crazy," Kraft said. "It's just part of being crazy."

"Having other lives isn't crazy," Hildy said.

Kraft drew in his breath and let it out slowly. He knew from experience that it didn't pay to hit this one head on. He had hoped that *this* summer Min might be off on some new branch of kookery and that his Hildy would find her former lives withering on the vine. No such luck.

"We have to understand," Min said gently to Hildy, "that some people have no sense of their former lives. They just can't feel it. No contact. It's natural for them to label what they don't understand as 'crazy.' We mustn't make them feel bad, love."

"We mustn't, mustn't we? You just keep that stuff in your own drafty skull, will you? Just keep your hands off my children."

Min opened her mouth with the shock of some southern belle who has heard an obscene word. "Why Kraft, what incredible things go through your head!"

"Are you two at it again?" Tammy's voice from the living room, clear as if she were beside them.

"Will you kindly tell your sister what she can do with her reincarnation theories?"

"Reincarnation?" Harry's disembodied voice.

"She believes in it," Kraft said. "Implicitly."

"Good Lord. Does this run in families? I mean, are the rest of you reincarnated?"

"I am," Hildy said.

"Are you really?" Harry's voice. "How do you know? I mean, how can you be sure?"

A snort of laughter from an invisible Weldon. "Because Aunt Min told her so."

"Don't be snide." Tammy's voice.

"Never mind my stupid brother," Hildy said to Harry, to Min, to everyone. "He wouldn't see his other lives even if we showed him photographs."

"They didn't even have photographs back then, silly."

"Weldon," Harry said, "how can you be sure it's all bunk?"

"Are you kidding?"

"Well, you've got to have some proof, you know. I mean, proof that there isn't . . . well, former lives and all."

"It's common sense."

"Sure, but that's not much of an argument. What if they said the same thing?"

"Then they'd be crazy."

"Right on," Kraft said. And then regretted it. He had hurt Hildy. Still, Weldon needed support. Anyone trying to be rational deserved support. Especially with crazies about.

"It's a proven fact," Min said. She spoke earnestly to empty space, her face aimed somewhere between Kraft and the semi-wall through which their voices came. "Certain people have the ability to see images of their former selves. Or future selves. Mostly in dreams, of course; but sometimes in waking life. Documented cases."

Kraft handed her a serving dish dripping with sudsy water. "Look," he said, "every hallucination by every patient in a booby hatch can be 'documented.' All you need is a fellow nut to say, 'Yes, yes, Jesus stood right there.' That's documentation. Take it from me, Min, history is full of that stuff—from walking on water right down to UFOs. 'Documentation' is the first thing you do to dress up a fraud."

Weldon's laugh drifted through the kitchen as if he were beside them. And from his brother, "Shut up, dummy."

"Hey, Ric"—a father's appeal—"you're not falling for this, are you?"

"No fair laughing at it."

So the black plague had broken out where least expected. Ric the outgoing, the healthy, the fisherman. Ric the incorruptible. Now suddenly showing symptoms.

"Laugh?" Kraft said. "I find it hilarious."

"No you don't," Min said. "Not at all."

A moment of silence. Kraft squinted to keep Min from going out of focus.

"Hilarious," he said, his voice steely. "A joke, a laugh; the funniest thing since the Ascension."

From the other room: "You know what Hildy thinks she was?" Weldon's voice turned nasty.

"No fair," Hildy said.

"A princess." Weldon's voice. "A little storybook princess."

"Well, it's true," Hildy said. Her eyes were brimming.

Kraft opened his mouth but said nothing, caught between loyalties. Weldon was right, of course, taking a solid, rational stand. But how could anyone strike out at Hildy, his beautiful little princess?

*"Prin*cess Hildy." Weldon's voice at its very worst.

"Shut *up,*" from Hildy.

"Come on now," Kraft said to her, his voice low. "Princesses don't cry."

The wrong move. "I'm not a princess *now,* dummy," and a flood of tears. Laughter from the other room. A shout of protest from Ric.

Kraft leaned against the sink, his head humming. Was this the only way to regenerate the world? Living like this? All these battles and alliances and struggles for position. Was it possible that all over the country at that very moment there were people like himself trying to be fathers, husbands, lovers, hosts, and intelligent citizens at the same time without any guidelines, without prepared scripts? Domestic anarchy! Nothing out there but a clutter of crazy cults. No social consensus. No agreement as to what was real and what was illusion, truth and fraud. No wonder marriages were breaking like eggshells. The whole society had been cast adrift, was being swept out to sea. No moorings. No landmarks. No charts.

Not even a war to oppose. For half a decade they had been held together opposing a stupid, blind, mad war—all right-thinking people in a single cause. And the opposition united in their own way. Now nothing. Bits and pieces of nothing. The ascension of the crazies.

It occurred to him with the suddenness of divine inspiration that the appeal of the socialist state was not economic at all; it was psychological—a rage for order (whose phrase was that?). Here he was, an adult already, adrift in this fractured decade. What chance did he have to see socialist order in his time? Christ, he was doomed to a lifetime of barnyard squabbling—cults, tribes, ethnics, each with its ordained loony in the pulpit. One of them right in his own house, corrupting his own children!

He put down a dripping pan and located his rum glass among the dirty dishes, drained the ice water, and poured himself another. Splash of fresh water from the ladle. Damn, no ice left. Nasty taste. He tried recalling a theory about roles to play without prepared scripts, without guidelines, but it had slipped its mooring, had drifted away with the currents.

What was it about his family and friends that made things so damn difficult? Why couldn't they be manageable, stay in place? There was something terribly wrong with the age he was living in—the worst decade of the worst century. In the thirties they would have been drawn together in poverty, the common cause, the collective agony. Earlier—nineteenth or eighteenth century—they could have shared the effort of agriculture, working in the fields by day, reading the Bible aloud in the evening around the single lamp. *Pilgrim's Progress* read in installments by the patriarch, family sitting in rapt attention. A better opiate than *things,* for God's sake.

Here they were, sniping, tearing at each other with crazy theories, flying apart like the cosmos after that great explosion. He had a sudden impulse to leave them all, to go up to his study, to lock the door, to plunge himself into the manuscript, into his psychohistorical analysis of Roosevelt, his fireside chats, those lessons in economics and fortitude delivered with calm assurance, the nation sitting by the radio in rapt attention.

"All right, kids." Tammy's voice, commanding. "Time to hit the sack." Army talk.

Like the cavalry, Kraft thought. In the nick of time. He glanced at his watch and saw that it was exactly ten o'clock, their summer bedtime. Why hadn't he thought of that? There he was trying to battle the age and defend himself against the tyranny of children and save his princess daughter from being torn to bits, when all he had to do was to order them to bed. Tammy had saved him: her respect for schedules and the order of the day's events matched his own reverence for dates and the intermeshing of history. Well, to hell with that. He should be able to fight his own battles, to wipe away the corruptions of a bourgeois society, to protect his family, to protect himself.

Upstairs he heard the boys complaining about the early hour and Hildy pleading for a reading. *Pilgrim's Progress?* Hardly. More likely *National Velvet.* In any case, it was going to be a long session for Tammy getting them down. He wished he could take the strap to them, but what the hell kind of wish was that? The kids had been raised to be protesters, to be civilly disobedient. How were they going to survive when they were getting two utterly opposed signals? How was *he* going to survive? Why did evenings like this produce nothing but questions?

The shadow image which was Harry crossed the living room and turned on the portable radio. A crackle of stations and then a Mahler symphony. That would be CBC. It was too romantic for Kraft's taste, but it did block out the sound of the children upstairs. Harry was a simple man of action.

The form crossed the room again and became visible in the doorway. "Poor Min!" he said. "All this work and no one offered you a drink." Poor Min, yet! "What will it be?"

She asked for a brandy and Harry went back to the living room to get a bottle, acting the host. Kraft, hearing him, seeing him, saw for an instant himself in Harry, saw what he could become or perhaps a hidden self—the Harry of charm, assurance, and no social conscience. Was it possible that everything Kraft imagined to be his convictions was really a malignancy, was really something that could be cut out?

He downed the remains of his rum. There were streaks of soapy water down the sides.

Min and Harry were talking about Lincoln Center, some pressing problem about the acoustics. They addressed each other through the wall as if it did not exist and walled Kraft off as if he were some nineteenth-century child, there to be seen and not heard. When Harry returned with a snifter for Min and his own drink, he apparently assumed that Kraft would not or should not have an after-dinner drink. Well, to hell with them both. Kraft poured himself another, casually turning his back, half expecting a reprimand.

"That's too bad," Harry said, "their being rounded up and herded off like that. I was just beginning to learn something. All that reincarnation stuff."

"It's no joke," Kraft said.

"I thought you thought it was."

"It's no joke the way Min has dumped all that psychic mumbo-jumbo on the children."

"It's not me," she said with a weary little shrug. "I just give words for what they sense intuitively from their unconscious. I'm just the catalyst. They're in better touch with their unconscious than you are." A nod at Kraft. "They're in tune. They can feel the pulse of the racial memory, get flickering images, catch the shapes that are shaping them. Oh, I'm not worried about *them*. Not at all." And to Harry,

"Children, as you know, are naturally psychic. They can let themselves go without"—she groped for a word—"the *retrogression* of alcohol."

Without a word of apology, the two of them left Kraft to finish up in the kitchen. He thought of quitting, leaving the place in a mess, but finishing was a part of the system; and system, Kraft reminded himself, was all that kept the place from turning into a loony bin.

He carried the scummy dishwater out to the back steps and slopped it into the dark; he mopped off the drainboard, hung up the sodden towels. How was it that someone who could gore *Time* into doing an outraged review of his first full-length book of historical analysis could not so much as prick the conscience of two self-invited houseguests?

When he finished, everything was in its place: pan hanging on the pan hook, ladle on the ladle nail, mixing bowls on the bowl shelf, nested, towels on the towel rack. It was a kitchen in which even Thea could take pride. Thea? His hand shook as he poured himself one absolutely final drink.

When he reentered the living room, the two of them were standing in front of the Franklin stove, speaking to each other in such intimate tones that they were no more than inches apart. Harry and Min!

"Hey!" Kraft said, a protest.

"What's the matter?" Harry said, stepping back from Min.

"A hell of a kitchen worker *you* are," Kraft said.

Min drew herself up. "I've never been deeply thrilled by that sort of work. Besides, I thought we were through."

"Well, I'm not through with all this . . . all this occult dream stuff. I want you to stop. . . ." He paused, felt his head go soft, start oozing; the couple before him blurred. He tried to remember who they were. It would have helped if he could be sure where he was. Time had slid—or was it place?

"Have a seat," one of them said.

"You're sick," the other said.

He was not sick and he would not take a seat. If the world was unsteady, it was hardly his fault. He managed to find the doorframe and grip it, cling to it.

But like everything else that evening, it failed him. It began to crumble, turning insubstantial. It swung to the left and was not even buoyant enough to support his weight. No damn good as a life raft. It must have sunk completely, because now they were negotiating the steps, one at a time, the water rising behind him, dark and turgid, cluttered with wreckage. Keep moving. His arms were over their shoulders. He could smell after-shave.

"Don't you worry," he said. "Head for higher ground."

The doorframe to the bedroom moved toward him, an archway. Somehow it slid around all three of them and disappeared behind. The bed rose to him and he lay there, spread-eagled while these two people removed his shirt and pants, talking to each other in brief, low phrases as if he were not quite there.

He reached up for contact, touched her face, kissed her. Then he saw the other figure standing at the foot of the bed, frowning. He lay back.

It was not surprising that he should be put to bed. That was a part of the order of things. And the feminine hand that now wiped the sweat from his brow was not unfamiliar. It was beautifully, reassuringly familiar. But how strange to have *him* up here too, to have him share in the ritual of going to bed. Strange to have his help, his concern.

What could have brought the two of them together like that? Made them all mellow. Gentle.

"Don't go," he said. "I'd like to talk. Really."

But by the time his eyes focused, they both were gone. He was very much alone.

14

Picture: A gleaming, eye-squinting chessboard. Large enough to walk on. A chessboard patio. Sunlit. The warmth is good, but he has advanced too far. He wants to move three spaces back, but he cannot. He is not directing his own moves.

The board on which he stands is transparent. There are layers beneath. It is a three-dimensional set—an incredibly complicated game even for experts, and he doesn't feel expert. He is only learning and there is no rulebook. *Blip!* He feels himself slip through the first level to the second. Another game going on here laterally; also connections up and down, vertical and on the diagonal. Bad enough on one plane. Where to move? And how?

"Sonofabitch," he said aloud. The image broke. He bobbed to the surface. Morning already. Real sunlight filled the room, window frame spreading a pattern of large squares across the floor and bed. Also, one hell of a headache.

Below him, people in the kitchen, others in the living room—the scrape of a chair, someone's cough, the click of a spoon against a dish, the slosh of water being poured from the bucket into the kettle. Coffee. The aroma seeped up through the hollow walls, wafted between floorboards, permeated the house. That meant there was no breeze, the outside air breathless. He imagined Thea bringing him a cup of coffee—not a word from her, just motion, silently setting it beside him, running a cool hand across his throbbing brow. Aid, solace, comfort, and no words; blessedly no words, nothing which would require response of any kind.

But no, that was unrealistic. If anyone appeared, it would be Tammy, and if Tammy came it would be with a wry comment on the evening. An answer required. He was not up to that kind of agility. If only he could forget the evening, retreat, slip back three, maybe four spaces, back to solitude, back before all this clutter of family and guests.

He got up and started dressing because the day demanded it. Besides, he didn't want to risk more dreams. The entire evening was now a dream in retrospect and he wanted to shake it, shake free. Getting to work was the only way. Work was always the way.

But he was not about to go down there. No, not yet. For one thing, he would have to deal with Tammy. Had she even slept with him? It was hard to say. It wasn't easy to construct a defense when he didn't know exactly what the charge would be. It never was.

"Oh, it's just marvelous. . . ." Min's voice drifting up through the floorboards, light as smoke. "Breathe in that ozone."

"Try some oxygen too," Kraft said, speaking genially to the floorboards.

"You're awake? Do come down. It's just vibrant."

"What is?"

"The day. Oh Kraft, don't be your usual sour self on a day like this. It's criminal. Come down and breathe it in."

"Have to work, Min. No time for breathing."

"Don't be sullen."

"Some of us have work to do. Can't all be idle rich."

That shut her up. Like her sister, she respected work. A rare overlap in values. Hamlet would not kill a man while he was at the altar; but here was a breed who wouldn't touch a man while at his desk. The moment he went down those stairs, he'd be fair game. The study as sanctuary; the mind as sanctum sanctorum.

The voice from below went on—faintly now, directed laterally, at someone on her own plane: "Absolute harmony of bird song . . . Crickets have such vitality . . . The caress of the sea sounds, the anima speaking to us all. How can you . . ."

He left his bedroom, crossed the hall, entered his study, closed the door carefully. Locked it. Thanks to an old rug, the clichés became muffled, garbled, the anima held at bay. What little seepage remained he could block out with his work, his concentration.

Mournfully he looked out at the panorama and longed for a three-day nor'easter, the Gothic phenomenon which two or three times a summer drove wind and rain in from the North Atlantic, wet and penetrating, unrelenting. But no, no such luck. The sky was cloudless, the sun Californian. He looked out on the rocky pastures with their outcroppings of ledge, nameless wild flowers all over the place, and then the marshland estuary, the roof of Thea's place. Ah, Thea. A part of his realm.

Would they really dare take all this away from him? Wrench it out from under him? After years of self-denial, this was the only indulgence he had allowed himself, and now they were after him as if he had established a dukedom. Shoddy politicians! Out to get him just because he was smart enough to seize it at the right time.

Sometimes it was awkward, owning all this. But his conscience was clear, absolutely clear. After all, this whole coast had lain dormant, almost abandoned for a generation. Some of it was even going for taxes. Worthless. He stood up and started pacing, his head still throbbing.

All I did was give it value. Found something lying around that no one wanted and gave it value. So they want to grab it back. Illegal and immoral. Breaking the social contract. Dictatorial.

He glowered at himself in an old, wavy-glass mirror. His image was twisted to the left, askew. If he moved a hair's breadth it twisted to the right, equally absurd. Well, if it came to confrontation, he was willing to go to the barricades, take up arms. He had dealt with fascists before.

He sat down at his desk again, but there right in front of him was that incredible view. Distracting. But soothing too. Tranquil from this distance; detached as a photograph. If he were downstairs he would have to go out on the front stoop with the others, ritualistically, breathing deeply, smothered in clichés. And ozone. No, it was much better from here. He was not going to let them spoil it for him.

Women's voices drifted up to him. Laughter. Startling to realize that those two sisters sometimes shared something, even a laugh. More than that, of course. They'd shared parents. Perhaps that's where it started—just as Min said. He remembered their father as a tough, demanding labor lawyer. Maybe he had seen Tammy as a son. In any case, he let Min drift free. And drift she had. Some pair!

". . . ordered it for you," he heard Tammy say. Ordered what? The weather, of course. What else?

"Looking out there . . ." Min's voice so clear she must be standing at the foot of the stairs at the open door; breathing more ozone, no doubt. "I tell you, perfect harmony."

Kraft snorted. Could she be looking down into the marshland? Had she ever waded along those estuaries? The bloodshed! Even now as she was standing there, fish snapping up the fry, their own included, herons after fish. No security ever, never safe. Perpetual threat. Worse than urban living any day. He imagined being seized in an enormous beak, carried with his back breaking, thousands of feet high, praying for death. Harmony, his ass!

If there was any harmony on earth, it was up here in

his study, protected by dusty glass, miles from that battle-ground where creatures copulated and snapped at each other, producing life and destroying it in one long, sustained battle. No, that was no place to learn anything. Only here, detached and yet concerned, disinterested but not uninterested, here he could meet with the past at his leisure, could speculate and make sense of it all. He had been no historian those decades he had spent down there fighting for good causes. Even if he had affected the outcome of history—which was doubtful—he hadn't been a competent observer. Entirely too partisan. Those in the battle know nothing. Those in the street see nothing.

He would remain in his study, would work on his manuscript, would make real progress this morning, would have something solid to show for it.

But first, a few moments with his father's journal. Later he would turn to the writing, would work double time. Just a few moments with the journal would clear his head, get the juices flowing.

He picked up the 1926 volume with pleasure and with guilt—his secret vice, his opium pipe, his pornographic masterwork.

> June 19, Sat., 1926. Moved to Croftham for the summer. Got staff up at 5.00 a.m. to complete packing and sent them down to station with trunks, hampers, and cases in three cabs. Henly in charge of my personal luggage; cook in charge of maids. Then Miss W. and I drove to Croftham at break-neck speed, racing the train to unload and hide booze in private. Later met staff at depot as if coming from Boston.
>
> Delivered them to the house in time for a quick sail in a stiff S.W. gale and then a swimming lesson for Miss W. Like almost all from fishing and farming families around here, she has never swum a stroke. Astonishing! Wind dropped at twilight for picnic on beach. Finished the evening with a canoe trip, following the coast by starlight. No sounds but paddles and whippoorwills from shore.

> June 20, Sun., 1926. Breakfast late—8.30—on acct. of be-
> ing Sunday. A pleasure to be at the Cottage again. Gave
> tennis lessons to Miss W. in early morning. Then took her
> out for golf. Miss W. a natural at sports though of course
> untrained. Chopped wood in afternoon. Miss W. brought
> picnic of my favorites—calf's tongue, pickled beets, and bot-
> tles of ice-cold Chablis. Found mossy bank secluded from
> staff. Spent much of afternoon there. Took Miss W. sailing
> in late afternoon and in evening had rum before roaring
> fire. Rum still a new and heady experience for Miss W.
> An extraordinary evening. Most pleased at turn of events.

Someone was coming upstairs and Kraft slammed the book shut. But that was absurd, of course. The door was locked.

Door locked? Against what? He was involved in legitimate and necessary research. Psychohistory. An intimate glimpse of . . . No, *socio*history, an objective examination of pre-depression life among the power elite.

"You awake?" Harry's voice.

"Of course."

"Going to join us?"

"Sorry. Working. See you all for lunch."

"Right."

Steps retreating. Checkmate. *Blip!* He felt himself slip from that level down into the journal again, skimming over the details: rhododendrons well out and bridal wreath. Quince came and went. Hardy azaleas out and doing well. First of the rose bugs spotted. (Kraft recalled picking them off, dropping them into kerosene—a penny for every ten.) Last year's blight on the ginkgo tree checked by heavy feeding. Dogwood winter-damaged.

From horticultural weekends the journal plunged back into the business week. Most of those three summer months he spent commuting by train just as *his* father had, two hours each way. But when the pressure was really on, he took the car for a predawn start.

June 28, Mon., 1926. Left for Boston by motor at 5.00 a.m. Miss W. up at 4.00 before cook to make liver and onions for me. Packed my things while I ate. A good start. Spent a long and hectic day at the office. Allied Packers revitalized with $16,000,000 and highly advantageous merger with Central States. Georgia Creosote Plant launched. Labor is cheap & docile. Potential is unlimited. May have to go public. Ralph Long just back from a week of negotiations in Rio and reports all in good hands there. Takeover is essentially complete. Only minor details remain. Local staff mostly incompetent & will be replaced w. U.S. personnel. I will stay here in Boston for a few days. Empty house is strange. I miss Croftham terribly.

June 29, Tue., 1926. At work by 7.00. No breakfast because staff is all at the shore. Miss W. managing things there. Mid-morning I had office boy bring up beef kidney stew from Durgin Park. Also three mugs of coffee, apple pie, cheese . . . .

"Breakfast?" Tammy's voice from downstairs. "Kraft, are you awake?"

"No."

"Want breakfast in your sleep?"

"No." Abrupt. Too abrupt. "Thanks, but I've got to work." The inviolable excuse. Asylum.

Harry's deep voice drifted through the house. He was asking Tammy if by any chance the general store carried the *Times.* The sound of Tammy's laughter. Lovely. No one he knew had a more genuine, melodious laugh. An old longing flushed through him. But no, this wasn't the time to join the crowd. This was work time.

He returned to 1926 and was locked into a scheme whereby a barge line to Cuba would be launched, barges soon replaced with freighters, line extended to S. America with federal assistance, one hand helping the other.

"Daddy . . ." Knocking at the door.

"Busy."

"Daddy, it's me." Hildy's voice. Hildy requesting a special dispensation. Requesting and getting. Kraft unlocking the door.

"Coffee?" she asked. Unfair tactics. They were treating him like a man bent on suicide. Getting him to say something every five minutes. Next they would be installing a one-way peephole in the door.

"Leave it there."

"Where? On all those papers? What *is* that?"

"The book I'm doing. The history book."

"This?" Her eyes drawn right to the journals, magnetic attraction. "That's an old book."

"That's something I'm using. Research. Written years ago. Look, put that coffee down over there before you spill it, will you?"

"You're copying the old book? That's not right."

Closed his eyes, drew in breath, clenched fists, then smiled at his daughter. "Not copying, honey, drawing from them. Building on them. Making use of them. That's what history is all about—reconstructing the past. Now look, just leave the coffee and say thanks to Mum."

"It was Aunt Min that sent me up. She said you were sending her thought waves."

"As indeed I was. But not the message she thought. Now look, tell your Aunt Min to take that coffee and . . . No, tell her thanks, but it's too strong a stimulant for me this morning. Tell her I want to be in complete harmony with nature."

"That doesn't make sense."

"Just tell her. She'll figure out something."

"Why are you mean to Aunt Min?"

"Mean? Me? I'm not being mean. It's just that she has . . . well, strange ideas."

"That's because she's the youngest in her family. Like me."

"Hildy, you have a much better grip on things."

"How come? She's old enough to be my mother. She *is* my spiritual mother, you know. She told me."

"Oh, she did? Ah. Well. Umm. Look, trust your own spirit, honey."

"Sorry, but I got to hurry. We're going to the beach."

She left, footsteps clattering down the stairs. Spiritual mother yet! Poor Hildy. One more clutter to untangle before she could grow up. What a laborious business, reaching adulthood!

Tammy's penetrating voice drifted up, asking Harry if he wanted milk in his coffee; Min's voice saying ". . . 'harmony'? He said that? Well, we're making progress. Now, next time you go up . . ." A conspiracy!

Footsteps to the front of the house. Mindless chatter. Screen door slamming—once, twice. Silence, sweet as music. Kraft stealthily slid back the bolt, opened his door, almost stepped on the coffee mug. Hildy had left it on the threshold, a kind of offering. It was lukewarm. Didn't Min know that he liked it scalding? He could do with Canadian bacon and three eggs too, but he didn't want to pay for it. He sipped the tepid stuff like medicine.

Then he wrote a note and posted it on the outside of his door. "Working," it said.

That should hold them. Keep the house between me and them. Out of sight, out of earshot. A sad day when a man has to sneak out of his own house. Privacy the scarcest commodity left on earth. If I can just get to the line of trees without being spotted. Escaping a goddamned concentration camp. Could get a bullet in my back any moment. Dogs set on me. My own house! There—behind the scrub oak. Another fifty feet and I'll be there. What's Tammy got in mind, anyway, bringing up the whole crew? People is one thing I don't want right now.

Furtive, darting from cover to cover, the figure slipped undetected from house to trees, from trees to the spruce grove. With a final, daring dash, he made the tallest one, and tucking a small volume in his belt, swung himself up the wooden slats.

Greatest risk right now. No cover. Take my chances. Thirteen more rungs. Quickly now. Five. Now, up now.

He tumbled into the tree house, breathing hard. For an instant he held his breath, listening. Not a sound. Not so much as a dog's bark. Perfect.

Strange that he hadn't thought of this before. An ideal retreat. Compact. Six feet by four feet. Walls almost high enough to hide him if he sat on the floor. A roof supported on four corner posts to keep the sun off.

He had not been up there for two years, not since the week they finished it. They had brought him up for one triumphant tour ("See—we didn't need your help at all!") and then he had honored their claim to privacy. It had begun with a family dispute about rights of property. The boys had insisted that their rooms were off bounds to adults ("We're citizens too"—echoes of adolescent liberation) and been refused ("The family is a social unit; all space shared"). The tree house was the negotiated settlement. Absolute privacy. A corner of their own.

But that was two years ago. Old issues fade quickly, old slogans disappear. Also enthusiasms. The crystal radio was there, attached to the aerial, forgotten, replaced by boating, riding, whatever. The place hadn't even been cleaned up: An old pillow chewed open by squirrels, a pile of acorn shells in the corner, three weathered playing cards, a tennis ball, a torn fatigue cap, two illicit bottles of Labatt ale (so much for liberation), some fishline with a rusty bucket tied to the end, a battered, coverless paperback entitled *The Pleasures of Bondage*, a Yo-Yo with a grinning face on each side. No compulsion, apparently, to tidy up the past.

Looking out, he could see back to the house, partially obscured by trees, a bit dark and brooding from his angle.

159

The gray of weathered wood and the long grass all about made it look like some outpost. Shabbier than he liked to think of it. But that was only appearance. In fact, it was everything he had wanted it to be—except when it was filled with a clutter of guests all out for a slice of his life. Except for that, it was serving its purpose. His fortress.

He had come here to work. He would not forget that. He hadn't come up here to play, certainly. He took out the journal from 1926 and opened it with determination, the willful motion of a man who has work to do. Not easy, really, after all that exertion. Out of shape. Still breathing hard. But never mind that. "Never mind that," he said.

> July 9, Fri., 1926. To Boston on the 7.10. Studied Alabama file *en route*. Ignored acquaintances with banal comments about the weather and state of the market. Mid-morning conference with delegation from Mobile Dockage. Subtle negotiations. Acquired 22% of the stock through Means office. Signed agreement shortly before lunch. Previously picked up 12% through a dummy corp. and 17% rather quietly through N. Y. office of Conti. Treated the four Alabama gentlemen and their counsel to a five-course dinner at Somerset Club and sent them on their way. It will be a week or so before they will be informed that I now have controlling interest. Company will benefit in the long run, though three of the four directors will have to go.

Ah, bloodshed among the gentry. Life cycles in the marshland.

> Tense and edgy when I got home so chopped wood for an hour in the rain. Felled two ailing oaks. Left clearing and bucking to Mr. Higgs and crew.
> Took Miss W. for a canoe trip around breakwater to cove. Gale force winds and heavy seas. Good fun but we almost didn't make it. Miss W. a bit pale on acct. of not knowing how to swim, but a great good sport. Finished up with a

swimming lesson in the surf and a run on the beach to
keep warm. Then a hot bath and rum. Dinner postponed
an hour. Miss W. a master at placating surly staff on such
occasions.

In evening I built a roaring fire and started teaching Miss
W. dancing with songs on Gramophone. Much laughter and
rum. Eventually she . . .

"Hey!" Shrill voice. "Hey, who's that?" Keep quiet. "Hey,
someone's in the tree house."

"Who's that in the tree house?"

"He ducked. Look, get around this way—you can see
him. See him?"

"Get Dad. Tell him to bring a gun."

"That *is* Daddy."

"Dad? Is that you?"

"That's Dad, all right."

"Hey, no fair. You're in our tree house. What are you
doing there?"

"No fair. That's our place. You're too big for it, anyhow.
Come on, that's our place."

15

"I hadn't intended to."

"Of course not."

"I had no other choice."

"None at all."

"You'd think with 953 acres I'd find some privacy. Well, that's why I'm here."

"Always welcome. You know that."

"You don't mind?"

"Of course not."

"I mean, with Tammy back and all."

"That has nothing to do with us. That's separate."

She reached over and ran her fingers through the hair on his chest and gave his neck a kiss. They were both naked, spent, lying in a rumpled nest of sheets and blankets. The room smelled of lovemaking. The old man was off scavenging and wouldn't be back for an hour. The air was still.

Idly he studied the clutter on the commode next to the bed: the kerosene lamp, the Bible, the copy of *Pilgrim's Progress*, and a package of Trojans. And now his father's two volumes bound in faded blue leather, one marked

"1926" and the other "1927." He had brought them to read in peace and quiet on her porch; he had taken them upstairs when they decided to read them together, aloud, in her bedroom. They had actually done this, he filling in the details about the cast of characters, reading and fondling, then more fondling than reading.

It was not a ruse on his part. He really did want to share those journals with her, whether she believed it or not. He wanted to help her cross through the glass like Alice, to enter that wonder world, to help him enter, to be there with him. To *be* those entries.

He was not used to feelings like these. They were strange, imprecise, not subject to argumentation, astonishingly strong. Nostalgia gone wrong, gone out of control. He wasn't used to that. Had no training in letting go. Fascinating but unnerving. A shiver of anxiety.

"Sometimes I miss politics," he said. "Wish I hadn't left it."

"What made you say that?"

He shrugged. "Just thinking. There was a time, you know, when it was central. Everything. It got me up in the morning. Even when students were doing nothing. Like in the fifties. And when they finally got going—the sixties—I just moved faster. Kept ahead of them. Until the bombings. Almost then too. Felt guilty about not pushing my convictions to the ultimate—blowing up buildings and all."

"But now? What about now?" She was lying back with her hands under her head, sheet across her chest on a bias, carelessly exposing one breast. Odd how she had no modesty. A country girl with her background should be shy, but she had no shame whatever. Walked around the room like a whore. No, like an Eve. Uncorrupted. "I want to know about now," she said softly.

"Now . . . it's like the war is over. I don't mean that the issues are over. I suppose they're all out there somewhere. Nothing really solved. But it's over for me. I've been discharged, sent home. Now I can do exactly what I've always wanted to do."

"And you do it very nicely."

"Yuh, well, thanks, but I didn't mean that."

"I know, I know." Resignation. "You meant your history book."

"My . . ." That was not where he had been spending his time. But what kind of historian admits to whiling away his time in Wonderland? "Yes, my history book."

"Men are different that way," she said. She lowered one arm from behind her head and idly massaged his stomach. Not an invitation, not even a conscious act. "Men have their work. That's the way they are. More drive."

He nodded. That was the way *he* was, and if she assumed the same about all men, it was all right with him. Somewhere women were struggling against that kind of thinking, and they were right, of course. Men had no monopoly on drive. He knew that. But here the two of them were insulated from political issues. This was his island and he was her Prospero. The one with drive.

"A fighter," she said. "That's what you are. All that political stuff and now the book. You get things done."

He nodded, shrugged modestly, smiled. He'd heard it before from students and others. Even from Tammy. He had his issues, his causes, his research. Now he had a manuscript to complete. His sustenance. Where was the pleasure? All he could feel was the tension, the deadlines, the weight of it all like chains.

"O.K.," he said, "but right now I don't feel like pushing for a while. I mean, I've put in my time. It's someone else's turn. Right now I feel like pulling back, getting out, doing a little thinking. I owe myself a little something. A little indulgence."

"Of course you do." she said, nuzzling his shoulder, nibbling. But that wasn't what he meant at all. How could he tell her he just wanted to read the journals, share them with her in a relaxed, nonanalytical way. That's all he wanted.

In the silence he discovered his fingers had been wandering, browsing, in the marshland below her stomach, drawn by moisture. Without his permission they had reached her inner thigh, working upward idly toward the headwaters.

He pulled them back. He was not at all ready for that. All the wrong signals.

"Look, I came down here to get some work done." He pulled the sheet over her.

"I thought you said . . . You mean your reading?"

"Those journals."

"Ah, the journals." Resignation. And an almost-smile. Disbelief? "It sure is hard for you to turn off."

"Who's turned off?"

"Sorry." She detached herself from him, slid to the far side of the bed, stared at the ceiling. "When we go for walks and sometimes in bed you're turned off. Just those times. But sometimes it's like you'd rather be in the thick of things than in bed with me. All those stories you tell—crowds and speeches and all that. You know?"

"I know." Silence. How could she imagine all that? The excitement of it. His mind flickered film clips from the previous decade, the active time. Fragments: a speakers' platform, an ocean of faces, a phalanx of white helmets off to the right, poised, waiting; a scuffle down front, a rush of figures trying to reach the microphone, a garble of obscenities, shoving, raiders repulsed. Speaking now close to the mike, caressing it, words rumbling out there, reverberating off sync, echoing across the park to city buildings and back. Slow build-up. Keep it paced. Inch it up. Not too much. Now the question, now the answer. "Do you want . . . ?" *"No!"* "And do you want . . . ?" "No!" Rising and falling, thrust and response, copulation in thunder.

"There were times," he said, smiling, half roused. "Oh, there were times."

"Like war," she said. He snorted. "What's wrong with that? You were the one who said it. 'Like war,' you said."

"Just a figure of speech. A way of talking."

"You talked that way about your father too. 'Going to battle,' and all that. Men are like that. My father used to . . ." Her voice trailed off.

"Used to what?"

"Never mind. He's not interesting." He realized he knew nothing about her father. Dead, he assumed. Otherwise, why with the grandfather? But she never talked about her family at all. He was on the edge of asking, when she said, "Tell me more about your father."

"You're really interested?"

"Of course. He's like in a storybook—made up."

"Well, he wasn't. Really. A man of great regularity. He'd take that train up to the city every morning. And that was some train—a kind of floating club. A men's club." He could remember—just barely—taking that train with his father, the old man sitting there in silence, absorbed in a sheaf of papers or the *Boston Herald*, hidden, unapproachable. More clearly, he could remember the sound of the steam locomotive, the creaking of the railway car, the chanting announcements of the conductors, the smell of cigar smoke. It was a male world, that commuter run.

He filled in for her all the details he could remember— the way it looked, the smells, the sound of it. But he was getting it confused with another train, his *grandfather's*. Eighteen ninety? Nineteen hundred? History now, a lingering racial memory: swinging kerosene lamps, Tiffany shades, spittoons of gleaming brass, red carpeting throughout, fresh flowers in brackets along the wall, stained glass in the men's room door (no ladies' room); mahogany paneling with gilt trim, plaster cupids in the corners, and at either end large paintings in the tradition of Ingres—heavy-lidded, supine nudes.

" 'Our Express' they called it. And it really was theirs.

Chartered. Not open to the public. Oh, Thea, you should have seen it."

"Seen what?"

"That train my grandfather and his friends chartered."

"We used to have trains here too."

He paused, shook his head. Nothing had reached her. Here she was picturing some miserable, soot-covered relic of public transportation dragging its way across Nova Scotia. Why did he bother?

But who else was there? He knew of no one else he could trust. For any normal, educated person this was all degenerate stuff, comic at best. And politically repugnant. Especially that train. An outrageously elitist statement, thundering by stations, flaunting class solidarity, a brazen display of economic and social power. Inexcusable. "Oh, Thea, you should have seen it."

"Are you talking about your father or your grandfather?"

"Never mind." He closed his eyes, weary. It was his grandfather's world that reached the peak. Downhill from there. All of it came to him by hearsay. Vivid as experience. And intense. The sense of membership, perhaps. A tribal unity. The train itself a kind of condensation.

Twenty-two passengers. No more. All male, all Protestant, all friends. To serve them, an engineer, a fireman, two conductors, a bar steward, three waiters, two cooks, and an ashtray boy. Eleven laborers for twenty-two able-bodied men.

As a train, it was short: one locomotive (brass trim shined each morning), one tender, one dining car with kitchen, one Pullman, and at the end a small green caboose for staff.

In the Pullman, a revolving overstuffed chair for each passenger—a kind of upholstered barber's seat—with the owner's name in brass on the back.

Newcomers by invitation only, subject to veto by blackball. Once in, in for life. If a member was late, departure was delayed. The older and more influential, the longer a

167

man could make time wait. The conductors knew the subtleties of hierarchy. Everything in its place. Every*one* in his place.

Midway on that trip from Croftham to Boston, the gentlemen had their breakfast in the dining car. Eggs, Canadian bacon, ham, kippers, sausage, hash-brown potatoes—the British tradition. At the proper moment the senior member would nod to the head conductor, who would nod to the assistant conductor, who would signal the fireman, who would respectfully tap the shoulder of the engineer. The train ground to a stop miles from anywhere in some wasteland of scrub pine while twenty-two distinguished gentlemen sipped their coffee. When the senior member finally finished and lit the first cigar of the day, the conductor would again nod to his assistant, activating the chain of communication, and within the minute the engineer would blow the whistle, a warning to tardy drinkers. With a lurch they would plunge forward to Boston.

Kraft closed his eyes, lulled by the hum of conversation, the easy laughter of close associates, the rumble of the railway car—all soothing as sea sounds, soothing as the whispering gentility of his father's Somerset Club, echoes of his own paneled Faculty Club. All inexcusable.

"An absurd thing," he said abruptly. "What can you do but laugh at it?" He was not laughing.

Nor was Thea. "Your grandfather? He's not absurd."

So perhaps she understood, after all. Accepted it all as a matter of course. Tolerant. After all, her family used to have acreage too, back when farming paid, when the sea was rich, back before the young men left, before lot after lot was sold for taxes and, finally, sold again to the man from Boston. But they had it once, and having had it breeds security, a sense of place. It can last a generation or two after the last acre is gone. So Thea had something no city girl can ever acquire—a sense of belonging on the land. She could accept what he was describing without derision, without political judgement. Right now she was nodding, understanding.

"Listen to this." Picking up the 1926 volume. But she put her hand gently on his lips.

"I have to get washed up and dressed. The old man will be back soon. I'll tell him you're working here today. For the quiet. He won't bother you. He respects work, you know. Even your kind."

She rolled over to his side and they kissed, bodies slithering together like two wet fish. Just when he was about to forget the journals, forget everything, she remembered her grandfather and pulled back. "Later," she said. Naked, she went down to the kitchen, to the pump, to sponge-wash and then dress. His Eve.

He stared at the daisies, the Bible, the little red-and-white carton, stared at the ceiling and then at the window, clouds swirled in the imperfect glass. When he was cool again, he picked up the journal. That was what he came here to do, surely. He was not going to pack up and run; no, he was going to do what he had come here to do.

He was into June 1926. He had only sampled scattered entries in that first look years ago. Now he moved painstakingly, deciphering each word, each phrase, like some Biblical scholar.

He slid into the entry.

Fishing with Miss W. at 5.45 this a.m. to catch the tide on the flood. Trolled in *Leona*. Managed to get motor going in less than five minutes. No need for a self-starter as long as I have the strength to turn the flywheel. *Leona* still the best motorboat of its type afloat.

Light easterlies. Managed to pick up two bluefish. Miss W. caught a third. Played it in without squeals or hysteria such as I get from Junior League types. Had cook clean and prepare them for breakfast at 8.00. Best part of the bluefish taste is its intensity.

Intensity? You get your share of that.

> Walked along breakwaters and out the length of the jetty
> with Miss W., checking for winter damage. Some erosion
> under west pier. Will require rock and gravel. Generally
> in good shape considering more than thirty years of battering
> by winter storms. Should last forever.

Eternity! Perhaps in some previous generation, some
deeper layer, they had put their stock in God and heaven,
but there was no trace of that here. Stone and gravel. Concrete and iron. Victorian confidence. The pharaohs' disdain
for time. Faith in time. And land.

Pausing, Kraft closed his eyes. Until he had come here
to Worwich, it had all been a frenzy. The struggle to elect
unelectable candidates, the struggle to stop an unstoppable
war, the struggle, earlier, to save two reasonable people
from unreasonable execution. No different, really, from the
struggle, earlier still, for a college degree, for a graduate
degree, for publication, for tenure. All frenzy. All insubstantial.

Now, at last, he had tranquillity. And substance. Substance? His work. Then what in hell was he doing in a
fisherman's shack, naked and smelling of semen? They had
driven him to it. Right now this was the only place he
could work. Work?

He flung himself out of bed, dry-washed himself with
a face cloth, dressed, threw the blanket over the bed, and
sat down at the bedside table. He was not going to run
out of here the first chance he had. He was going to stick
with his research. That was what he had come for and
that was what he was going to do.

> July 16, Fri., 1926. Boston hotter than hinges of hell. Re-
> turned to Croftham wilted. Strong S.W. wind revived me
> at once. Changed and chopped out deadwood and bullbrier
> back of bathhouses. Miss W. a great good help, hauling

brush down to beach for burning. Two of us well scratched and exhausted by dinner.

July 17, Sat., 1926. Up early to burn brush on beach in calm of early morning. Chopped firewood while tending bonfire. Miss W. added driftwood etc. Fire hot enough to melt glass by noon. Tide extinguished it by 1.00. Cleared trail to Gen. Weldon's place before lunch. Felt good to get that much done in a.m. Gave golf lesson to Miss W. in p.m. Will stick to our own course this summer, but she will be ready for Club course in a year. Thunder storm at twilight. Walked along shore path in rain to watch lightning over the bay. Got soaked. Marvelous time. All in all, an ideal Croftham day full of simple pleasures.

Simplicity. For all the elegance in his father's world—even in *his* father's Victorian world—they admired simplicity. Elegance in its place, but never ostentation. It was not good to be poor, but it was worse to be rich and ostentatious. How could he ever explain such subtleties to Thea?

For generations they had worked hard at keeping things simple. They drank their rum with rusty local water. Perrier and soda were for city living. They sailed in the rain, played golf in gales, and chopped their own firewood. The servants, half of Eden's population, were kept busy with the more monotonous occupations.

When golfing they never hired a caddy. That was for New Yorkers with their affectations. They tended their own gardens, leaving only the watering and weeding to old Sean. It was considered affected to take a towel to the beach or apply lotions, though of course the sand was raked each day.

In the name of simplicity, they held the telephone at bay for years. When they finally did give in, they installed only one for the three houses, and that in the boathouse, well beyond earshot.

"Only a Means would consider that clever," his mother

said to him years later. Those who are born poor don't fear conveniences. "They all agreed not to let the number out, but of course your Great-Uncle Frederick did. He couldn't stand the idea of not being reached. No, not friendships; fear of business crises. And there were always crises. So they would call and let it ring an hour or more until one of the groundsmen would answer and ask them to hold the line. Your Great-Uncle Frederick lived across the cove, so they would come up to tell me and I would walk down to the cove and row across—it took a good twenty minutes—and climb up the hill and tell your Uncle Frederick. For some reason it always enraged him to have anyone actually use the number he had given out, so naturally he took it out on me. Then he would walk with me down the hill and I would row him across the cove, with him directing me from the stern.

"Well, he would talk to the person, bellowing into the receiver as if his voice had to reach all the way to Boston unassisted. When he was through I would row him back across the cove again, and all the time he would complain about how we should never have put in a telephone, how imbecilic it was for anyone to call, how pointless the call had been. By the time I delivered him at his landing, he would be bellowing as if I were on the other end of the receiver. And then, of course, I would have to row myself back again. It wasn't an ideal arrangement."

Kraft moved on, entry by entry, picking up speed toward the end of July 1926. The social season was cresting. Kraft Senior, out of mourning, began to join in: his sister, Christina Clarendon, and her family on the same beach, his Great-Uncle Frederick across the cove, the Weldons down the coast, imported friends. A small, active, articulate set.

July 27, Tue., 1926. Returned to Croftham after two-day series of meetings with Conti home office in N. Y. Explosive potential there. The only risk is Samuel Conti's boundless optimism. Had time for a quick swim before dinner at Cousin Lydia's. Miss W. reluctant to go with me. The usual arguments about preserving my reputation intensified because of Cousin L.'s age and matriarchal status. Convinced Miss W. to go and all was as successful as could be under the circumstances. No drinks, of course, and a tedium of anecdotes to which I added my mandatory share. Miss W. very quiet but radiantly beautiful.

Home relatively early. Had hot rum with jIEMB to ease the strain and then gave her another swimming lesson in moonlight sans suits. Had many laughs at Cousin L.'s expense. The water warm and provocative.

July 28, Wed., 1926. A long day divided between the two offices. Hope to take a week off this summer. Running both Conti office and my own keeps me in a frenzy of activity, but somehow it works. Enormous satisfaction.

Returned to tennis match already in progress. Postponed dinner and played two sets of doubles and three of singles. Most everyone there, playing or watching. Almost like good old days. Iced tea served in tennis house. I beat all comers in all combinations—singles and doubles. Miss W. not yet ready for women's doubles, but we will surprise them by end of season.

July 29, Thur., 1926. Cuban barge line now a reality. It is typical of Conti's schemes. Bond issue doing surprisingly well. Eleven conferences and two board meetings without time for lunch or tea. For first time in my life I found my mind wandering on occasion, thinking of coming weekend. Miss W. to blame. Keep thinking of the sound of her voice and her form. A remarkable creature.

Returned ready for peace and quiet and found Miss W. had accepted dinner invitation for me at Clarendons. Again she hung back, but not as long. Appearing with her socially disturbs some, no doubt; but this is family. Christina is kindly and entertaining, which offsets arch reserve in Howard. Evening went well. Rum helped.

173

July 30, Fri., 1926. End of the week at last. Thought for a while that I would have to go back on Saturday, but simply rejected the idea. Will probably pay for it. But prospect of two full days with Miss W. is major concern. Had secretary spend a valuable hour reaching her on the telephone. No real message, of course. Just needed to hear her voice. Damn foolish business, this.

Faked a touch of influenza on train on way home to fend off golf invitation with Howard. Arrived to dinner invitation with Uncle Frederick but used same excuse. Sent staff into village for movies, driven by Mr. Higgs. Had cozy supper with Miss W. in kitchen. Rum neat with beef kidneys done in Burgundy. For dessert we made up our own rhubarb sweetened with Cointreau.

After supper we went down cellar and bottled wine from hogshead. Sampled liberally. Resembles a lowly Bordeaux. Quality improved as evening progressed. Experimented with herbs and rum fortifier to see if we could produce a good vermouth. Kept increasing the fortification to kill the grape taste. Managed to break a few bottles. Drank mock toasts to Cousin Lydia and threw glasses against the wall. Lovely sound. Threw bottles too. Finally left cellar in total mess and helped each other up stairs in good spirits before staff returned. Played Wagner records on Gramophone and had outrageously good time together on living room rug. An extraordinary evening.

Kraft snapped the book shut. His face felt hot. He tried laughing. "You lucky sonofabitch," he said, trying to play older brother. The trouble was that he *wasn't* an older brother. "You've got no right to do that," he said, "to my mother."

16

Tammy, head in refrigerator, giving instructions to Harry and Min: They were to get bread from the cupboard and spread six slices with mayonnaise and six with peanut butter. Tammy out of refrigerator, arms stacked with little jars and plastic dishes, a can of fruit juice, a glass bottle of milk, telling Hildy to hurry up and please get the eggs mopped up from the floor and Ric, would he and Weldon mix fruit juices and pour them into Thermoses.

Kraft stood in the doorway watching this woman, this wife. Early-morning voltage shimmered from her. Those within touching distance were vibrating with her energy. Kraft hung back. They had generated a little of that energy last night, he and Tammy—a flurry of combat, a grapple of sex. Not bad, really; but right now he wanted to start the day gently. Softly.

He had spent the entire previous day in beleaguered isolation, hounded from his study to the tree house, from there to the McKnight place. It was one hell of a way to sustain his research.

He had rejoined the family and guests for drinks before dinner. Came back voluntarily. Played the host. He was sure they would understand his absence. The right of scholars to be inhospitable during the working day—surely that was universally accepted.

But no, something dark hung in the air. They treated him like some kind of defective, a patient just home from the mental hospital. They made polite conversation, a conspicuous act in that circle; they kept their voices low. When Hildy complained that they would have gone on a picnic and would have had a super time if he hadn't been off somewhere hiding, they shushed her.

A subdued dinner; coffee on the front porch, some on chairs and some on the steps, examining stars, listening to crickets, swatting mosquitoes; drinks back in the living room, sitting around an indifferent fire. Conversationally they threaded their way through the minefields: the publishing business (nothing about deadlines, contracts, agreements); the State of the Economy (not a word about the radical reordering of priorities he supported); the quality of living in London (Labour Party ignored); relations with China (a State Department commitment to generalities).

At an all-too-proper time, Min drifted off—not to sleep but to her "other life." And then Harry. "Have to stay in touch with the nether world, you know"—a tone which hovered deftly between irony and conviction.

Kraft and Tammy were the last to retire, lingering there, at first in silence. When she started talking, it was trivia. Somehow the drinks and the fire had turned her soft, had released a hidden vein of nostalgia.

"Times like this," she said, "it seems as if the rest of the world has gone on without us."

"Good feeling?"

"Yes and no. Good but a little spooky. Like being dropped on the moon. Makes you wonder about getting back." Pause. Then, "Remember the week you organzied the march from the Green to City Hall? All those negotiations about the parade permit? The *Catch-22* bit with the commissioner?"

Nod.

"It all seems so far from here."

Nod.

"And setting up the Dixon Street group, pushing them into the coalition?"

Nod.

"Jesus, you were great."

Flicker.

Flicker of what? Love for her, this woman sitting beside him? Excitement? A moment of energy recovered? The sound of bullhorns, distant sirens, the surge of crowds, mounting the platform again, his voice out there again; he felt a stirring in his groin. But no, that was years ago and in a different world. He had left it by choice.

"That's behind us," he said. No more stirring, the fire dying. "Dixon Street is unchanged," he said. "Back to where they started. Bought off." Pause. "And the war went on until *they* were willing to shut it down. For economic reasons. Too expensive. Nothing to do with us. Same with the War on Poverty. Same fate, when you come to think of it. No money for the good wars or the bad wars. Stalemate. Then we treated ourselves to a half-assed birthday celebration. How's that for greatness?"

"It's not that bad," she said softly. "You're out of touch."

"What do you expect? Up here with no newspaper. I *wanted* to be out of touch."

"Come on." She stood, held out her hands to him. "Touch something."

He stood, a little unsteady with the rum again. But not bad. Just slightly off balance. Just enough to catch hold of her hands.

"Now I'm in touch," he said.

They went upstairs, arms awkwardly around each other. He wondered if he was up to it—twice in one day and him in poor condition. He'd better be up to it. How else could he prove that he was really in control?

He wondered, step by step, whether this was really at the heart of it all. Sex. Perhaps this was all there was, the rest a clutter of disguises. Perhaps after all the class struggle, the tribal rape, after all the wars and the wars against wars, after all that, it came down to this. Two adults; with luck, both consenting. Both up to it.

By the time they reached the top of the stairs, he had his hand on her buttock, a friendly hold. He was not thinking about class struggle or wars or wars against wars. Some minority voice within him, some watchdog, growled that this was no way to deal with life, this hand-on-buttock routine again. But the voice was faint, distant.

A slight tussle getting through the door, two abreast. Women's rights here working in tandem with tradition, the two sending her through first. In the dark room, door shut, all lamps extinguished, they stood there and massaged each other's backs.

A ritual of theirs from way back when. That end-of-the-day exhaustion which left them both light-headed, dizzy; a kind of sober drunkenness. She having spent a day divided between court appearances and her own office, he having split his energies between teaching and perhaps testifying before a state legislative committee, attending a hearing on police brutality, and ending with a precinct organizational meeting, the two of them finally orbiting together for the first time in seventeen hours, paying off the sitter, checking the sleeping children, and then, discovering each other, standing in the kitchen or the bedroom, massaging each other's backs and replaying the tapes from the day: the events, the protests, the complaints, the retorts, yard after yard, the day verbatim.

Now, once again, they began making that leisurely trip up and down each other's vertebrae, a circular swirl on each disk, kneading the muscles on either side, working down to the hips. But no playback of tapes. Not a word.

That great sieve of a house stood ready to amplify every syllable in full quadraphonic. Here they were always silenced.

Kraft's fingers continued to work, but he was not sure he liked this. Too many associations with that other world. He had come close to tranquillity up here, and now she was bringing back old rituals, reminders so strong he could feel the residue of tension in his stomach.

Still, the place was keeping her quiet. That was an improvement. He had come to appreciate silence, wordlessness. It was a part of this place. He could never change her, but the house could.

"Things aren't so bad," she said, whispering, playing the old game. "Congress just passed . . ."

"Shh."

Fingers working down across the hips, pressing from both sides, then slowly up again to the neck, brows touching, fingers loosening the taut neck muscles, then down again.

"Maybe you should subscribe to . . ."

"Shh."

"This shitty house . . ."

"Shh."

It was always this way, shifting to wordlessness each spring; but this time he was taking more pleasure in it. That was one of the problems of the world out there: too much talk, like too much booze, too much smoking, too much frenzy. A clutter of words, a nervous proliferation. Only in this house, here, could he impose silence on Tammy.

"Look," she said, a fierce whisper, "if you think . . ."

"Shh." He ended it with a kiss as strong as a hand pressed against her mouth. He had forgotten until now, but that was how he used to muffle her in coitus—a kiss like a hand over her mouth.

She shook loose, but he was ready for her now, pleased not to be playing the old game, dimly aware that they were into a new one.

"Look," she said, a harsh whisper. "I've changed my . . ."

"Shh. The children."

She was struggling, but not convincingly. No finger holds, no knee to the groin, no shoulder flips; a simple spoken word would have stopped him dead; hers was a burlesque of protest.

He pulled her toward the bed, they tripped on the rug, were down, stage-falling so gracefully as to be silent and painless. Still she protested, muttering, twisting her head so he could not kiss her, writhing like a caught fish, the two of them pulling at buttons, at fabric.

There in a clutter of arms, legs, pants, shirts, breasts, elbows, hair, he somehow managed to enter her, she biting him, slashing at him, swinging with him right into the climax.

That had been last evening. Hard, looking back, to distinguish the game from true feelings—hers *or* his. He wasn't sure he wanted to know. In any case, he wasn't going to find out from her. She was back to her competent self, cool-voiced and managerial.

"Hey," she said, catching sight of him. "The master has risen." A flash of a smile. "Will he join us?"

In that smile a high-frequency radio beam sent in his direction. A "tentative feeler," as they say in diplomatic circles. Kraft stood in the doorway and nodded, weighing—futilely—the exact weight of her irony.

There had been a historical period, he reminded himself, when the word "master" could have been uttered by a woman without the slightest touch of irony. He was dead set against it, of course, as was every other liberated member of his generation. But there it was as a historical fact.

"Are you," Hildy asked, "are you coming on the picnic?"

He nodded. Hildy cheered. The boys joined.

And then there was a more recent period—up into the mid sixties—when a wife could use that word with only gentle irony. She knew it wasn't true literally, but it was an acceptable game to play. But come the seventies, there were new rules. He had lectured on that. *(Although sexual words no longer have the force of obscenities, there are a number of formerly neutral words which have become essentially forbidden in serious, nonironic conversation.)* "Master," of course, was one. Only in the far reaches of southern and Canadian rural areas had the old ways been maintained.

"You going to help?" Ric asked.

"He doesn't have to if he doesn't want to." Hildy's lovely voice.

There had been a time, years ago, when Tammy would have said that too. As his student, she gave him privileges. Even when she evolved her own career, his vote broke ties. But recently . . .

"Everyone helps," Tammy said briskly. And with a smile for Kraft, "Because they want to."

Had she really been his adoring student? Of course that was years ago. And of course she was right—everyone should help. No special status. He would have agreed, said yes, but she was turned already, her back to him, adding oil to the pan of frying chicken, flipping pieces like a short-order cook, directing Harry to take towels out of the freezer (towels in the *freezer?)* and newspapers from the pantry shelf and wrap the Chablis in the stiff cloth, old *New York Times* over that, and please do it quickly so as not to lose the chill. Hardly finished the sentence before sending Weldon out for more water and telling Ric to work with his sister rinsing the floor mop out and to stop describing the raw egg mix as yucky and to wash their hands just as soon as they were through and start scraping carrots and splitting them into quarters and to watch out for the knife which she had just sharpened and how on earth had Kraft survived all those weeks with kitchen cutlery as dull as a bunch of letter openers?

It was, he knew, absurd to be standing there without helping. Unconscionable. This was no time for introspection. It was picnic time. A ritual of preparation. A cooperative enterprise which he had supported from the beginning as a periodic reward for the workers, an act of solidarity, a time of sharing, a venture he used to lead with exhortations.

She had made the right decision, selecting this rare, perfect morning, the early air still crisp. Sun untouched by cloud or haze. It might not happen again for weeks. This was a moment to be seized.

Still he hung back. Wasn't there some danger in stepping close to radioactivity? A risk of impotency, perhaps, a shriveling up of one's vital and favorite organs.

"Kraft makes the most marvelous clam dip," she announced to everyone over her shoulder, lining up before her a great feast for rabbits—garden lettuce (exempted from the lingering boycott), raw carrots (scraped and quartered), cauliflower, celery, endive. "Clam with a lot of hot things. He invented it." And to him, "How about it?"

Diplomatic feeler was now a direct communication. Escalation.

"Oh, curry?" from Min. Always hungry for the scent of India. "Would you?" Enticement.

"Hey," sudden discovery by Weldon. His contemporaries stopped, looked up. "How come Dad's not working?"

"Hey," from Ric. "How about that?"

A sudden radical awakening. Students activated. Spontaneous solidarity. Traditional diplomacy swept aside. A rush to the streets. Chanting of slogans. A rounding up of fat cats, laggards, intellectuals. Public trials in the marketplace. Revisionism exposed. Taunts, ridicule. Confession of error. Pledge of penance. Enter the work force.

"Thought maybe I'd make some clam dip."

He stepped within range of the collective energy and felt his marrow humming. Mustard, she told him, was in the refrigerator, powdered variety on the shelf, the canned clams were in the pantry, and the curry might be above them or next the stove near the pepper, or had he been using it in her absence?

It was he who had taught her—decades ago—the old Communist organizational technique: give everyone something to do even if it is sweeping out a clean hall or delivering empty envelopes as messenger. *He* had told *her* and she had branded it cynical.

Still, it wasn't bad. Here he was at the table, mixing the dip, in the middle of a swirl of activity. It was almost like the old days, the Golden Age of Worwich, when they did things easily, cooperatively, when they held the past and the future captive. Perfect harmony it was then. The activity justified itself. Didn't it?

If it did not justify itself, he was in trouble. They were all in trouble. They were turning soft, turning their back on the revolution.

Kraft rises above the room, a dark angel, the frown of a Jonathan Edwards, and sees a group of adults and children acting childishly, scurrying about as if building sand castles, playing games, laughing with each other.

He sees that it is all an elitist game, adults playing children, escapists withdrawing from the world of class hatreds and exploitation. He is offended by the whole scene, but he is outraged most of all by the man in British khaki shorts and safari jacket, the costume of Colonial oppressors. The man is a student of history, a master of dialectics, a partisan; why is he standing there mixing a curry clam dip?

The woman, the organizer with the sandy-colored mini-Afro and the springy step, pours him a Bloody Mary and adds ice cubes and hands it to him wth a sprightly harlequin gesture. She can afford to joke; she has won. He toasts her. His adulthood flickers out, its image fades. He has descended, has joined them.

17

Picture: A procession in festive attire. First the horse, a bouquet of wild rose and dusty miller in his brow band, a girl on his back, a two-wheeled donkey cart in tow loaded with hampers of food and wine, beach umbrellas (one raised), blankets, Oriental carpets, an inflated rubber swan, beach balls, badminton rackets, deck chairs, flags raised on bamboo fish poles (one UFW eagle, one reading "Save the Whale"); also two passengers, a gypsy queen and an Edwardian gentleman in white pants, open white shirt; and on foot behind, a woman in a striped caftan, a gentleman in British safari costume, a boy in khaki shorts, and another in long, narrow Victorian bathing trunks and striped shirt tied at the waist, and a small, jaunty, floppy-eared dog trotting with his tongue hanging out in what appears to be a grin.

Down from the old house, through the tall grass, left along the ocean trail, away from the river and along the coast. They splashed across the rocky beach at the head of Rosenberg Cove, then headed inland around Deep Six Cove, finally out to the shore again, along the sandy beach, dunes to the left and eye-squinting sea to the right.

The sun was intense, the air crisp and vitalized with a sea breeze; the sky entirely blue but for streaks of mare's hair in the stratosphere. And the sea: no sign of movement except at the very edge, where smooth rollers curled in slow motion and fell on the beach. In the far distance, where the land ended in a ledge, there was from time to time a spume of white spray rising and then falling again, an unexpected, soundless release of energy.

Looking forward down the length of that eternal beach, right down to the distant point in the haze, and looking back from where they had come, past the rocky inlet of Rosenberg Cove, past Front Beach, right to the marshy estuary of the Styx, not a house or a person or a dog or as much as a solitary beer can. And out to sea, not a sail, not even a lobsterman.

A procession, Kraft thought, not through space but through time. A sensation of release, of escape, a touch of giddiness. Surely this was what divers call "rapture of the deep."

They walked for the rest of the morning. There was no need, of course. They passed enough space for ten thousand to spread out blankets and enjoy the warmth of the sun and the soothings of the sea. But with such enormous riches, they raised their standards. The goal was to reach the end of the beach, a slight indentation before the way was blocked with that rocky point and, inland, a great tangle of brier. They had seen it from a distance, had watched the gentle undulation of the sea break in surf against those rocks, but they had never traveled that far. Reason enough to make it their destination.

There were times when the sand was too soft. Harry and Min had to descend and help push. And twice they gave their royal places to Tammy and Kraft. Sitting there amongst all that paraphernalia, high above the beach, the walkers, and the sound of cart wheels and hoofs muffled

185

in the sand, nothing to conflict with the gentle breathing of the sea, Kraft decided that he would without question sell his eternal soul to keep from going back.

It must have been after noon when they finally reached the spot, but no one knew for sure, no one had a watch. A timeless moment.

They stopped, looked about them without speaking. A great hush. It was hotter than he had expected: the rocks and ledge which barred the beach, extending to the point, cut them off from what breeze there was and flattened the water. Inland, to the left, the dunes were high. Behind them a barrier of bullbrier tough as barbed wire. No man's land. There was satisfaction in knowing that this was as far as they could go.

Then they broke the silence: shouts, laughter, talk. Like nomads they began to build their settlement in the wilderness. T.R. was freed from the cart, the cart was emptied and upended, shafts pointing skyward. To these the boys attached a large striped tent, open on one side, protection against the Arabian sun.

Within they spread blankets and a threadbare Oriental rug which Kraft had bought in a Halifax junk shop to keep the wind from blowing up through the cracks in the living room floor. Hildy had packed a broom and began sweeping sand from the rug. "Like in Persia," she said, sweeping needlessly.

"There is no Persia," Weldon said, moving the hampers of food and wine into the shelter.

"Of course there is," Hildy said. "It's here."

"O.K.," he said cheerfully, the lion befriending the lamb.

T.R. was tethered, watered, and given his hat, a large-brimmed forest-green Allagash type with holes for his ears. Normally he balked at the tether, what Kraft took to be a flickering memory of his life as a spirited stallion. But now, gelded and aging and tired from the trip, he stood quietly, blinking at the glare of the sand and sea.

No one was in the mood for badminton or volleyball. What energy they had went into preparing their Arabian fantasy.

"This is the kitchen," Ric said.

"And this here is the bar," Harry said, setting up the ice bucket and arranging the hamper of chilled bottles. These he kept in reserve, opening three types of vermouth.

"The throne room," Min said, arranging pillows and blankets in the corner formed by the upended cart and the wheel. She struck a pose, half reclined, hand raised in languid greeting—a raven-haired vamp from *Desert Idylls.*

Harry offered her a choice of vermouths, three glasses served on a silver tray. She took the sweet and Tammy took dry. The children had grenadine and ginger ale. They all sat or reclined in Roman style around the perimeters of the blanket. Even Trotsky the irrepressible was spent, spread out with legs fore and aft, happily panting and drooling.

"Here's to good spirits," Kraft said, raising his glass.

"Alcoholic spirits?" Harry asked.

"No, spooks," Weldon said.

"Never sneer at spirits," Min said gently. "They're all around you, listening."

"Hey," Tammy said "let's leave the dead out of this. How about a moratorium on spirit talk, O.K.?"

"Cheers," Kraft said, raising his glass a second time. "I only meant a toast to good cheer."

"But you said spirits," Min said.

"Hey," Tammy said, "tell us a story, Kraft. Come on, tell us a story."

"Yes," Hildy said. "Tell us a story."

"Well, did I ever tell you about my Great-Uncle Frederick?"

"Never," Tammy said, eyes wide in mock sincerity. She had heard all about Great-Uncle Frederick, though not recently. Such stories had been a mixed pleasure for Kraft, part embarrassment and part scorn; by the mid sixties they had become outrageous. He had stored them away like a collection of gilt-framed portraits. Relics from an earlier age. Buried.

But here in this tent, miles from anywhere, old rules did not apply. The sea air, perhaps, the wine, the eager audience . . .

"Well, this is a naughty story. Not a dirty story, but a naughty one. It goes back to the P.L. days." Pause.

"All right," Harry said, "what *is* 'P.L. days'? Progressive Labor?"

"Pre-liberation. The bad old days."

"When you were a boy?" Ric asked.

"Well, that was P.L. too, but this was even before that. This was in the days of yachts and commodores and all that."

"What's a commodore?" Hildy asked.

"Oh, let him go on," Ric said.

"Actually, it's essential that you know what a commodore is," Kraft said. "Because he's extinct. Like the dodo and kings. And emperors and all that."

"And witches," Weldon said. "And spirits, and . . ."

"No more of that. Remember? This is about a real live person. . . ."

"Live?"

"Well, he *was* alive. Your Great-Uncle Frederick, a real person who used to live on the North Shore—back before he built his place in Croftham. He was commodore of the Corinthian Yatch Club."

"But you haven't told us what a commodore is," Hildy said.

"O.K., O.K. A commodore is like a little king. A duke. The yacht club was his dukedom. And the harbor too. The harbor was a part of his dukedom, so he could set up rules and everyone had to obey them."

"Why?" Weldon asked.

"Because they wanted to. A nice sense of order."

"Like having bishops," Harry said. "And drama critics."

"Exactly."Yes, Harry would understand this perfectly. But the young ones would have difficulty.

"What if they weren't members of the club?" Weldon asked.

"Those that weren't wanted to be. So they went along. Whatever the commodore said went."

"Crazy," Ric said.

"Shut *up*," Hildy said. "He's telling a story."

Harry filled the vermouth glasses all around.

"Anyway, your Great-Uncle Frederick was a striking man with a full black beard. A bachelor. Very handsome. And he had a yawl, a kind of sailboat, one which took a crew of six to sail. And in the summer months he often lived on board.

"Now, your Great-Uncle Harry—I mean *Frederick*—was a man of great energy even when he was living on his yacht and not working. And he was also an orderly man. Precise. He had a habit of rising at seven A.M. and going for a swim. In the nude.

"But of course this was a crowded harbor. In those days there was no income tax and so there were a lot of yachts which were quite large and lots of people lived on board. So your Great-Uncle Frederick issued an order that no woman on any vessel was to come up on deck before seven-fifteen in the morning."

"I like your Great-Uncle Frederick," Harry said.

"I knew you would. Well, one beautiful August morning he came on deck in his red and gold bathrobe at precisely seven o'clock as he always did, and there on the very next ship—a two-masted schooner almost but not quite as large as his own—were three ladies sitting on the afterdeck in green wicker chairs, having their morning coffee served to them.

"Now, a lesser man might have spoken to them. On a

calm August morning you can even whisper to people on the next boat. But not your Great-Uncle Frederick. He looked in their direction and they looked at him. He then reached into the pocket of his bathrobe and pulled out his great gold watch and verified that it was 7:02. He placed the watch back in the pocket and then removed his robe, standing there dressed only in his beard. And then, after a slight pause to breathe the morning air, he dove in, assuming, of course, that what *appeared* to be three ladies sitting in wicker chairs sipping their morning coffee and now fleeing with gasps and cries *could not exist. That* is being a commodore."

Applause. More wine. More grenadine and ginger ale for the children. Beer for the boys? Why not? "More."

"More what?"

"More about Uncle Frederick."

"Uncle Frederick and his electric launch?" Applause. Ah, yes, his own design. Batteries under the deck, along both sides, three deep in the stern. Kraft could see it in its most minute detail—the Corinthian pennant at the bow, the ensign in the stern, brass railing all around, brass wheel for steering amidships. Smooth enough for ladies to board in their Sunday finery; quiet enough for easy conversation; steady enough to serve tea; buoyant enough for a flat-calm sea. "But rather like all men of privilege, the launch was not equipped for a change in weather. It was swamped one day by a six-inch wave and sank to the bottom like a millstone."

More applause. Cries for food. Throw the children cold cuts. Carrots. Tomatoes. Pour the wine. A niblet of cheese for Min, for Tammy. "More, more."

"And the private planetarium." Was that in Marblehead or Croftham? "In Croftham—set into the ceiling of his living room. Thousands of tiny lights which were lit in patterns by sliding enormous cardboard disks into a circuit selector."

The drama of showmanship. " 'And here,' "—Uncle Frederick's booming voice projected through Kraft to a different audience—" 'are the stars as they were on the night Charlemagne was born.' " Gasps. " 'And here—with verified historical accuracy—the stars the night the Christ child was born. And now, time to guess. There! What of that? Planets, stars, the heavens at what personage's birth? A hint: the summer solstice at three in the morning. Queen Victoria? No. Kublai Khan? No, not quite. Give up? At risk of appearing immodest—yes, *me!* " "

Cheers, laughter, cries of protest—echoing from one century to the next, from one audience to another, both timeless.

Min spilled wine on her arm; Harry kissed it dry, his hand pressed ever so carelessly against her breast. Tammy put her head in Kraft's lap and he inserted a grape between her gleaming parted teeth.

"And did you know he was a personal friend of the Stanley brothers, the motorcar builders? With their help he designed and had built a brass and nickel-plate steam-powered velocipede which was clocked on Beacon Street early one Sunday morning at a devastating sixty-eight miles per hour!"

With difficulty, Tammy started handing out food. "We must eat," she muttered, half smiling, half clinging to her organizational self. "Kids, help out. Please? We must eat." Suspended, drifting like space-walkers, they handed out chicken and cucumbers, French bread, passing and taking with giggling and fragments of talk, colliding with each other on hands and knees, watching food drift from person to person, from hands to mouths, spilling, being caught, being passed, being eaten.

Outside, out beyond the flaps of the tent, the desert sands glowed red hot. Except for their voices, there were no sounds whatever. Even the sea hushed, the sun hung motionless.

A cog slipped in Kraft's mind and he recalled a trick he had learned from boarding school. "Watch this," he said.

How was it that this should come back to him at this moment after decades? He mounted a pad of butter on the handle of a fork, set the fork on a breadboard, and with his fist struck hard at the tines. The butter catapulted, climbed upward in a great arc, struck and clung to the tent roof. Shrieks of laughter.

He launched a second, then a third. As he was preparing the fourth, the heat from the sun released one of the lumps and it fell, striking Min a greasy slap across the face. More laughter; Hildy doubled up, gasping for air. A second pad dropped, *splat,* on Trotsky, who lunged for it as if for a flea.

Min went for Kraft, fierce as a paper tiger, but it ended in a mock tussle, him licking her cheek clean. She returned to her Edwardian gentleman in white, the two of them settling back against pillows, becoming an Impressionist painting.

Tammy flipped a grape in Kraft's direction and he snapped at it but missed. The dog pounced on it. Tammy tossed another and it, too, missed. She put another in her mouth, holding it between her lovely teeth, and delivered it personally. She deposited it between his lips—grape, wine, and kiss all mixed. Children giggling, now flipping cherry tomatoes, bit of cauliflower, missiles of cheese—children's liberation.

The adults, paired now and entwined, moved on from apéritifs to champagne. Kraft taught the children how to perform the ritual, firing the corks down the beach. Weldon's reached the sea. Applause. Another toast, this one to liberation. A fine one, Kraft is told, to be toasting liberation. But of course, his stories are about the bad old days.

"More about Uncle Frederick," some child says.

"*Great*-Uncle Frederick. In fact, to you, Great-*Great*-Uncle Frederick."

"Tell us a story."

"But *not* about Great-Uncle Frederick," Tammy said. "Pretty please?"

"In deference to the women's caucus, Great-Uncle Frederick will go back in the closet. He's nothing but trouble, anyhow. Speaking of trouble . . ." Kraft slipped into his country accent, the rural speech he had learned from his mother and tried for most of a lifetime to repress. Less of an imitation than a release.

"Speaking of trouble, did I ever tell you about old Captain McEldridge's fifth child? You never knew Captain McEldridge, but he had a little house right down the coast from here. Now, the first four children were all normal. And I guess you could say the fifth one was too. Normal, that is—right number of fingers and all. Good-looking feller. But there was just one thing a mite different, though. The kid was black as tar. . . ."

18

"Kraft." Tammy's voice. "Are you with us or not?"

"I'm here, aren't I?"

"I don't know exactly." He looked at her across the campfire. Campfire? He hadn't been sleeping, yet here it was night and a campfire burning. Tammy's form now robed in a blanket. And beside her Harry and Min, he lying with his head in her lap. She with some kerchief arrangement over her head, a Greek peasant woman sheltering the exiled king.

The old agony: a block of time missing. A paragraph of history—his own—torn out, lost. Not a trace. Like losing an arm or an ear. A part of him gone. He detested it out of proportion.

Direct questioning was impossible. An admission of incompetence. A resignation of leadership. Once again he would have to be devious—wily as that old police inspector Porfiry Petrovich. Or was he Raskolnikov instead? Could a man be both criminal and detective?

They had apparently decided to stay the night. A bad decision. They had come too far—like fishermen on a good day who had drifted too far, drawn by the stillness, the simplicity of it all. A beautiful withdrawal from the world, a retreat from responsibility, from caring. But too far. They were in trouble. Here it was night and they were unprepared. Too far out. He would have reminded them: no sleeping bags, no ax for firewood, no weather report, no real shelter. Totally unprepared.

Yet somehow they had found firewood, stacks of it. No memory of that. They must have gathered sticks, searched the beach and dunes. Total blank. The children, perhaps. Clear-headed and energetic. So much healthier than adults. Hope of the future. Yes, the children had gathered firewood. Had they, too, made the decision to stay? A teen-age takeover? Red Guard in power? Adults to the wall? No, more likely Tammy did the organizing. Probably she had stayed cold sober, watching him, taking notes for future recriminations, and directing the workers in wry, sardonic tones. She had grown more managerial in her tenure as commissar of the home. Yes, he could see it now: Tammy directing and the children doing the hard work. Now the laborers were exhausted, wrapped in rags, towels, blankets, sound asleep and scattered about the shelter like the poor waifs of Manchester after a ten-hour day in the pits.

Children . . . He could half recall a less tragic scene, a volleyball game. Here? In the hot sun? Adults on one side and children on the other. Laughter. At him? Or had he only watched? It might have been that day or perhaps a memory retrieved from the previous summer, or the one before that, an undated photo from the wrong file.

And, yes, he could recall now children and adults, too, staggering back to camp from forays over the dunes, arms loaded with branches, bits of driftwood washed up there in the winter storms. An exercise in communal survival.

Not a retreat at all, not an indulgence, not an evasion; a reclaiming of their earliest heritage, a rediscovery of their frontier skills.

"A good idea," he said. "This campfire and all."

"I'm glad you like it," Tammy said, "since it was yours."

A slight edge to her voice, a gentle mockery. Gentle and annoying. A heavy price to pay for a mild indulgence. Two and one half months of dedicated, puritanical labor: he deserved one slight celebration. A civilized one at that. A few vermouths, a bit of champagne, a good Chablis with the chicken, and then no doubt that Spanish port with fruit and assorted cheeses. Perhaps just a taste of Cointreau, judging by the empty bottle in the sand. All good, civilized wines and cordials. No cheap American booze. Neither ostentatious nor raw. Yet they had destroyed his memory. It was hardly fair.

He had been looking forward to the grapes and cheese. Now they were gone. No, that was impossible. Weren't they still boycotting grapes, still defending the United Farm Workers? Probably the last family in America who were. Or was that over? No, that vivid memory of grapes and cheese on a warm summer's day must have been washed up from some previous summer. Perhaps from his childhood. Or some photograph from his *father's* childhood, them all gathered about the enormous fitted picnic hamper, service laid out on a tablecloth. Great bunches of grapes. Bottles of fine wine. There, in the upper right corner, you can just make out the front wheel of Uncle Frederick's steam velocipede. Kraft feels himself slide through the chessboard again, landing lightly on the next level, two moves back, diagonal to the right. He is sitting next to the picnic hamper. Is there wine?

No! Back up again a jounce. Night scene. Chill. He noticed with disgust a bottle of rum set in the sand next to him. His? Next to it there was an incriminating enamel tin cup from the picnic set. And a half-filled bottle of Perrier. She had got him that, had she? A nice thought. But he had lost hold of the afternoon. There was no telling what kind of an ass he had made of himself.

"Welcome back," Harry said. More gentle irony.

"From where?" Take a chance.

"We were wondering the same thing. You weren't sleeping, were you?"

"I told you," Tammy said, "he couldn't be sleeping. Not sitting up. I mean, he's talented. An erratic genius, yet. But he can't sleep sitting up." And to Kraft, "I don't mind a guy staring into a campfire for an evening, but all your little mumbled monologues get a bit unnerving."

Kraft poured himself some rum and Perrier. The first sip tasted terrible, as he knew it would, but it generated warmth and smoothed off the rough edges of the evening. He realized that he had been cold. He threw another stick on the fire.

"Communing with his spirits," Min said. "I told them you were communing with your spirits, but they didn't believe me. Tammy insists you don't believe in such, but there are things Tammy doesn't know about you. You *were* communing with spirits, weren't you?"

There was a harshness in her voice. He was coming in on the end of an argument. Well, he wouldn't get sucked into it.

"Just this spirit," he said, raising his cup of rum.

Tammy laughed. "Atta boy."

"Don't encourage him," Min said.

"To do what?"

"To joke about his unconscious."

"God, Min, let go. This is the first time he's relaxed in over a year. Let him be."

"Let him be *what?* You'd rather have him drunk than in tune with his spirits."

"Leave him alone. I'm fed up with all that spirit crap, Min. I mean that. It's a cute affectation for a kid, but you're all grown up, Min. Old enough to have children. Here you are playing games."

"Games? That's what you think it is? The soul as games? You keep thinking that and you'll end up losing your husband."

"Matrimonial advice! Now, isn't that something?" She turned to Harry. "The great expert on marriage here. Marries a poor lost soul and pushes him to the brink. He was a sick man. He needed someone to hang on to. He certainly didn't need a crock full of mysticism."

"Easy does it," Harry said. "That's all over with, right?"

"Don't pat me on the head, Harry. I knew the guy. Not a bad type considering all the crazy ideas they pumped into him as a kid—bits and pieces of Hindu and Christian and Jamaican voodoo. . . ."

"That's a lie."

"I knew the guy. I know what I'm . . ."

"My husband! He was my husband, Tammy. He had nothing but scorn for voodoo. You've got no right to lie, to make up filthy . . ."

"Some wife you were. He was just hanging on—figuring out how to live in New York and all—and you had to dump all this Jung stuff on him: the anima, the unconscious, spirits, racial memories, contact with Mother India. Jesus, he was drowning and you shoved his head under. I wouldn't do that to a dog."

"What do you think you're doing to Kraft?"

"Kraft?"

"You're gelding him."

Tammy was on her, quick as a panther; the two of them struggling and ripping at each other. The men pulling them apart.

"Good God," Harry muttered. They all settled down, spaced out.

"Don't worry." Tammy said, catching her breath. "It's a once-a-year thing."

"Usually at Christmas," Kraft said.

A pause. A tamping down of passions. A child stirred but did not wake. Min moved over to Harry's side. "Forgive me?" she said to him in a tone Kraft had never heard her use—a little girl's voice. Harry's arm was around her now and he smoothed the hair back from her temples. They were, Kraft decided, two other people when they were together, two people he hadn't met yet.

"I love campfires," this other Harry said at last. "Haven't sat in front of a campfire since I was a kid. In Wyoming."

"You?" Tammy asked. "In Wyoming?"

"So surprising?"

"You in the saddle? Yes, surprising."

"It was my idea, really. At stormy fifteen. I wanted to get out of Manhattan for once in my life and escape my parents and all that. The usual. So I ended up in this private school with a lot of horses. Some classes, but mostly riding and camping out. I've always liked traveling about."

His voice was calm and sure. It had neutralized Min's rage as no other's could.

"You were happy?" she asked. "It was a good time?"

"I was involved. Wrapped up in it. Maybe that's the same thing. It was the right thing to be doing then, but I wouldn't go through it again. I mean, we'd go on these long treks by horseback and it was hot and there were terrible flies and the food was always burned or raw. But it was the right thing to be doing at that age. It made me feel good.

"I remember once we went out to the Haystack Mountains on horseback. They stick right up from nothing, right out of the scrubland. No roads for miles around. The mountains themselves are all clay—almost no vegetation except at the top. Lots of ravines. You can't get up them by horse, so we camped at the base and explored all day on foot. I found some petrified wood, I remember. Beautiful samples. But then two of our group got separated and didn't make it back to camp and we had to hang around there for three days looking for them. We finally found them, but we were running out of food and water and all that and of course the horses were in terrible shape. We were lucky to get back."

"Sounds like hell," Tammy said.

"It was marvelous. Heaven. For us at that age, I mean. We generated such an energy. We needed to be tested. You know? We needed to push against something. We acted like a bunch of heroes. That's something, being fifteen and heroic."

"So why aren't you still out there?" Kraft said, sipping his rum, his hand still trembling. "Being heroic."

"Oh, you can't keep that stuff up. Don't need to. It was an antidote, I guess. Just getting the poisons out of my system."

"What poisons?"

"Seventy-second Street. I was raised on East Seventy-second Street. That was a good district then, but still city. You have to neutralize all that. Or build up antidotes. Something like that."

"But you went back."

"Sure. One always goes back. Everyone does. One way or another. When I got back to New York I announced that I never wanted to smell horse manure again. Or the smell of people either. God, we stunk. I reverted to the clean little urbanite they raised me to be. Overreaction, I guess. Strange, sitting here, looking at that campfire. I'd forgotten how good it all was."

"Oh, Harry!" Min's voice, alarmed now. "You should have stayed out there, listened to your own inner voice."

"Hush now," Harry said. "That was all years ago. Ancient history."

"Oh, but you should have stayed there." This in a stage whisper, still intense. "Out there you could have worn silver and leather and a kerchief around your neck."

"Min!" He was laughing, sitting up looking at her in astonishment. "That's not me."

"Well, neither is this." She plucked at his white flannels, now rumpled and sandy. "We both go around in costume. Ridiculous costumes . . ." Her voice trailed off, crying now; a sniffling, whimpering, little girl's crying.

Harry wiped her eyes, bent over her, whispering or kissing her, rocking her. "That's all right, that's all right," he kept saying.

"Sorry," she said to him. "Sorry," to the others. "I mean, your going out there and being yourself and then getting pulled back in. Like putting you on a long leash and then . . . snap! They could have broken your neck."

"My choice, though."

"That's the worst kind. When they pull you back in and you *think* it's your own choice. If you don't watch out . . . if you don't watch out, you end up worse than before. A caricature of what you were. A cartoon. You step out of line and they'll get you. Make you a freak."

"They?" Tammy asked, sisterly now. "Who they?"

"I don't know. Everyone. I mean, you try to shape yourself—go out West or something—and somehow they make you bounce right back. Make you pay for it. I mean . . . oh, like getting married outside what everyone expects. They swing with it, you know? They go along, finally. They give presents, the hypocrites. They don't block things, because this is the twentieth century. I mean, you can't go out and annul your daughter's marriage just because her husband's a Jamaican Indian, right? I mean, we're all modern and tolerant and *liberal*. Oh, God, are we liberal. But somehow it ends up just like it used to a hundred years ago. I don't know how they do it. They put the poison in you from the start, maybe. Because it comes from inside. It isn't that you can't get an apartment. You *think* things like that are going on, but you find out that everyone in the city is having trouble getting an apartment. Same with jobs.

And you get used to being looked at. Maybe you even get to like it. I don't know. But it isn't all that. There's something inside. You step out too far and there's a kind of acid that starts seeping into your system. There's nothing you can do about it. Your whole life seems out of balance. You can't set it back. You think it's racism, and then you figure it's capitalism with people owning people, and then you blame the chauvinist pigs who think you're dying for a white man. You do everything you can to put it outside yourself. But they've got this leash around your neck and they'll keep the pressure on, pulling you back, right back to where you started. And if you don't pull hard against it, real hard, you end up being a cartoon of what you were—worse. I mean, that's the way they make you pay." Pause. Then very softly, "Do you know what I mean, Harry? Do you know?"

There was a long silence. In the dying fire, Kraft could see Min's back, Harry's arms around her, rocking her; he could hear low sounds, the two of them mumble-talking.

Was it possible that Harry really did understand all that, had put it together? It wasn't easy for Kraft and he had known her much longer. But then she had never talked this way before. He had always supposed that she *liked* being odd, being stared at, being smiled at. A touch of exhibitionism. Perhaps all this time she had only been putting up with it, tolerating it. That he could understand. It wouldn't be so different from his own life—always on exhibit.

What he was hearing now seemed like a hidden longing to be normal, to blend in. A longing and a fear. Both. What could one make of that? Perhaps none of it should be counted. After all, she'd been drinking and was muddled—more than her usual muddle.

Harry seemed to think she was making sense. He was consoling her as if they shared the same nightmares. A most unlikely couple, divided by age and spirit. Hard to imagine how they could take each other seriously. Worlds apart. Yet there they were, reaching each other in some shared language, creating their own private garden, walling out the rest of the world.

Kraft looked away, embarrassed. He shouldn't be watching, shouldn't be listening. He should never have brought the two together. It was getting out of hand, becoming a cosmic event, particles in space being drawn toward each other. But why not? Surely no astronomer would feel so involved, so much a part of it. He picked up a pointed stick and rammed the fire, watching the spray of sparks.

So Min hadn't really got rid of that poor Indian. Still squatting there in her memory somewhere. Kraft could hardly recall him at all. What was his first name?

If the man had been at all political, had worked with the Socialist Labor Party, the Black Caucus, the radical Jamaicans, done something valuable, Kraft would probably have helped. Most assuredly would have helped. But a religious nut—what could you do with that? From a Hindu upbringing to Christianity to some kind of cultism in New York, and Min compounding his problems, holding séances, getting him in touch with his spiritual ancestors from Calcutta, yet. What was Kraft supposed to do? What could anyone do?

A hopeless marriage from the very start. He could have told them. But they didn't ask. An independent sort of girl, Min, always trying to get out from under the shadow of her older sister. Tammy had taken over almost every area: tops in grades even in a selective high school; tops in journalism—editor, in fact; tops in friendships. Worst of all, she was tops in the mind of her father. He trained her to be a winner. What was left for Min but to go underground, to create her own realm? She pieced together her own symbols, her own religious system. She adopted the traditional costume of outcasts, of gypsies. The more she asserted her identity, the more she was excluded from the tribal membership of school and home. She began raiding the works of Hesse, Gibran, and the Upanishads in haphazard fashion, like a Goth picking over rubble; but she drew the most from Carl Jung, not so much for his theory as for his mystical suggestion. She never read any book from front to back, preferring always to browse here and there, guided by what she described as cosmic vibrations.

She needed a man she could depend on, but instead she found another lost soul. T'sali the Jamaican-Indian outcast, a man with no country, no notion of what he was. Driven from his home by a merchant family who couldn't stand a dreamer, driven from the island by black radicals who found him a misfit, he came to New York as a fellow gypsy. That was her first choice. Until he died of food poisoning from his own cooking. And now Harry!

Kraft had decided to say something light-heartedly cynical; something to break the mood and break up the lovers; but they were already standing, the two of them, and brushing sand from one another. She was smiling, ruffling his hair.

"We're going to walk down the beach a bit," Harry said, his tone so self-consciously offhand that it was barely audible.

"Don't wait up for us," Min said.

Kraft wanted to tell them to sit down, to behave themselves; but he couldn't. He remained by the fire, mere spectator, watched them go without a word.

The sky was overcast and the wind beginning to pick up; their forms and their voices were swallowed in the darkness almost at once. After they disappeared he realized that they had not been walking down the beach; they had been heading for the dunes.

He turned to Tammy. She was propped up on the pillows—the throne Min had abdicated. "Ah ha!" she said. "Alone at last!"

It would have been good to match her mood, to enter

the game. A perfect culmination to the expedition. But Harry was on his mind. Harry and Min.

"He shouldn't be doing that," Kraft said, standing, swaying, pacing unsteadily, muscles stiff. "You never should have brought them up here together."

"Why not? They're getting along marvelously."

"They're . . ." No, he couldn't say they were too old for that. Absurd. Harry was barely older than Kraft himself. But somehow there seemed to be a full generation between them. No way to explain that. He shrugged.

"Look," she said, "they're old enough to make decisions."

"It's so . . . well, blatant."

She turned to look at him squarely, leaning back as if to take in all of him. "Jesus, Kraft, let them be."

"Be what?"

"You're one hell of a prude."

"It's not that."

"What then?"

"Well, for one thing, it feels like rain. If that wind has shifted into the northeast, we're in for it. Can't you feel it? That dampness. And the chill. Straight in from the Grand Banks. Let's wake the kids and harness the horse and get the hell back."

"What?"

"Head back. I've got a flashlight. We'll just follow the hard sand. The kids could sleep in the cart. It won't take long to get T.R. hitched and all. Look, Tammy, I don't like being out here. We've come out too far. Let's head back right now."

"Are you crazy? Love, you're still drunk as a coot. You have been most of the afternoon. You'd never find the way." She started to giggle. "I can see it all, a drunken Moses leading his tribe right into the sea. And for us it wouldn't open."

"Not funny. We'll put it to a vote. I'll ask the others."

He grabbed the flashlight and stumbled out of the shelter.

The energy Harry was talking about—all that energy of that western adventure. He'd apply that right now. Create it. There was no amount of liquor he couldn't will away if he focused his mind.

Out in the dark, he pitched forward onto the sand, cursing the hole or the footprint or whatever that had thrown him to his knees. Never mind that; he would find Harry and Min and they would agree, would help harness the horse; it would be done in minutes. And none too soon. Things were getting out of hand. Someone had to take control.

He headed for the sand dunes, walking and running alternately, stumbling and cursing. He would burn off the alcohol, create energy, get things moving again. He would get them all back before they were in deep trouble.

The sand was softer here, back from the sea. The waves were more distant. A hush. The air warmer. Warm and black. He would not use his light until he was upon them. He would save the batteries for the great trek back.

Laughter. He stopped. A man laughing. A woman making wordless sounds, throaty. He raised the flashlight and pressed the button like a trigger. In two sweeps he found the forms—one form, really. A clutter of feet, a tangle of legs, someone's knees raised, white skin, a rump, no clothes whatever, motion frozen with the light. For an instant they were not on a dune but in tall marsh grass at the head of a great estuary.

The light went out, quick as an eyelid. He backed off, face and neck tingling.

Back to camp. Retreat. Retrogression. Weak knees, heavy stomach, tight throat: reduced to a child at his ripe age!

The tent was empty except for the sprawled bodies of children—the aftermath of a disaster. A sense of isolation there in the darkness; desolation. Miles from anywhere.

"Tammy?" he called, a stage whisper so as not to wake the children, so as not to wake the child in him. "Tammy?" His light beam swept the blackness of the beach. Empty.

He headed down toward the sea. "Tammy?" The tube of light caught nothing but an occasional ghostly white line of a wave breaking. Then something. A form?

"Kraft? Is that you?" Her voice was unfamiliar, muffled in low sea sounds and dank night air. Softer, it seemed. Malleable.

"Tammy?"

He headed for her with such longing that he almost turned and retreated. An unmanageable need.

She stood there, uncertain, not reading his voice, not seeing his face in the glare of his light. In the instant of contact he was clinging to her, drowning, sliding down, hands seizing her buttocks, face against her groin, burrowing into fabric.

"Hey!" A crisp, brisk response to an exhibitionist. "What *is* this?"

Was there no way to melt this woman? Just once he wanted her to dissolve without a word—bone to flesh, flesh to syrup, a great pool, warm and deep, he drinking until his half-self was made whole, diving in, sinking deep, descending, descending. . . .

"Are you crazy?"

Mouthing the answer right there at the source, but not in words, his mouth full of fabric, his fingers groping for that switch which would loosen all those splendid muscles, melt the marrow, smother the questions.

"O.K., O.K.," she said, trying a laugh. "But Jesus, Kraft, not on your *knees.*" She tried a quick step back, but she was also undoing buttons, sliding zippers, half pulling him up, urging him up.

In the struggle they were both down in the sand, wrenching at clothes, she beginning to gain spirit and he losing it. At the moment when the last shred of cloth disappeared in the blackness, she sprang up, laughing now, he stumbling to his feet, she shoving him down, an adolescent romp, she leaping just beyond reach. The wrong game; altogether wrong. The sight of her, some ghost of a gray sea bird, darting by him, nudging him, laughing, drove him past love to anger. Furious now, he lunged, missed, ran after her, caught her arm, lost her, caught her again, was down on her hard, rolling in sand, she laughing, he locked silent in rage.

Suddenly he forced her, dry and abrasive. She cried out. The peak, climax, discharge. Done.

He rolled off her almost at once. She rolled in the other direction, a quick spasm, widening the gap. In the sudden quiet, his skin, rubbed raw, burned—knees, elbows, groin. Even his eyelids scratched.

They lay there in the dark, just beyond touching, motionless, two bruised bodies from a wreck. Then he heard, faintly, almost lost in the sound of the sea, her crying. He reached out as far as he could, but all he could feel was sand.

19

For a moment he paused, one hand on the bridle, face against the horse's neck. The hide was warm, the only warm surface left in the world.

For most of the night a chill drizzle had drifted in from the North Atlantic, had penetrated the tent, had worked through the blankets, had made its way to the marrow. The beginning of a nor'easter. His prediction. But what good was it being a prophet?

His stomach was in bad shape. From time to time it rose, graceful and silent as an ocean wave, acid reaching his throat, returning with a hiss. And his head—brow now against the warmth of T.R.'s hide—his head was damaged. An iron spike had been driven through it, temple to temple. It is not easy to harness a horse with a spike in one's head.

Hanging there as if for life, he turned to see how the rest of them were surviving. A sad flock! The whole scene was in shades of gray, a grainy newspaper photo: Slate beach stretching to a hazy blur. Trackless. Beside it, a roiled and slate-gray sea to match, blending. Around them, where they had camped, a circle of sodden possessions—towels and rugs half buried in wet sand, plastic glasses, bottles. Artifacts from the world's greatest civilization.

Silent forms poked about in the ruins—adults, children, and a mangy dog. Some wore blankets over their heads, others were wrapped in tablecloths.

Picture: Dazed survivors probe ruins of their bomb-leveled town. Dressed in rags, stunned and speechless, residents search in vain for treasured possessions. Rescue operations hampered by lack of food and water.

Where were the American helicopters? The hearty GIs dishing out rations of rice? The free rides back to safety, back to central heat, hot meals, and plumbing?

Picture: POW camp discovered. In a ghastly echo from WW II, one last prisoner-of-war camp was found on a forgotten mist-shrouded island in the Aleutians. Like a perversion of nostalgia, the small band dressed, talked, and lived as they had during the 1940s. Cut off from all news, they were convinced that the United States had been defeated and lay in ruins.

"Kraft." Tammy's voice. "We need help." A plea. None of the old punch. The damp had reached her marrow too. Like him, she had salvaged her clothes from the beach, had put them on, dew-soaked and sandy. Like him, she must have been sandpapered all night as she turned in her sleep. They were too old for games like this. No, it wasn't that. The children were quelled too. Even the horse.

Poor old T.R.! Willing in his day to try to charge up San Juan Hill, now standing there, head low, eyes red, coat mottled from a winter of confinement. Brought out of retirement for this. Poor old fool of a horse.

There was so much between them and shelter, between this moonscape and the simple protection of a roof and a bed; farther still to a hot bath, a thermostat. They were cut off not just by miles but by years, decades, and no way to speed up the trek back. No magic carpets, no whirlybirds. Just that miserable, red-eyed horse.

With numb hands— almost fingerless—he began working

with the harness, fitting the collar in place, snapping on the hame tugs, attaching the traces. Slow and dull work, a ritual never hinted at in nostalgic films or noticed by conventional historians. *(Instant accessibility, not speed, was the original appeal of the horseless carriage.)* Oh for a car with a self-starter! And a heater.

Behind him, Harry's voice directing children to pick up rubbish and pile it in buckets, in baskets, in blankets; suggesting to Min and Tammy in the same tone—low-keyed authority—to fold the tent. His professional voice, imported for the occasion; his managerial self. A clear, clean mind, uncluttered with historical significances. Effective. Practical. And naïve.

"Poor old T.R.," Hildy said. "Out all night in the rain. It's not good for horses, you know."

"*I* didn't make the rain."

"Well, you brought us out here."

"That was stupid," Ric said. "Staying out here."

"Come on," Weldon said. "Let's keep working."

He should have left it there, let the defense rest. But the accusation hung in the air—not just for the picnic, but for moving to Worwich, leading them into the wilderness.

"You agreed. Right?"

"Ah, but it was your idea in the first place," Min said, emerging from the mists like one of the weird sisters, arms draped with bathing suits and sodden towels, head shrouded in a blue-gray blanket. "As I remember it, you wanted to establish a commune right here on the beach and never go back."

She looked at him, her large, circular eyes made larger still with lack of sleep. Was this the woman he had seen last night? Was she really with Harry, the two of them like a couple of white lizards on the sand dune, pinned for that moment in the glare of his flashlight? Or was that a dream? Perhaps a memory from childhood or just a fantasy.

He looked at her a moment too long. A gentle smile flickered across her face, quick but just enough to make her look two decades younger, two decades more attractive. He reached out to touch her, then pulled his hand back.

"Come on," he said. "Let's hitch the cart."

"You were the one, weren't you?"

"The one which?"

"The one with the flashlight."

"Let's get to the cart. . . ."

"In a second. You *were* the one, weren't you, flashing the light on us?"

"So what if I was?"

"I just wanted to let you know that it's not what you think."

"Jesus, Min, what else?"

"I know what you think, but it's not like that. The drinks had nothing to do with it. We have a beautiful and spiritual thing, Kraft. Don't spoil it with your thoughts."

"Min, I . . ."

"Oh come on." Tammy's voice. "Can't you leave off talking *ever?* Help me with the damn cart."

They all joined her, tugging at the shafts, trying to turn the wheels in the sand, grunting like a gang of field hands. Here we are, Kraft thought, exiles reduced to common labor, slave labor. Even the children pressed into service, sullen as migratory workers. And for what?

He left the cart and went to T.R., tried to back him between the shafts. He had forgotten that T.R. never backed. It was a matter of principle with him. Kraft tugged at the bridle, hoping to break tradition, but it did no good. The others had to push the cart up behind him, grunting and sweating, rational humans subservient to that wretched old creature's inflexible will.

Shafts finally in place, collar attached, shaft tugs adjusted, backstrap threaded through—mindless, brute work. There had been a day, of course, when all this would have been done by servants, but that was no answer—then or now.

212

"All right now"—Harry's executive voice—"everything in the wagon. Just toss it in. We'll sort it out later."

A great flurry of throwing and heaving. Everything went. No effort to fold blankets or separate garbage from clothing. What had been a delicate little pony cart now became a refuse wagon. The air was filled with flying junk—bottles, bones, beach balls, sodden magazines, picnic hampers, plastic plates, badminton rackets, knives, forks, dripping pillows, towels, cigar butts, an unending supply of plastic glasses.

Incredibly, the boys drew some pleasure from this. They moved faster, tossed higher, even grinned at the grossness of it all. Thrilled, no doubt, at the whiff of anarchy.

The rug, their Arabian floor, was now saturated, heavy with sand. The boys rolled it like a great tortilla stuffed with pillows and garbage, but they couldn't lift it. Everyone helped. "All together now!"—heaving, grunting, swearing, until they tipped the great mass over the side into the cart, where it collapsed, crushing everything else like the corpse of a dead ox.

The cart wheels sank into the sand with the weight of it all. It was clear that no one could ride. Kraft looked down the length of that gray, rain-streaked beach and wondered how they would all make it. Especially him.

They started off in sullen silence, Kraft leading T.R. by the bridle. His head had not improved and they had no pills, so he tried walking with his eyes shut. Somehow the darkness was preferable to that great expanse of beach and the gray desolation of a northeast gale sweeping in from the sea.

He was almost able to forget the scene, forget himself, when "Hey!" "Jesus!" "Holy Mo!" ricocheted off his skull. Eyes open, he felt a rush of cold water around his ankles. He looked down and saw the dark, foamy swirl of a wave rush past his sneakers and then out to sea again. His feet were too numb to respond. They belonged to someone else.

The cart had come to a stop, sand piled around each wheel. T.R., his ears back, lunged sideways. Kraft steadied him and everyone else pushed the cart. They were on their way again, but this time it was Tammy who led the horse. Kraft walked at the rear, his hand on the backboard of the cart, sunk in his blackness again.

Defeat. Retreat from Moscow. No, not Napoleon; one of his lieutenants, perhaps, deprived of his vision and his mount, guiding himself at the rear of a gun carriage, counting the steps back from Moscow.

Napoleonic officer? Now, there was a fascist image! No one could accuse him of that. A lifetime of antifascist work. At least his conscience was free.

Good training in defeat too. A steady diet for any radical in America. Habitual. Wouldn't know what to do with success if it came. Probably would go all to pieces. Hell, he was battered numb with defeat—one lost cause after another. Toughened, he was.

But this was different. Nonpolitical. Had nothing to do with politics. A picnic. Some bad weather. Nothing more than that. A picnic and a bad decision. Pushed their luck. Well, maybe the picnic itself was the bad decision. All those drinks. The pretension of it all. Arabian dream, yet.

That's what he got for letting go of it, for letting Harry and Min set the tone. Let go for a minute and everything reverts. Retrogression. They had gone on picnics before, but not like this. Those were rewards for work, a time to study the environment—types of beach grass, bird life, mollusks. Lessons in weather prediction, campfire building, food gathering. Frontier training. Survival training.

Something had gone wrong this time from the very start. All that equipment—a decadent elegance. A Victorian opulence. All that wine. What the hell made him spew out all those anecdotes? The wine? Absurd stories, class-ridden and sexist. Echoes from childhood. Telling them to his own children right in their formative . . .

Kraft counted his steps. Let the numbers block out memory. Getting back was the main thing. Back to the house and the pure life—hard work and an ordered day. Get rid of these guests. Counting, 52, 53, 54. Get rid of these urban affectations—spiritualism, elegance, nostalgia for earlier times. Counting, 58, 59, 60. Get the family back on the track. Clear them from entanglements, 61, 62, '63, '64, '65. Back to the rigor of a working commune, '66, '67, '68. An American kibbutz, '69, '70. No, a Canadian kibbutz, '71, '72, '73. A Canadian frontier, a fresh start, moving unencumbered through the seventies, '71, '72, '73.

Kraft counted through the seventies, then into the eighties, lost count and ran through the seventies again, one count for every *two* steps now to make them last, to do them right. Then back to '62 and up through the seventies again, one for every three steps, more deliberate. Do them right.

The cart lurched to a stop. He slammed his chest against the tailgate. "Look at that!" "Oh, hey!" "Je-sus!"

They were back to Rosenberg Cove. A quarter mile from home. But the tide was high, covering the section they had crossed the previous day; a stream had formed, draining from the marshland above. They would have to ford an ugly, rocky section of the beach where the outgoing, rain-fed stream met the incoming waves.

"We can't get across that."

"Have to."

"No way."

"Leave him here?"

"T.R.? After a night in the rain?"

"And no food. No fodder for him."

"We can do it."

"Down there."

"No, up here."

"An angle; cut at an angle like that."

Kraft listened to their strategies and stared dumbly at

the water, the surging swirls coming in from the sea to his left, the stream boiling down from the right. No way of knowing which way the tide was going. No one had even asked. If coming in, they'd better move fast.

He shook his head. The consensus was to cross it. What else? A hell of a thing, though.

"Everyone help push," Weldon said. Enthusiasm in his voice. Enthusiasm! The lure of adventure. For Kraft there was only a dead weight in his stomach.

Now they were all behind the cart except for Tammy, who guided the horse, hand on his bridle. One step forward, then a balk. "I don't blame him," Kraft said. "I wouldn't take a step if I were him."

Then a lunge forward. Everyone shouting and pushing, the water rising ankle to knee, swirling. A sudden stop, caught on a rock. Shouts, a great tugging. Free. Plunging forward, rocking. Then caught again. Solid. Jammed tight on a steep angle.

An impossible damn situation. They couldn't leave everything there. No way of telling about the tide. Can't move the cart without T.R., can't move it with him. Can't leave him there. No going back even if T.R. were willing. Kraft stumbled through the water past the cart and pulled the belt out of his pants, doubled it over and brought it down as hard as he could on T.R.'s hindquarters, once, twice. Cries from children. A release of fury.

The horse vanished. The scene flipped to gray, a solid overcast, molded lead. Kraft lying in the water, gasping; everyone shouting, someone screaming. He struggled to his knees and saw the cart overturned, the horse on his side. He was galloping madly, but on his side, head raised on a crazy angle, just out of water. A jumble of people slipping and falling and getting up again in the water, pulling on reins, pulling on each other, sliding into the water, clinging to the cart. The horse kept galloping.

Something odd with T.R.'s left front leg. Kraft lunged

for it, tried to seize it. A joint where there should be no joint, bone pressing against skin. "Get the children out of here," he shouted.

No one heard him. The horse raced on, stationary, churning the water.

Kraft had been on his knees; he now tried to stand. Something burning his leg. No, it couldn't be burning. Not in the water. Pain? Had he been kicked? He, too, had broken a leg? The two of them?

Tammy coming toward him and the horse with a kitchen knife, slipping and stumbling in the water.

"No!" he shouted. Slit the horse's throat right there in front of the children? Scar Hildy for life? Had Tammy gone mad?

He stumbed forward and tried to wrestle the knife out of her hand. She was screaming in his ear. He tried to get his leg behind hers, to throw her down.

She was shouting something about the harness. "The harness. Get the harness. . . ."

So she wasn't going for the horse. She was trying to free him.

He shook his head and dragged her toward T. R., forcing her to look at that wretched front leg. She looked up at him, her face twisted. "Oh, Jesus," she said. "Poor you." And for the first time he realized that it was up to him to shoot the animal.

He would have to get his father's shotgun. Would a shotgun kill a horse? Could he pull the trigger? And if he did, would shells from another generation still fire?

For an instant they both looked at the children. With Harry and Min, they were wildly lunging for possessions as they spilled from the cart and were swept in with the end of a wave and then out with the current—beach balls, rackets, sneakers, cameras, sweaters. "Get them to the house," he said. Then, louder, to the rest, "Leave that and get up to the house. Go on now."

But he would have to get there first. "Get them out of here," he said to Tammy. He heaved himself up on the bank and ran for the house, shoes slopping water. He ran hard without tiring, an enormous energy returning to him.

Inside, it took him a while to find the keys to the chest. It was the only corner of that house he kept locked. Where were Tammy and the children?

There in the bottom of the chest, under fly rods, nets— milder forms of killing—were the firearms: the shotgun and, yes, he had forgotten, the .30-30. What on earth had the old man used that for? It would pass through a house, he had been told, and kill a man on the other side. That had impressed him.

Oiled, wrapped, waiting. Waiting for this. A thunder of sounds, someone crying—all at the back door. Of course, Tammy would have herded them in that way to avoid the executioner. Kraft fumbled with the rifle, trying to recall loading it thirty years before, trying to remember his father's instructions.

He was out in the rain again, oily sheets wrapping the rifle again, an old raincoat over that. Clumsy. Not at all the image of a killer. But how else does one go armed in the rain?

For one beautiful moment he thought that the horse's head was under the water, that the poor old beast had died, had done the job himself. But no, he raised his head, hearing Kraft. In trust? Kraft refused to believe it.

It would have to be a shot to the head. A single shot. And from an angle at which T.R. would not see him. That was important.

As he circled his prey, the horse kept looking. "I've never liked you," Kraft said. "Not for one minute." He found a point at which the horse could not see him. "I've never liked you." He felt sick to his stomach, a great welling of love. "I have to." The recoil threw him back into the water.

20

Aug. 27, Fri., 1926. The beginning of a new life for me. Am overwhelmed at the fact that jIEMB has agreed to BNSSZ me. Have kept this secret from staff for obvious reasons. Also from family. It will be easier to tell Christina and Howard by letter. Same for Uncle Frederick, who moved back to Boston last week. He will not be pleased.

Weather is shimmering. Returned from Boston early for long sail with Miss W. Then tennis and a swim. Dinner of kidney stew with excellent Burgundy. Hot rum by the fire. Then off to the finest feast of all.

Clumsy euphemism. Coy and sentimental. Heavy-handed.

Kraft grunted his disgust, then plunged into a spasm of coughing. Still sandy from yesterday's trauma on the beach, stubble-bearded, itching, he was racked with a chest cold. Divine retribution, no doubt. For one sunny, carefree day, two of rain and horror. The damn Puritans were right all along.

Aug. 28, Sat., 1926. Fresh westerlies & suprisingly warm. Weather and our mood both Edenic. Only annoyance is necessity to avoid staff. Indoors or around the place, they act as stealthy chaperones. Up early this morning to outwit them. We sailed to Nashawena Island. Explored deserted headland and ponds & then camped out for night. Bonfire of driftwood. Perfect evening.

No mosquitoes? No rain? No hangover? Unfair. All the luck and good fortune beaming down on them like sun-rays—had they used it up?

Kraft sneezed; spittle splattered on the page; he wiped it and the print smeared. Some historian he was, destroying the evidence just as he was uncovering it.

He started to close the book but couldn't. What else did he have? Besides, he had decided to stick with the journals until he finished them. No interruptions. Being sick was the perfect excuse. Being sick and "getting back to work." One as good as the other.

He had remained in his study since shooting the horse the day before. What he thought at first was an embarrassing psychological reaction happily turned into a solid, defensible virus complete with chills. Tammy kept enticing him back from his study to the bedroom, but then the coughing started. It would never do to keep her awake.

They had come by on various occasions—bringing soup, urging him to come down by the fire. But he was content there. Until the weather cleared. No, until his cough cleared.

Actually, they were doing surprisingly well without him. He could hear them below, trying to establish the normal order again. Harry asking where the firewood was, Tammy telling someone to heat soup, Min asking someone to help mop up the leaks of rain water. No mention of Kraft by name, but occasional comments about someone having the flu, having a virus, feeling rotten. That must be him.

No laughter, of course. They were aware that there had

been a death. But competent. Helpful. Was it possible that only the day before he had shot a horse with a .30-30? Somehow he had expected hysteria, recriminations against him, the birth of terrible hatreds requiring years of psychiatric treatment. Especially Hildy. Yet here they were being perfectly normal. Was that natural?

He stared blankly out the window, hoping hopelessly to see some break. None. Poor old T.R. left out in all that! Not even a decent burial.

Decent burial? For a horse? Now there was a comic reflex! A knee jerk from his bourgeois heritage. How many generations of rationality would it take to wipe out this nostalgic longing for ritual? He tried grinning at himself, but the muscles of his face were still caked with salt.

Two habitual leaks dropped into containers which were left permanently in the correct spots, one a chipped enamel wash basin, *pong;* the other a sugar crock, *chunk-chunk.*

"Will keep the wedding as simple as possible."

Pong.

"Service and reception at the house."

Chunk-chunk.

". . . favored with another ideal day. Light easterlies and crisp. Service in the living room." *Pong.* "Dr. Sears from King's Chapel, still a high-church Unitarian . . ." *Chunk-chunk.* "His robes would be the envy of any Anglican." *Pong.*

The sparse details on the page, mere fragments, revived what his mother had told him over the years. The place was still clear to him from his own childhood memories; now he added the players. The scene began unfolding for him, history and invention blending.

Over there next the piano is Hilda Winslow's stolid mother, a rural Baptist, widowed parent of five, member of the Women's Christian Temperance Union, and a tight-lipped opponent of any marriage which crossed lines of class or religion—up or down. Close beside her, Hilda's sister, round-eyed and round-faced, silent not in disapproval but from instinctive and habitual reticence.

The rest, all Meanses. An awkward mix, but everyone trying, especially Aunt Christina. She softens the heart of the venerable Mrs. Winslow with questions about each of her five sons and daughters. Christina has the ability to bring charm and decorum to a revolution.

Deftly, she puts the Winslows at ease and continues the conversation to keep Uncle Frederick from pontificating. He never indulges in small talk. Once launched in a topic, though, there is no stopping him.

Christina, nimble, skips from Winslow children to a verbal tour of the gardens as seen through the French doors—the roses clinging to final buds, the scattering of marigolds, the Chinese lanterns, a few chrysanthemums, lower leaves already frost-killed, and beyond these the ginkgo tree which her father-in-law had brought back to the Meanses from the China, where he had served first as missionary and then as a successful exporter of jade and tea. If pressed, Christina has anecdotes about every plant on the place. "And the larch beyond that was brought as a seedling from Sweden by my own father. . . ."

"I can prove," Uncle Frederick says abruptly, staring out to sea, "that the slums of Boston could be eliminated with a stroke of the legislative pen."

Pause. Silence. Though his days as a commodore are over, he still wears the uniform—white flannels and blue blazer. His weathered face is half hidden behind a great bush of a black beard. No one speaks. He continues: "If next Monday we cleared everyone out of South Boston and Charleston too, right up to the Mystic River, and simply resettled them in some new territory like Jamaica Plain and blew up those rotting triple-deckers—which my nephew now manages with such consummate skill—and allowed the sea to reclaim the area as tidelands, a great salt marsh, the city and the Commonwealth of Massachusetts would be repaid in a single decade in increased tax revenue, reduced crime, reduced fire and health hazards. It is a fiscally provable fact that poverty is a liability to any society. The solution is simply to banish it. Export it. And if good people like dear Kraft find some hardship in the loss of income property, we can simply give them title to the new colonies of Jamaica Plain. It's as simple as that." He turns to the bride, extending his cigar for emphasis. "Your first lesson in economic philosophy, my dear child: the solution to poverty is dynamite."

"My uncle's rhetoric," Christina says gently, "is, fortunately, more explosive than his practice. Come, Mrs. Winslow, let me show you a set of jade elephants which my husband's father brought from . . ."

"Alfred Bernhard *No*bel," Frederick says, pronouncing the last name as "noble," as he always does. The announcement hangs motionless in the air. He, poised, cigar in hand, holds the initiative of conversation even in silence. He aims his cigar at his nephew, finally breaking the silence like an aerialist who has reached the other trapeze. "The explosives man."

"No *bel?*" his nephew asks.

"*No*bel, yes, of course. That's what I said. *No*bel. Alfred Bernhard *No*bel. Holds the key to global power."

"In South Boston?"

"South Boston? Who's talking about South Boston? *I'm* not talking about South Boston. Get your mind out of petty real estate if you want to grasp whole principles, Kraft my boy. Whole principles are global principles. Like the Great Northern Dam."

Pause. Another death-defying leap through space. "Yes, the Great Northern Dam." He turns his attention on Mrs. Winslow, who is transfixed. "It would run from Cape Dyer, Baffin Island, to the town of Itivdleq, Greenland, a distance of only one hundred ninety-seven miles. Difficult? Easier than the Panama Canal. No malaria. And far more valuable. Far. For one thing, Mrs. Winslow, it would employ one hundred thousand laborers, who for a decade would live happily either on Baffin Island or in Itivdleq, Greenland. Brisk, healthy climate either side. And their absence from our cities would improve the domestic scene, reduce undesirable elements, and, Mrs. Winslow, remove one hundred thousand hard-working men from the temptation of unlawful alcoholic beverages." He turns to the Reverend Doctor Sears. "Improve character."

Pause. "In addition to the civilian settlements, we would construct on the dam itself settlements every fifteen miles—twelve in all—each populated with volunteers from U.S. prisons. Volunteers, mind you. It would save the taxpayers some thirteen million six hundred a year. And safe enough. I dare say it would be difficult indeed to escape from a five-hundred yard strip of land across the coldest sea on earth."

"But the dam, Uncle. What . . . ?"

"These are but peripheral benefits. Peripheral. The real function of the Great Northern Dam is its ability to control ocean currents. It would block the Arctic current, which normally moves southward along our Atlantic coast until it reaches the Gulf Stream, forcing the latter out to sea, eastward, where it eventually warms England and Western Europe. When completed, the dam would allow the Gulf Stream to continue directly up the Atlantic coast, as God intended, without veering out to sea, giving Maine the climate of Southern France and transforming Labrador into our own Emerald Isle.

"Meanwhile, England, France, Holland, and Belgium would be chest-deep in snow. Chest-deep. The very weather presently endured by Labrador. Imagine it, dog sleds in Dublin!"

Cries of delight and amazement. Except for Hilda. "Cruel," she says. "Very cruel."

Frederick appears to smile. "See what happens," he says to the Reverend Doctor Sears, "when you give women the vote? Rampant sentimentality." And to the bride, "You're not to worry. Blizzards would be only a last resort. The dam is to be fitted with sluice gates. They would open or close the flow of the Arctic current, controlling the European climate week by week. In this way, we would have considerable influence over European politics. Indeed, with a simple turn of a valve we could, you might say, cool the most heated argument."

Preposterous man! Kraft rose to the surface as if out of a dream, struggling against the magnetic attraction. Astonishing power. Yet the two had never even met. All those anecdotes told and retold with skill had taken on the force of memory.

No entry for the following day—one of the few gaps. Self-censorship by omission. Then brief notations about his new life there briefly without staff.

> Close to Paradise. We rise when we wish and take to our bed again when we are inclined. I dine in my shirtsleeves for the first time in my life. Why is such freedom so rare?
>
> My Hilda is radiant. She has taken to rum and to the other splendid indulgences of life, discovering for the first time the full range of what this world has to offer, entering each new venture with wonder and delight. My Miranda.

Wonder? Delight? Are these terms for adults? Kraft looked for some hint of irony, some slight touch of self-mockery. None. Not a trace. He shivered with envy, joining his parents on their wedding trip.

A little surprise for Hilda: a private railway car waiting for them at the Croftham depot. On loan from a Mr. Gambridge of Allied Packers. A Victorian gem—a parlor with overstuffed chairs, love seats, hanging plants, potted palms and rubber trees; a dining room area with bar; bedroom with oversized carved mahogany bed; and at the other end, behind two soundproofing doors, a small room for the butler and cook. Twenty-four-hour service. Just ring the bell.

These details, too, had come to him from his mother. Even at the close of her life she retained her sense of wonder. The sound of her voice recalling it all blended with the blunt handwriting on the page and drew Kraft back into the entire voyage, a voyage on which he had been a secret, uninvited companion, a stowaway, quietly taking shape.

From Boston west through Albany, Rochester, and Buffalo. Then along the lake to Cleveland (one day off for board meeting of Western Electric), Sandusky, Toledo, South Bend, Gary (conferences "on board" with organizers for the Chicago—Port Arthur barge line), and Chicago. Two nights there. Gave cook and butler a vacation.

> Her first speakeasy with a live floor show. Tears of delight in her eyes. Returned at three in morning. Had car to ourselves. Maintained high spirits. Danced to the Gramophone sans clothing. Managed some astonishing gymnastics. Drank excellent champagne both before and during the act.

This was getting out of hand. How could one draw general conclusions, see significant patterns in social history, with entries cluttered with personal intimacies?

Still, he had sworn off browsing. If he was going to march through, determined as Sherman, he would have to take each entry in turn, each line and each word. His obligation as a social historian.

From Chicago southwest through Joliet, Galesburg, Kansas City for an extended meeting with Mr. Lucian R. Gambridge. The bride entertained by Mrs. Gambridge and her sister while the men "went on the town."

From Kansas City west through Topeka, Junction City, Hays, and finally the long ascent to Denver.

A suite at the Brown Palace. Hilda's silent wonder at the glittering galleries around the central court. During the day, hiking, snowshoeing; in the evening, back in the city, dancing, drinks. "And lovingly to bed." A city of delights.

After the return East, there was less time for intimacy,

226

more time for commerce. Kraft read faster. A backload of work at both offices, quick trips to Norfolk, to Charleston. Trouble with the Havana barge line. Success with the Savannah turpentine plant. Nineteen twenty-seven: trouble with Hilda's pregnancy, success with the birth.

Sickly child? Kraft? He hadn't heard that. Constant crying. Nurses. Special medical examination. A constant complainer. Nineteen twenty-seven and 1928 slipping by with redoubled effort to ride the economic wave. Disapproval at the wild spending throughout the nation, but particularly in the West.

The dark day sank into darker evening and Kraft lit his lamp. The hunger pains which had doubled him up in midafternoon had now passed. A new, light-headed energy. Perhaps there was something to fasting after all.

From time to time, visitations. Tammy twice, straightforward and not pleading. Hildy's more plaintive. Harry's gently paternal. And at twilight, his father's voice.

"Don't be an ass," it said.

"Why not?"

"It's bad form. Are you sick or something?"

"Working. And sick too. Both."

Same excuse for them all. Silence would never do. And it would be a mistake to tell them the truth—that he wanted to be alone. Just that. Solitude for its own sake was a bad sign, a mark of neurosis, the forewarning of psychosis. It was the wrong century to play St. Simeon Stylites. As a captive in this miserable age of reason, the only acceptable behavior was intellectual effort, research, scholarship.

"Hush." Tammy's voice to some child. "Your father's finally got back to work."

Ha!

By the winter of '28, Kraft realized that the house had gone quiet. The rain outside continued, but the wind had abated. The steady hiss was soothing. And back in Boston, the baby—himself—had ended its "colicky complaining," which was a relief to all, though the infant, always "the infant," remained "rather spleeny."

The year flashed before him, entry by entry. The writer and the country—in tandem now—moving faster. Confidence was energy, energy was motion. When the others caught up with Samuel Conti, he pushed further: Brazilian coffee, Nicaraguan pineapple plantations, Venezuelan oil. The barge line to Cuba expanded into a steamship company, seized a good share of the Caribbean freight, and pushed forward a new line to Rio. There were absolutely no limits.

A metallic streak of light appeared in the sky as Kraft entered the summer of 1929. Whatever fatigue he had felt earlier in '28 now passed. New energy. Hilda Means was ready for "the first fully social season we have allowed ourselves."

> Until now our summers at Croftham have been mostly a time for learning the essentials—sailing, tennis, golf, and giving small dinners. But this summer we will match what my father must have had for himself in the '80s. There is no limit.

Kraft the infant was barely mentioned; Kraft the reader found himself drawn into the scene through the pages as if he were another weekend guest, playing tennis in white ducks, skeet shooting off the front lawn; drinks on the patio in the evening with the sea below lit for swimming, aglitter with floating torches. Nothing wild, nothing hinting of New York bad taste; but all with more style than anyone in Croftham had mustered since before the war.

At last, the final house party of the year. Labor Day weekend. The guests begin arriving on Thursday and continue into Friday. They fill the house and then the Clarendons'. Those who are not close to the family—clients and the young bachelors—are rowed across the cove to Uncle Frederick's. Barges with canopies in bright stripes are constructed for the weekend and rowed by unemployed cranberry pickers dressed like Venetian gondoliers. Mandolin players on both docks.

Friday the tennis matches. Preliminaries run the length of the day. Friday evening they gather for a variety show put on by members of the Vincent Club, then a midnight buffet on the lawn.

Saturday the tennis is limited to the finalists in each category—singles and doubles for men, then for women. Losers sail, fish from the pier with long bamboo rods, go skimming across the bay on aquaplanes. A younger set has a kite-flying contest with equipment brought in cartons and hampers from the city. A dissolute clique drinks gin in the rose garden and later sets the horses free for a lark.

At four in the afternoon the ship's bell is rung and all activities stop. A great hush. Time to rest and then prepare for the evening.

Cocktails at six o'clock and dinner at eight at the Clarendons'. The dance itself at the Meanses'. Every piece of furniture has been removed from the first floor, stored in neighboring barns and boathouses. That great space is decorated with peacock feathers; two orchestras play alternately in the living room—continuous dancing music for the entire night. The lawns and the beach are lit with torches. At two in the morning an enormous bonfire of railroad ties soaked in gasoline is lit on the front lawn. Some dance, others sing, others roast lobsters in the flames, dangling them live on wires from the ends of fish rods.

"Kraft." Pause. *"Kraft!"* Tammy's voice. "Hey, you've got to wake up. You've got to come down. Kraft, do you hear me? He has a writ. Kraft, there's this man here and he has a writ. The Reclamation Man. He's not kidding. Listen, say something. You've *got* to pull out of this. If you don't, he'll send the CMP. Kraft? He'll send the police. For real, Kraft. No games. For real."

21

He stood, ran his hand through his hair, squared
his shoulders, breathed deep, opened the door.
Tammy gasped. "Jesus," she said.

"Jesus what?"

"Jesus you look terrible. You really are in awful shape,
you know that?"

He felt the stubble of his cheek. "I need a shave."

"Oh, Kraft." She reached out. He stook a step back.
"Where is he?"

"Who?"

"This Reclamation Man."

"Down there. Kraft . . ."

"What?"

"Look, don't get feisty with him, O.K.? I mean, he's got
a case, you know. A legal case. We can fight it, but not
here. He's just got . . ."

"A job to do?"

". . . a job to do."

"Kind of a Canadian Eichmann."

She closed her eyes a moment, took a breath, opened

them again. "Kraft . . ." She started to put her hand on his shoulder, but he turned slightly, just out of reach, and brushed by her.

At the foot of the stairs everyone was gathered. Had they been listening? More likely they had been talking with the one they called the Reclamation Man. He was standing by the front door, still in his black slicker, rain pants, and rubber boots. He could have been a local lobsterman.

"What is this?" Kraft said.

"Sorry, sir, but it's something I'm required to do." There was a faint burr in his accent, a fading echo of a heritage.

"You don't *have* to at all." Take the offensive; move fast. "And don't tell me you're sorry."

"I wanted to explain." He started to rummage about in an old leather satchel.

"There's nothing to explain," Kraft said. "The land just sat here unused until I bought it. And now all of a sudden you want it back. It's a political thing to do—grabbing it back because we're aliens."

"Here are the topographical maps. The master plan."

"Purely political. What we call a play to the grandstands."

"Is there a table where I can spread these out?"

There was a chorus of muttered agreements, all the rest of them saying, "yes, yes," and "right here," moving into the dining room, all speaking softly as if this were a funeral, all cooing agreement, nodding, fluttering like a bunch of doves.

"Don't bother with maps. They have nothing to do with it. This is a political power play. Put the maps away."

"Here it is," the Reclamation Man said. Perhaps he was deaf. Perhaps they were *all* deaf. "Your land starts here . . ."

"I know."

". . . at the stream."

"You don't have to tell . . ."

"And this here's all marshland."

231

"I *know* where the marshland is."

"And the high ground here. With the wooded section starting back from the house, here."

"Look, I live here. It's mine. I know all this."

"This here's where the new public tract will be. From here, across the stream, down the coast, including the next two tracts as well."

"Both owned by noncitizens, right?"

"No, I don't believe so." So he wasn't deaf. "One is a gentleman from Toronto, a developer; and the other property is going for taxes. And of course, the acre or so between—the McKnight place. That too. The feeling is, if the province doesn't move fairly rapidly, there won't be sections like this left."

"You think I'm a developer? Look, you could zone this so as to keep me from building a rabbit hutch. Do you know that? One house for every thousand acres. You could do that. Cheaper. If this isn't a political game, why not do that and keep collecting taxes? Why don't you do that?"

"It's not me, Mr. Means. Surely you understand that. I don't make policy. I'm here only to explain it. As I said, you can appeal this in court. A figure has been set for compensation, based roughly on what you paid for it originally. . . ."

"Which at this point is an outright theft."

"Kraft." It was Harry. "This is to be *public* land."

"So?"

"I thought you were big on public lands."

"A thousand goddamned miles of coastline and they have to pick *my* little section. Nationalize the whole coast—great; but this . . . this is just getting back at outsiders. Pure politics. And who's to say this is really going public? Watch them grab it back and then sell out to upright local citizens."

"They wouldn't." The Reclamation Man looked hurt.

"But they *might.*"

"Perhaps it's different in the United States," he said quietly. He looked ruffled now, a cornered hedgehog. "But the province isn't going about playing tricks and games. This land is needed." He paused and looked around the room. In the hush, a melody of drips into bowls and pans. "And it isn't as if you had invested heavily in the place."

"Invested heavily? We've put hours of work into this place. It was a wreck."

"I'm sure. But even now it's not what you'd call 'improved,' now is it? I mean, having no direct access to the highway, having to ford that stream and all. Cut off. No utilities. What we call 'unimproved' property."

"Improved enough for me. What the hell is the province planning to do with all this if they succeed in stealing it back?"

"Mr. Means . . ." He was almost inaudible now. "I'm not the planning board and I'm not a judge. You'll have your appeal, you know. With full rights and all that. My job is simply to explain. And to serve this"—rummaging in the satchel again—"writ."

A writ! Kraft stared at the back of the man, watched him burrow among papers, felt rage fill his body, tingle his neck, his arms, knot his stomach. The arrogance of this little bastard, the arrogance of the whole system. Taking all this from him just at the point when it had become the most solid, sensible thing in his life, the answer to all those unanswered questions.

Protest poured through him too fast for speech, almost instantaneous, too complex, too personal for utterance: Look, this isn't summer property, you know. This isn't a vacation spot. It's the place where I'll be when the revolution starts. There's going to be one hell of a fight and it's going to be bloody. I don't want my children in it. I don't want to be in it myself. I'm too old for that stuff. I'm fed up with street action. Dazed with defeats. I've got things to do here. Besides, I never did like that stuff. Always had to force myself. Against my nature. *This* is my nature, this place, this spot. I *need* this place.

All of us need it. We'll be living here year round soon. They don't know it, but they will too. We'll all be refugees from the inferno. Rural citizens. Pioneers. Starting all over. Can't you see that? Can't the judge see that? How in hell can I put all that in words? Tell me that. How in hell can I put my case in words?

The man's back was turned. He was rummaging through that black bag. Had he heard? Had any of them? Kraft was trembling with shackled energy—a surging need for street action.

Picture: He saw himself pick up a chair, strike the man down, two more blows to the head. Drag the body down the field to the stream. Dump it. Watch it bob in the current and out to the gray sea. An outgoing tide. Writ server? Never saw him. Perhaps he lost his way. Kidnapped, perhaps. Suicide. No, sorry. Terrible shame. Keep an eye out for him.

Head buzzing, muscles aching to be tested; but he only stood there. Was he really considering it? Impossible. But that's what he thought about the horse until he'd gone ahead and done it. Action. It was just a matter of taking action. Perhaps this time he wouldn't have to pull the trigger. Perhaps a gesture would be enough. Whatever, it had to be done right now.

"My glasses," he said, and ducked across the hall to the chart room. There in the chest below the extra blankets was the .30–30 he had so recently used, and the shotgun. The rifle gave him a sick feeling in his stomach. Was that old horse still lying there on the beach? Had the tide got him yet? No he didn't want to touch the .30–30 again.

He took the shotgun instead. Two barrels. Undetermined bore. Was this the very piece he had been taught to fire as a child? And for what purpose? Quail hunt? Deer? It looked like the type police used for riot work. He'd seen that, knew what pellets could do to the face. Well, this was only a gesture. A statement. He slipped the old shells in just for authenticity. For authority.

For some reason his hands were trembling, but surely there was no arguing with what he was doing. This was the only way to signal to the provincial government that they would have to look elsewhere for their damn land. A gesture, a signal—that's all he intended.

The logic was so apparent, so solid, that he didn't hesitate. Not for an instant. As a family they could argue for weeks as to whether the boat should be painted blue or white; he and Tammy could as a couple spend the length of a winter debating whether or not to subscribe to the *Washington Post;* but this matter was not debatable. The little Napoleon must be shown to the door as quickly as possible and he could shove the writ wherever he wished.

"Kraft!" Tammy's voice. He hadn't expected that. This was between the Reclamation Man and him.

"Jeez!" Ric.

"Put it down." Harry's voice, low and so steely calm that it made him wince.

Kraft had forgotten that the others would be present. He had pictured himself and the Reclamation Man alone, the latter quietly backing out of the house. But this was a different scene. Tammy looking as if he, Kraft, were in some kind of danger. She had it all wrong. And Min a strange shade of unhealthy gray. None of them enjoying the spectacle, none of them appreciating what he was doing for them. Where was their revolutionary spirit? Little Hildy with her two hands over her mouth. Didn't she trust him to do this right?

He couldn't quit now, couldn't lean his gun up against the wall and mutter something about a duck hunt. There were situations which had to be played out.

"Look," he said. He wasn't sure he could keep his voice

from trembling. "I don't want a writ. I don't know what it is, but I don't want it. So I want you to go back there. To wherever they sent you from. Tell them whatever you want. That I am uncooperative. Or violent. Or whatever. But tell them I don't want that writ. And I don't want to see anyone else coming around.

"I didn't buy this place the way most people buy land. I mean, it wasn't just a summer place, you know. It wasn't . . . Just tell them that this place is legally mine and I don't like the idea of anyone taking it away from me."

"I'll tell them all that," the Reclamation Man said, stuffing things back into his satchel. He was flustered, no doubt about it. But he was doing his best to maintain that air of Scottish control. "I'll tell them all that," he said again. "But it's not right, you know. I mean, they won't just leave things as they are. This is very serious."

He said this looking Kraft right in the eye. "Very serious," he said again, as if Kraft thought it was a joke, a play of some sort.

"You don't have to tell me how serious it is," Kraft said. Surely the drama was over now.

But incredibly the man took a step forward, a long Manila envelope in his hand. "I'm leaving," he said, "but it's my obligation to deliver . . ."

Kraft raised the shotgun to his shoulder and squeezed the first of the two triggers. The sound was far louder than from the .30–30. It struck his ears and left them ringing, a high, steady whistle. But he had been braced for the kick. It didn't throw him off balance this time. He had done that much right. He was learning.

Over the whine in his ears he thought he heard a long scream. Excessive hysteria. Unwarranted. Unexpected. And so was the smoke. Hadn't planned on that.

The scream stopped, the smoke cleared, and he was alone. He had a quick sense of relief. Now he could get some work done. He had erased the problems; he could concentrate on essentials now. That's what this place was all about. . . .

But no, the place was populated. Everyone was hiding. Tammy had pulled the children down behind the dining room table; Harry and Min were behind a chair. In the humming silence—the white sound of radio—he could smell gunpowder, a good smell. It was clear that he was in complete control.

Wind blew through the room, clearing the rest of the smoke. For the first time he realized that the dining room window had vanished—glass, molding, everything. A hole. Shredded curtains—ribbons—waved inward, driving in on an angle like the rain. That was where he had aimed. A demonstration shot. An expression of his absolute sincerity.

The only movement in the room was the Reclamation Man. He was on his hands and knees, crawling toward the door, dragging his satchel. His boots dragged on the floor. There was no need for that.

"Oh, for Christ sake," Kraft said. "Get up. I'm not going to shoot you. Just walk out that door."

The Reclamation Man stood and brushed his raincoat as if it were his Sunday suit. And there it would have ended—simply and neatly—if Tammy hadn't lost her nerve.

"Kraft," she said, "put that damn thing up and let me get the children out of here."

There was such fury in her voice that he broke the shotgun, releasing the catch so that the barrel hung down as if limp. He continued to hold it easily in his right arm the way hunters are supposed to when not on the alert.

So what was going on in her head? What did she think he planned to do?

"Hey," he said, "what's the matter with you?"

"Come along," she said to the children.

"What's the point of that? The man is leaving. That's all I asked. That's all I wanted."

"Can they get raincoats?" she asked him. "Or are they to go out in the rain as they are?"

"Tammy, for God's sake."

She herded them into the chart room. Min and Harry too. Much shuffling about, all of them putting on slickers and boots and rain hats, but not a word from anyone. No regrets. No apologies. No hesitations. They headed for the open door, sneaking past him, keeping their eyes averted, not so much as a glance back—as if he had the power to turn them to salt.

"Hey, Tammy." The sound of hasty footsteps. "Tammy?" He wanted to tell her how he had just won his case. He had beaten the Reclamation Man, sent him packing. An extraordinary victory. For him and the family too. For them all. But there she was, going down the steps, sweeping the children—his children—before her. Something had gone very wrong in Tammy's head.

They were all out and swallowed up in the rain and mists. If they said anything to each other on the way to the car, their words were muffled by the ringing in his ears and swept away in the winds which moaned through the house. The shredded curtains fluttered darkly. The place was abandoned. Haunted.

Kraft was so thoroughly charged with adrenaline that it seemed as if his arms and legs would fly off in four directions, cartoon fashion. He could have run ten miles down the beach without breathing hard, but there was nowhere to run. Nowhere at all.

He went from the dining room to the kitchen, poured himself half a dirty glass of rum, added a ladle of water. He drank it as if he were thirsty.

He closed his eyes. If he had left them open, they would have popped like corks. The amber of the liquor spread across the backs of his lids, rising upward in a line; he was sinking gratefully under the surface, sinking like a bottle into the sea, descending to depths.

It was all right. It was all right. The Reclamation Man would go back to wherever he came from and tell them that seizure was impossible. Too much resistance. Not worth the trouble; a risk to life. They would select another section of the coast. Some abandoned section. Hadn't he said that there was a tract going for taxes? There must be others.

The family would drive to Yarmouth and spend the night in some dreary little rooming house—no, she would put them all in a motel on his Master Charge and have a drink in the bar, cool as a cucumber. The next day she'd see the sense of his action, would see the logic. She would put Harry and Min on the ferry—they had nothing to do with this—and then she would drive back with the children. No apology from her, of course. That was not her way. But she'd make a good meal and they'd talk about other things and the summer would go on as before. No, better. He had cleared the air. Literally.

Or perhaps she would take them all up to Halifax, a larger city, where she could do some shopping and take the children to see the fort again and come back as if that was the only reason for going. Together they could erase the entire incident. And so would the provincial government. Strike it from the record. A bad venture all around. Hardly worth the risks. The bad publicity. Secretly they must be ashamed of the fact that they were taking land from foreigners. That was not the Canadian way, after all. They would not risk exposure. They would erase the entire affair from the records.

Tammy would be on the road now, driving with that sure competence of hers. The road? Driving?

Kraft opened his eyes. The stream which they had to ford would be flooded with all this rain. If she took her goddamned Detroit-built imitation Jeep, she'd stall midway. With the children.

He set down the empty glass hard on the table and ran down the hall to the front door. The house rose and fell under him, an old steamer in heavy seas. Steadying himself against the frame, he looked through the rain and the mists to the barn and saw that both the Scout and the Jeep were there. No sight of Tammy and the others. Were they hiding in the barn? *Walking* to town?

He lurched down the steps and ran across the cemetery, stumbling on stones in the tall wet grass, hurrying to where he could see the stream. Yes, he could just make them out, fording. On foot. Knee deep. A bunch of sodden wetbacks. Were they crazy? There was no place to stay within twenty miles. She was going to walk them all the way to Yarmouth? A children's crusade? She had gone absolutely bonkers.

He started after them, but that would do no good. He ran back for the Jeep. The seat was beaded with water. Was nothing dry in all of Canada? He started it with difficulty, stalled it, started it again. It balked like an old horse. The windows were wet on the inside as well. He cleared a streaky sweep across the glass and turned on the wipers. Except for that hand-wide path, he had no visibility whatever, neither to the sides nor to the rear.

"Tunnel," he said aloud. "Tunnel vision." He grinned for the first time all day. He was feeling much better. He still had an excess of energy, but the sharp edges had been dissolved. He knew exactly what to do. He would meet them on the road and point out to them how absurd all this was, how crazy they were being, and they would clamber into the Jeep, sitting on each other's laps, poking each other and laughing, and they would all go back to the house and light a big fire and have hot grogs. The Reclamation Man would become a family joke. And after lunch Kraft would take Tammy to bed.

A crash and the sound of breaking wood. He jerked the Jeep forward again and got out. Splintered boarding and part of a wheel. Jesus, his wheelbarrow. The hand-carved wheel. Old McKnight's winter of labor. It was supposed to last a generation. Two with luck. Already in pieces. Two lousy years.

Down on his knees, Kraft picked up pieces of the six oak crescents which the old man had carved to fashion the wheel. Split and broken. Beyond repair. McKnight had said this was going to be his last. No one else knew how; no one else would take the time to learn. Kraft let the pieces drop.

"Only a goddamned wheelbarrow."

He moved the pieces aside, arranging them carefully for no reason. Back in the driver's seat, he rammed the shift into reverse again and spun the wheels. Out, he plunged down the hill along the familiar ruts.

"Damn," he said. "Damn, damn, damn." No, the damn barrow had nothing to do with it. Tammy was to blame. Why hadn't she stood by him? What kind of crazy idea . . . ? He'd been defending her and the children. They were all in this together. And she'd sided with some small-time politician, a *Canadian* politician at that. No logic in that. No logic anywhere.

He paused above the stream they called the Styx. He'd been right about the rain. What was normally four or five inches deep here, rippling across sand and gravel, was now knee deep and ugly. Tammy had taken a chance leading the children over. One of them could have slipped. . . .

The swirling water—just like the beach at Rosenberg Cove. T.R. Surely the tide had taken him by now. He hoped to God it had. Even gelded and old, there was something admirable there. Sticking power. Stubborn bastard. No compromise—except at the end. Yes, that was compromise. A big one. But until then, admirable—in a stupid sort of way.

And now washed out to sea. Would he sink? A terrible thing, having him rot on the surface. An eyesore. Navigational hazard. Bloated whales they shot at sea to make them sink. Coast Guard spots dead horse on high seas. Deck guns used. Wry comments about killing a dead horse.

Well, maybe T.R. would be more obliging. Sink by himself the way he was supposed to. Once he was under the surface, they could remember him as he once was—not bright, not really defensible, but . . . oh, shit.

He shoved the transmission into four-wheel drive and plunged down toward the stream in second, engine roaring. He would let momentum work for him, ram that Jeep through the water and up on the other side. A glorious charge!

He hit the water like a Boston Whaler in heavy seas, great and satisfying waves curling up on either side.

His face went down hard on the steering wheel. He saw red. Had he hit a rock? No, he was still moving. He gripped the wheel as if it were a life ring.

The Jeep lurched to the left and stalled. He tried starting it, but there was no response. Not even a click. He beat on the wheel, but the damn thing was lifeless. His feet were cold—no, wet. His feet were submerged. Incredibly, throttle, brake, and clutch were all hidden in dark swirls. He couldn't even see his own boots. When he opened the door, he slid at once into fast-moving water.

He was down in it for a moment and then regained his footing. When he stood, the water was up to his waist. The Jeep had slid into a deeper section; water was up to the hood. The current rose on the far side, sweeping around the ends as if it were a rock. He tried to work his way back upstream to it, reaching for it, thinking that if he could try the starter once more perhaps the battery would have one more thrust, one last beat.

The family. He turned and saw that they had disappeared. But there to his right, where the road began to climb from the beach inland, he saw a panel truck, the large type used to transport road crews. The goddamned Reclamation Man had taken the whole family. Spirited them off.

Standing there in midstream, barely remaining upright

against the stream, he watched the truck disappear into the gray of the woodland.

He made a megaphone of his two hands and drew in his breath for one last argument, one last call to reason, but no sound came. He had run out of words.

22

Cold. The place was incredibly cold. Being soaked didn't help. He would have to get a fire going. All those other problems could wait out there somewhere in the rain. Right now it was just a matter of fire.

To the back door, shoes going *schlop, schlop.* No kindling. Hell, they'd burned the last of the wood too. He hadn't stocked much. Hadn't stocked any. What they used was left from last year. Gone now.

He wasn't about to go out in the wet again, trudging along the beach looking for driftwood. No sir, not out in that damn mess again. Wood wouldn't burn, anyway.

Kraft rubbed his face, sandy hand against stubble. Well, there was wood enough here. The bench to start. The ax. Legs off. Kindling. Planks split. Warmth enough for an hour.

Paper? A couple of novels. A volume of poetry. What was verse if it couldn't warm a man's soul?

The crumpled pages burned sullenly. More needed. Wood resisted the flames. The natural perversion of nature. Stumble once and it's out to get you. More paper. Books. Slim little volumes. Must be Tammy's. *Dreams Songs,* it says. So

give me a decent dream just this once. *Nightmare Factory*—
who needs it? *The Lice.* Lovely stuff.

Pages ignite slivers; slivers start bench legs. A fire of sorts.
Reluctant but hungry. Feed it with a lobster-trap end table.
A fitting end for a table. Still, damn little return for the
payment. Meager warmth. What choice was there? Bad
times.

And what is a man to do waiting for warmth to return?
Research. That's what he was here for. That was the whole
idea. Walled off. Isolated. Get the job done. It was working
all right before they all crashed in on him. He's been doing
all right. So now he could return to it. A perfect chance.
He'd be crazy not to.

Upstairs two steps at a time, feet pounding, giving a little
life to the place. The journals, all of them. Back down to
the living room for the warmth. No interruptions now. He'd
mastered the handwriting, could read it like print—almost.
Those volumes had become entirely too important. The
main job now was to finish them off. Finish *him* off. Once
and for all.

Picture: A padded, bundled man in sweaters, jacket, and
blanket, head covered with a tassled cap, bunched up in
a chair pulled next a smoky fire, red-rimmed eyes fixed
on his reading. A nineteenth-century comic etching, a cartoon: "Winter Scholar."

Kraft, picturing this picture, seeing this image of himself,
shook his head—an absurd state of affairs. How had he
gotten here? In little steps, that's how. Little steps so trivial
he could not distinguish one from the other. Step by step,
one following the next. Like journal entries.

Read, he told himself. Even if there was nothing to learn,
the entries would wall him off from where he was, as in
a waiting room, reading to muffle time. To warp it.

He read for three years—the length of 1930, '31, and
'32. All downhill. Energy ebbing. The writer, the nation,
the reader.

Somewhere in the middle of 1930 he swung an ax through the bottom of two kitchen chairs, the action warming him more than the flames. In '32 the bookcase went. Pine, unfortunately. No lasting value. Oak was what he needed. It was not easy prying up the kitchen counters, but there, at least, was wood with some durable heat to it. If Tammy didn't care, why should he?

In February 1933, close to the end of the last kitchen counter, the governor of Michigan closed the banks of that state for a week. Gangs raided self-service grocery stores in Detroit, dismantled them. In Seattle, a mob seized city hall. In Boston, vandals burned the Lowell Building. Where was it all going to end?

"Never mind how *it* is going to end; how about *you?*"

He wouldn't answer that one. Almost nothing about himself. Selfless? Somehow that didn't seem the right word.

> Means office practically dead. No rents coming in. Banks pressing hard. Conti office is far worse because of recent tragedy and scandal. I'd shut down Boston branch except for court order pending litigation.

"But how about you? You've only got five years, you know."

> Home life in shambles. Cook and one maid sick in bed. Hilda nursing them and young Kraft. We eat in kitchen now. Hilda competent but hard. No laughter in this house.

The other chairs went, all but two metal ones and the overstuffed one in which he sat.

The great genius, Conti, had shot himself in the stomach. Sloppy aim, but in six hours he was dead. Branch managers left to deal with the courts and the press. Unfair? The entries gave no hint of judgment. Just facts. Numbed facts. No, sometimes closer to flickering dreams.

246

Feb. 23, Thurs., 1933. Stayed at office late. Walked home after dark past ruins of the old Lowell Building, which was burned out last week. An open shell now. Six or seven bums inside charred walls, warming selves around a campfire of old boards and tires. They turned and looked at me as I passed. Not a word. Just stares. Hollow-eyed. Terrible hatred and envy. Can we survive against such hatred? Felt on the very edge of the abyss.

Attended *Aida* with Searses and their niece. Fifth or sixth production I have seen over the years. Best opera around.

After-theater party at a new and elegant speakeasy on Tremont Street. Everyone in high spirits. Just a touch of hysteria.

The next day he was badly hung over. The situation was complicated by recurrence of gout. Pain in his left toe and also his elbow. "Work at office made very difficult as result. Am greatly impressed with the fact that I am growing old. . . ."

"Old? You're forty-eight. One year younger than me, for Chrissake!"

Hangovers much worse than in past; gout returns regularly. Bifocals are a horror. Declining energy in all areas but lovemaking. When that goes, I'll be "finished."

Conti office now being formally prosecuted by Justice Dept. and I'll be tarred with it as branch manager. Means office was always kept separate, thank God, but investigations loom there too. Every prosecutor in country now thinks he's a little F.D.R. Today was typical of late: 10% of time spent running the business such as it is, and 90% conferring with lawyers. Goddamn radical gov't is out to grab all private property.

"Radical? *Roosevelt?*"
"Radical. Half-crazy radical."
"*Liberal,* for Chrissake. At best, bland liberal. Just trying

to protect property. Working for you. If it weren't for those rich liberals trying to keep the thing afloat, you *would* have lost the whole bag."

"Out to get every last acre. End of free enterprise system in three years; end of personal freedom in five. We're on the route to Moscow."

"Crazy. You've gone completely crazy."

An uneasy silence. "Jesus," Kraft muttered.

Back in the journal, he moved down to Croftham late that spring, delayed by "that boy," who was "sick again." He could remember that: being driven down, wrapped in blankets, his mother reading Dreiser to him—something set in Russia. His father must have gone by train.

In August, an entry about a costume party. Faint memories there, too, of guarded talk. No details until now.

Wasted entire afternoon in sordid theatrical costume shop. Felt like perfect fool. Had to have alterations on G.D. costume for what promises to be the worst social affair of the decade. Cousin Lydia Weldon is having "surprise party" for the General, who will be 60. Costumes required. She should be committed.

Costume shop caters to theatre people. Place also sells jokes, tasteless novelties, off-color novels (Joyce, Miller, etc.), French playing cards, and dildos. Various individuals there of uncertain sexual persuasion who took *me* to be the variant!

Took late train down to Croftham in perfect fury. Dread the thought of being in costume tomorrow. What is the appeal of pretending to be something one is not? Strikes me as a kind of madness. Spent evening in silence, a man condemned to an asylum.

Aug. 5, Sat., 1933. Sulked about most of the day, brooding about party. As it turned out, it was worse than I had imagined. About 60-odd people there all in idiotic "get-ups." Clowns, bums, and bomb-throwing "Bolshies" in great profusion. Hilda was better than most—a Swiss peasant costume I found for her. She was a ray of beauty among chattering lunatics.

My own disguise was as a Chinese Mandarin—one hundred pounds of brocade, with gilt dragons across front and back and enormous headgear. New lining added by costumer added to weight. Felt like a millstone. Damn thing belonged to my father, who in turn received it from *his* father. A G.D. curse on three generations.

No choice, of course. One can't *not* use a costume which must have cost a "King's ransom" in its day, and one can't *not* accept an invitation to the major social event of the season. Am baffled by iron-clad demands made by so-called free society. If I had my way, I'd move family to Tahiti and start over."

Kraft recalled a flickering memory: in the attic with his mother, being shown an extraordinary costume, she holding it up. Dragons in gold thread. He was not to tell. A secret.

Hilda had almost convinced me that the damn costume had some dignity. It is genuine Cantonese work, after all, except for two-ton lining added by fairy tailor. Has historical value—a remnant of the China trade. But treatment by old friends at party dispelled any flicker of pride. Most shrieked with laughter, pointed, called others over, etc. Younger ones used Yahoo expressions like "Cat's meow" and "Razzmatazz," knowing how I hate them. Suddenly realized what it must have been to have faced screaming mobs during French Revolution.

Drank too much punch, naturally. Tried dancing with young Cynthia Talbot dressed as Apple Mary and spilled her apples. Made some caustic remarks about military mentality to the General, who came in his own service uniform. Reprimanded by his daughter in absurd kitty-cat costume; pulled her tail; she scratched with real claws. Was shoved by some blotto pirate against the table; fell back into punch bowl; table fell; landed in pile of broken glass. Lay there dripping and bleeding while entire party went mad with laughter. Wagnerian nightmare.

On into the winter of '33. January with nothing hopeful to celebrate. Bitter cold. Kraft shivered. The damn house was a sieve. Winds were sweeping through the place like Mongolian hordes. More wood needed.

The upstairs—untapped reserves. Chairs, bedside tables. Three trips brought a decent pile. Swinging the ax kept the circulation going. Chips in all directions.

In his upholstered chair again, breathing hard. Winded like an old man. Should exercise more. But not right now. Right now, the journals.

Feb. 20, Tues., 1934. Terrific Blizzard, tying up most trains and closing city streets. $-14°$ below in Boston and in Maine it was $-56°$. Terrible consumption of coal. Pipes in the maids' bathroom on fourth floor froze. Ruined third-floor ceiling.

Civil Works Admin. plans to spend a billion dollars before spring; has more than 4 mil. on payroll. So much for hope that Roosevelt plans to balance budget or follow any sane fiscal policy. Work projects by CWA generally absurd. In N. Y. C. they had 150 men making block prints and woven belts which they called "Boondoggles." My tax money going for "Boondoggles"!

Took Hilda to Club Touraine for lobster and Champagne dinner and then to a fine musical comedy, "Anina" with opera singer Jeritza being star. Lovely music and fine dancing, etc. On to Copley Plaza after that. On arrival home, some drinks and more dancing and much love stuff. A great time!

Feb. 28, Wed., 1934. Terrible shape. Gout again. Right knee and right toe. Considerable pain. Unable to get to office. Began reading history of France (Guizot) to keep mind off the pain. Much interested in 18th century—growing symptoms of social decay and portents of revolution. Cozy eve-

ning in front of fire with my Hilda reading aloud from Guizot, pain softened with good homemade rum.

The next day the doctor told him he must avoid all alcohol
and go on a diet described as "totally inedible baby food.
Reduced to infancy." Hilda enforced the new regulations,
but he was able to hire his seven-year-old son to sneak
rum-grog drinks to him several times each day. "First decent
thing that boy has done for his father since moment of
conception."

Since conception? Kraft paused, face prickling. Once
again, in a shiver of nostalgia, he could see the estuaries
before him, could smell the saline musk of that salt marsh,
hear the rhythm of his paddles, *schlop, schlop,* feel the dampness and the warmth. The place was still vivid from personal
experience, from memory; the event became real from the
entries, himself now as observer; place and event now super-
imposed, made one. Unsettling to be thanked for his part,
his father's voice as real as anything of late.

The rum drinks—yes, the rum grogs; he remembered
those. An illicit pleasure, serving his father, providing secret
services known only to the two of them. An initiation; a
secret bond. Inexcusable and delicious.

He could smell the fumes from the hot water mixed with
the warmed rum ("Never boil it—it'll lose its kick") and
one spoonful of sugar ("In the water first before the booze")
and the squeeze of half a lemon ("throw the other half
away so the damn cook won't tell on us") and a final squirt
of bitters. Cleaning out the saucepan, hiding the lemon
halves deep in the rubbish, then sneaking up the back stairs,
up from the kitchen to the first floor, half running, checking
both ways, coast clear, up from first floor to second, hand
on the top of the mug, wet and hot with the grog, slithering
along corridors, darting to avoid servants, mother, intercep-
tors. Finally into the sickroom, mug dripping.

"Ah!" from the old man there in the bed. "Ah!"

Gratitude, warmth, perhaps even love in that single syllable. Kraft went soft with the memory of it, then hard again:
was one word all the old man could spare?

End of March his gout improved. "Doc thinks it is due
to no drinks. So much for medical know-how."

But no improvement in the outer world.

> Spending most of my time with legal defense now. State
> and Congressional investigations come in waves—Goths
> against the city gates. The press just as bad. Attacks from
> all sides. Country on the edge of total collapse. General
> W. has acquired a case of automatic rifles for home defense
> and has offered me some. Makes sense.
>
> Am working up a Schumann String Quartet for next musi-
> cale. Spent Sunday on "Drei Quartette" Opus 41. A marvel-
> ous piece. Worth great effort and time.

"Fiddling?"

"Playing."

"Like Nero?"

"Nero never played Schumann."

In the spring of '34 Kraft appropriated the children's bureaus. It was too bad, but they had renounced the place,
left with their mother, had no more interest. And he had
to stay warm. Couldn't risk pneumonia. He'd have to dis-
mantle the whole place if the weather didn't turn soon.

By the time he got back to the journals, his father had
lost two court cases and settled three others privately but
at great cost. The creditors from the corrupt Conti firm
had moved in on his family firm, threatening to consume
the remains of both.

That summer he learned that his application for tax abate-
ment had been refused.

> A bitter blow. Am forced to unload acreage and liquidate
> holdings in a bad market. A dismantling of the entire trust.
> What on earth can I leave the boy?

He does not look like the type who could recoup, either. Dreamy and lacks interest in the place. Spends hours in his jerry-built Kayak. Likes to explore stinking marshes all day. Also spends too much time with his mother. Lovely as she is, she has odd notions of History and Social Justice. Am afraid she will pervert his values. This place is too isolated for children.

Stinking marshes? Is that how he remembered them? The very spot on which he had conceived his son?

Kraft floated up from the entries for a moment. The light in the room had begun to fade, the day coming to a close. Had he eaten nothing? No hunger. Light-headed, but no pangs. He would not take the time to eat or light lamps. Only four years to go. Then three. The country giving some signs of recovery, but not the Senior Means.

Nineteen thirty-eight. The last year. Twilight. Kraft paused at each phrase. Surely there would be intimations of death. When he, the reader, could count the remaining entries, wouldn't the author have felt it coming? Wouldn't there have been signs? Visions? A man does not simply step off into nothing.

Jan. 1, Sat., 1938. Combination of heavy snows and quick thaws have caused leaks. Much plaster ruined. No one can find trouble spot. G.D. house is crumbling on me.

"The *house?* You have three and a half months to go and you're worried about the *house?* Wake up! Look around you! What about your wife? And your son? What about them? Reach out, damn it, before it's too late!"

Jan. 20, Thur., 1938. Stricken with gout again. Toe, left knee, and sometimes elbow. G.D. ailment for a man of 55. Makes me walk like a centenarian. Doc. tells me there's uric acid in my system. Told him to get rid of it. Told me to give up all meat, all good food, all liquor. Might as well be dead. . . .

253

Feb. 23, Wed., 1938. Hilda is going through a strict teetotal stage and is stiff, severe, and chilly. Tries to be pleasant and keeps very busy, playing nurse to me and housekeeper as well, but she is taut as a violin string. No arguments, but she has slept in a separate room for 3 nights which for me is like giving up rum and meat. I practice violin late into the night. Quality declining steadily due to bum elbow and rum, latter a necessary antidote to general chill around here.

"You've only got two months!"

Weather and health, weather and health, right into the final month.

April 4, Mon., 1938. Winter is still with us. Hard to imagine that we usually go to Croftham on Patriots' Day, April 19, to transplant trees. Will never make it this year. Frost is still in ground and filthy snow remains everywhere. Something strange is affecting the seasons. Solar disturbances.

Plan to turn in the Marmon for a tinny little Ford—the new economy. How splendid that Marmon was when new! It was a revolution in car design. Now poor old car is miserable hulk, worn out and burning oil. Not worth a damn to anyone. Junk.

April 5, Tues., 1938. F.D.R. and his gang growing steadily worse. A mad house of Crazy Men.

Something is very wrong. General population seems content to slide toward Socialist State and loss of all Freedom; Germans doing same under a man we thought a clown. Italians slightly better off, but gov't. there is taking over means of production to run military machine. Russia beyond all hope. All about me I see attempts to obliterate the past, to establish new orders. Have we done so poorly that nothing is salvageable? This must be the most baffling moment of all history. . . .

April 15, Fri., 1938. End of hideous week. Gout giving

real trouble. Would walk with two canes but for the humiliation of it.

Only bright spot of the week was Hilda's willingness to go off wagon. Had Cocktails and a splendid meal. Contrary to Doc.'s warning, beef with plenty of fat did me no harm. Felt fine after meal. Played Victrola and danced, well fortified with pain killer. Off to bed in fine spirits just like in old days. Played a variety of games. Great abundance of love and comedy. Kept at it until well into night.

April 16, Sat., 1938. Terrible hangover. Joints swollen. Hilda in bad shape too. Canceled breakfast and let maid take care of young Kraft. Excused selves as having flu.

Finally organized ourselves by noon; had chicken broth laced with bitters. Decided that the only way to clear my head was to exercise—burn off the alcohol. Hilda unwilling to join me because of rain. Urged me to stay home. More nurse than wife these days.

Drove out to Country Club alone. May be last drive in old Marmon. Running on five cylinders & leaves trail of smoke, but still gives me pleasure—like being at wheel of a fine old motor launch.

Played 18 holes by self in drizzle. Tried to jog trot between strokes to keep warm but system was not up to it. Shoes heavy with water. Felt oddly weak. Muscles gave considerable pain, but exercise is only way to keep them limber. Must keep moving.

Paused on 18th green. Entire course deserted and gray in sweeping rain. Branches littered fairway. Looked abandoned. Realized that this is the way it will be when Sociallists finally take over: Country Clubs outlawed, abandoned. No more private cars, no private property. Estates seized. End of good life. And for what?

April 17, Sun., 1938. Felt rotten this morning. Chills. Took long walk along Esplanade. Weather still terrible. Odd drowsy spells and coughing which I do my best to ignore.

April 18, Mon., 1938. Went to office with some difficulty. Dizzy spells. Chills and hot flashes. Evidentally passed out at Board meeting. Brought home in cab. Doc. and some specialist here. Nurse at night. Great fuss. Needless expense.

Young Kraft brought in to say good night. A stranger to me. Must have long talk with him soon.

April 19, Tues., 1938. Feel like hell. Something is very wrong."

The next page was blank. Just faint blue lines. No words. Kraft turned more pages. Blank. All blank.

The journal blurred. Kraft, astonished at the first tears of his adult life, let go, gave in at last to the secret grief of decades.

23

Morning. He reached over to touch Tammy. Gone. Ah, all gone.

From where he lay he could see a section of sky. The rain had stopped, the wind had blown itself out. Overcast broken. Marvelous patches of early-morning blue. Not clear yet, but getting there.

Ah, yes, he had eaten hunks of chicken and pieces of bread, drunk water, and stumbled up here in the dark. Exhausted with reading. No, exhausted with feeling. Dreamless sleep.

Except for the iron bed on which he lay, the room was stripped. Ah, the fire. Crazy business. Enough of that. First step, out of bed and shave. No more looking like a bum.

He had slept soundly without rum. He'd forgotten what it was like to wake clearheaded, with energy to spare. He sat up, put his feet on the sandy floor, shivered, breathed deeply. And then froze.

Noises downstairs. A moving about. Cooking pans. The smell of coffee. Fresh-brewed coffee in this abandoned shell of a house?

He stood up and paused, listening. Yes, unmistakable. The slam of the oven door, the scrape of a chair. Not a family; just one person. Cooking. No greeting. That was strange. You don't just move into a place—or back into a place—without greetings. "Hi! I'm back," at least, or a familiar "Hey, mister, how goes it?" None of that; just moving about. A specter in the kitchen. A spirit.

He went to the door and stood there, hands on the frame. "Who's there?"

Pause. Then from below, "You awake? Want coffee?"

Thea! He'd forgotten about her. A jolting complication. What right had she, barging in like this? It was enough to sort things out without having her to deal with.

He clomped downstairs, barefooted, hair a tangle, unshaved. She'd take one look and leave.

"Thea," he said at the kitchen door, using his parental voice. And then, entering, he stopped, caught for an instant. There she was by the stove, hand on the kettle, head turned in his direction, a hint of a smile, a sepia print. The old-photo trick.

"Will you have some coffee? I've made some pancakes too."

"What are you doing here?"

"I thought maybe you'd be wanting a decent breakfast."

He shook his head. "Things are . . ."

"Never mind the way things are."

"Never mind? Look around you."

She didn't. She was taking pancakes out of the oven. Adding fresh ones from the fry pan, pouring coffee, setting things up on a little tray he had missed.

"I was aiming to have things ready when you came down." A smile of apology for the moment's delay, and she was moving into the other room where, fortunately, he had left the table. The table and the two metal chairs. Other than those, the place was stripped and she hadn't asked any questions, hadn't *seen* it. Crazy as a loon. "Have a seat," just as if they'd been married for years. Spooky.

She sat, poured coffee, gestured to the other metal chair. He stood.

"Look," he said, "what is this? What's going through that head of yours?"

She let go of the coffeepot; looked up at him. "She is *gone*, Kraft. They've all gone." She spoke slowly, distinctly, as if he were foreign. "I saw them go. It's not like before, with her about to come back. She's gone. I don't imagine she'll be coming back this time." Pause. A look around. Just a little smile. "It doesn't look like you expect her back."

He shrugged. He wasn't about to confirm or deny. She continued in that modulated way of hers. "I figured maybe you'd like a real breakfast."

He wasn't prepared for this. Not at all. There was so much to solve out there across the river—wife, children, friends. He hadn't planned on Thea too. Was this really the woman with whom he had shared chapters of his life? Some other life, that was. She gestured for him to sit down with her, join her, share this echoing house with her. A voice in him kept saying, Don't sit; stay clear. Watch out.

"Look," he said, "I'm leaving." When had he decided? "Getting out of here." No response. That calm, almost blank look. "It has nothing to do with you. I decided . . . I decided last night. This whole thing is wrong. I've got to get out of here. I mean, thanks for all this. But look, I've got to get out of here. Fast." Surprise at the squall of panic running through him. "It's just one of those intuitive things. Something's very wrong here."

She nodded. "I know," she said. She smiled, and for a moment the smile broke into a grin. A tooth was missing at one end of that grin. Odd, he had never noticed. "I expected that sooner or later. Place like this will drive you crazy after a while. I don't like it either, you know."

"Of course you do."

"Hate it, Kraft."

"It's your whole life, Thea. Yours . . . Not mine."

A slight tightening of her mouth. She stood up and faced him, leaning her buttocks against the table, bending slightly forward at the waist, a more intense Thea than he was used to. More assertive.

"It was just a matter of time," she said. "You had a funny kind of view of this place. And now you don't. That simple. It's a good thing, Kraft, getting out of here. People can go crazy around here. Believe me. I'd rather be anywhere but here. I'm ready to go anytime."

Uh-oh. Watch out. "What about the old man?"

"There's nothing that says I have to take care of him for the rest of my life. Is there?"

"Just that he means a lot to you."

She shrugged. "Love and hate. About equal. It wouldn't be right to go through life like a cripple just because of him, would it? Besides, we may get thrown out of here, anyway. There's talk about a provincial park. It's O.K. with me. Godforsaken strip of land."

"But what about him?"

"He's got people in Halifax. And if they won't take him, there's homes."

"It would kill him."

"I've done my part."

"It would kill him, Thea."

"It wouldn't be my fault. It would be time, not me, that took him. I'm not going to get all riled up over what time does. I've tithed my share to him; now he has to face time on his own. That's the way it is. So how about it, Kraft?" Looking him right in the eye—not like her at all. "Well?"

"What's come over you?"

"I've had plenty of time to think, living here. That's one thing I got plenty of. And Mrs. Means—Tammy, I mean—has really opened my eyes."

"Tammy?"

"Well, we've been talking a lot. When I was working

here. A lot. There's more things in this life for me than serving up meals to an old man. You don't have to go through life as a servant, you know. Not nowadays. Not even out here. It's not right. So . . ." Hands on hips, head tilted, a little smile. "I'm ready to go." Silence. A big breath. "You said you wanted to go, and I'm willing. Now that the others have left you." Silence. Hands down, smile fading, face hardening. "You weren't figuring on just sneaking out of here, were you?"

"This is your home, Thea, here. You've told me that yourself."

"My prison, is more like it."

"You've never said that. Never even hinted."

"You've got this picture of me, Kraft."

"What I see is what you are, Thea. No pretense to you. No 'picture.' "

She shook her head sharply. He'd never seen her do that. "You had this picture of me when we first met. That first day. Made me out to be the country girl."

"But you *are* a country girl."

She started to shake her head again, denying it; then shifted: "What does that mean, anyway? 'Country girl.' You keep calling me that. Kind of insulting, really. I mean, I could learn to drive a car and drink liquor and dance. All of that. Or use a washing machine and shop at supermarkets and wear slacks and learn all about history—I told you I wanted to learn about history. I did all right in school. I can read. I'd learn fast. I'm not dumb, you know. It's not right that you treat me dumb. Tammy says I've got the brains to do anything I want . . ."

"Tammy . . ."

". . . and go anywhere I want, and she's right, you know."

"Leave Tammy out of this. Look, I never for a minute meant . . ." But of course he had. He'd meant it all. She his Miranda, his creation. He the magician. The magic was to keep her just where she was. But now he was tired of it, wanted out. A rotten game to have played. And her defenseless.

She had slumped back in her seat as if he had hit her. "Never meant it? Never meant any of it?"

Long pause. Silence magnified in the emptiness. He sat in the other chair and reached out to place his hand on her arm, to steady her. She drew back. Then softly, with astonishment: "You cruddy son of a bitch."

"Hey!"

"Hey what?"

"That's . . . I've never heard you . . ."

"Game's over, *Mr.* Means. Those rules don't apply any more. And you are, you know, a cruddy . . ."

"O.*K*. Look, think what you want of me, but don't go calling it all games. Not you, anyway. Maybe me, but not you."

"No? You set up the rules and I played them. Stupid of me, but I played them just the way you wanted me to. When was it we met? Three years ago? When you first bought this place—that first spring. May fifteenth. Early morning. You came over and introduced yourself. Just you by yourself. Started talking about country living, about old values, 'lost values.' The whole bit. I thought it was kind of weird at first. Really. But you kept at it. Before long, you got me playing the part."

"Part? What part? You were just being yourself, for Chrissake. Just yourself."

"You think? Still?" Bitter lines in her face, muscles pulling vertically from cheek to neck, adding another five years to her, reminding him of that missing tooth. How old was she, anyway? "You still think I was born and raised out on this Godforsaken coast, don't you?"

"Weren't you?"

"You never asked, did you? You had it all figured in that head of yours, so you didn't have to ask. We talked about *your* childhood, but mine you knew all about. Well, maybe just this once we'll talk about mine. O.K.? First of all . . ." She paused, shoved a hunk of cold pancake in her mouth and chewed it. "First of all, I've only been out here four years. Just one more year than you. Surprised?"

He nodded. She swallowed and wiped syrup from her mouth with the back of her hand. "My father was a day laborer in Halifax. He hung around the docks, mostly. Some winters he'd go off and work at the coal mines in Pictou. Until they closed. He'd come back a stranger to us. He was a silent, beaten old guy. It was like I had no father.

"We lived in one of those clapboard tenements you see all over that damn city, trying to keep warm with kerosene heaters, not starving but never eating good either, and bored out of our heads, learning nothing in school and then quitting and not finding work and spending summers sitting on the curb giggling with guys or maybe wandering off with them down to the dump. That's where I learned about men. Some of the guys had little shacks—tin roofs and dirt floors. I don't mean to live in; just to mess around in. For privacy. None of us could afford cars. So a lot of them had these shacks—sometimes with a broken-down chair and a mattress. Always the mattress. I learned a lot down there."

"Never mind the details."

"Always smelled of smoke. Always. I guess *we* smelled like it after an evening down there. We kids called it 'getting smoked.' Maybe you can put that in one of your books. 'Getting smoked.' A fine old-world expression. Except I got burned. I ended up pregnant. At seventeen. How do you like that? Went through the whole nine months at an aunt's house over in Dartmouth and then lost the kid in a clinic. Dead on arrival, as they say. After something like that in these parts, they give you a real simple choice—you can live like a whore or live like a saint. Six 'friends' must have told me that. And they were right. There's nothing between. Nothing regular like getting married and raising a family. Not for the likes of me. Not around Halifax. There's one of those 'old values' for you. Right out of the 'good old days.'

"I took care of my aunt for four years—she was sickly; then I went home and looked after my mother for another six; a proper spinster, I was. When she died they sort of sent me out here to look after my grandfather. It's not that I chose sainthood, really; it's just that I couldn't forget the smell of that damn dump. Every guy I met smelled of ashes. And I guess I must have smelled that way to them too. I mean, around these parts, everyone knows everything.

"So I'm no country girl and this place would have left me walleyed if a crazy American hadn't come up here and started playing games." She paused, going soft for a moment. "Maybe I was in the mood for playing make-believe." Words stopped, lips parted, lower rims of her eyes filling. Then tough again:

"What were you trying to make me into, anyway? You dressed me like you owned me, you know that? Like I was property. Approved one costume, frowned on another. I learned quick. You know, I've got jeans like everyone else, but you gave me a lecture on it and I figured you were maybe a Catholic and went along, but you're not. You've got something in that head of yours about me and"—sweep of her hand—"this whole house. It's weird. You know that? You know anyone else who would live in a spook place like this that didn't have to? Do you?"

He was shaking his head, but it didn't stop her. "Do you think anyone else gets along without electricity unless they really have to? You could afford plaster, couldn't you? And running water? It's playacting. The whole place is weird. And what you do with people is weird too. It's not right, Kraft, it's not right."

"Then why did you play?"

A long pause, a shrug. Then, anger gone, "Maybe I've

been a servant girl too damn long. Just doing what I'm told. That's what Mrs. . . . that's what Tammy says." She paused. Then she shook her head. "No, I liked it. It was beautiful. Like turning time back for me. I don't understand half what you say, but for me it's like going back to . . . back before."

"Before you got smoked?"

"Before I got burned. Oh, Christ, things . . . were . . . so . . . simple."

Her head went down on the table, face hidden in her arms. She was crying. He reached out, his hand on her shoulder, an absurd gesture—but what else?

"Thea," he said softly. "Thea."

She looked up, eyes red. "What do you want? What do you want *now?*"

"Just . . ." What *did* he want? "Just to end this thing on good terms. Friends."

She stared at him a moment, face blank. Thinking, perhaps. Then she shook her head.

"Not that easy. You want to end like nothing happened? Well, something did happen. I haven't felt like this since I was seventeen. You know what I mean? I mean, I can smell the ashes again. I'm not going to be your sweet little country girl and kiss you goodbye. No sir. You got to hurt a little."

"Jesus, Thea, I feel . . ."

"For once, don't put it all in words. Just feel rotten. Because you are." Pause. Her face went soft again. "No, I don't mean that. Not really. Sorry."

In embarrassment and confusion, she stood up and stacked the dishes, added the mugs and the silver, picked the stack up, took one step toward the kitchen, and then froze.

"Look at this!" Sudden exasperation. "Look what you've got me doing. All of you. You and the old man, two of a kind. Got me cleaning up your mess. Your little servant girl. You know he won't let me put on lipstick? Or listen to music on a lousy little radio I have to keep hidden? You're like that too. You'd have me smothered in no time. Well, I've got to do some growing, you know. Everybody's got to grow. I thought you knew that, being a teacher, but I guess not. You're as bad as he is. Well, to hell with you both. I can't stop time for you—either of you. I'm not going to feel guilty, because no one can do that."

"He's not trying to stop time. He's . . ."

"He's not? You notice he won't have a calendar in that house? Did you know he never celebrates birthdays or mentions age? You know why? 'Cause he doesn't even know what *century* it is. The good old days . . . The good old days . . . Christ, they were never good and it's only *men* that think they were and that's only because they were king of the dung pile then and . . . Oh, shit on you both."

She let go the plates. They fell with the mugs and the silver. The crockery shattered, mixed with the syrup, the coffee.

Pause. They stared at the mess. "Sorry. I am, you know. Sorry and mad. You've got a lot of cleaning up to do. I wish you luck. I really do."

24

She was gone. That's what he wanted, wasn't it?

She'd have to clean up her own life and he his. There was still a portion of him that wanted to follow her. Just a fragment.

As for him, he'd have to start right here. He found a dustpan and cardboard from a cereal box and began scraping up hunks of pancake and broken crockery and syrup and coffee. Absurd, really. He knew that. Empty house. Dying house. He wouldn't be back. At some point that decision had been made. Still, this seemed like the place to start.

He recalled wryly a scene from some Conrad story: the captain of a burned-out hulk of a ship, about to abandon it, sending the astonished crew up to furl the sails before the damn thing sank. Crazy act. Or maybe an antidote.

He could hear Thea's voice—soft, angry, soft again—as he dumped the mess. Dreamlike, the words were indistinct. Just the resonance, an echo of her presence. She wouldn't let go of him for a while; she'd haunt him for a while. A kind of sentence.

He stood up and wiped his hands on his filthy pants.

He wished he could throw everything in a washer and himself in a long shower.

The word "sentence" stuck with him. He'd probably be charged with assault with a dangerous weapon. Fair enough. He'd have to pay up—a fine, perhaps. Even if it were a month in jail, it couldn't be any worse than what he had already been through. He'd face that when it came, and there would be no pretending that it hadn't happened. Somehow that was important.

There would be other trials. More subtle. He couldn't ask the children to forget him holding that shotgun; he could only wait for the image to fade and for trust to rebuild. In time. A good reason for staying alive. Odd to have time on his side for a change.

The worst would be with Tammy. He had taken some terrible risks. Done real damage. No telling how much. She might not accept him back. Well, he'd just have to deal with it. Stay nearby. Stay active. Drop by for dinner. Share concerns. Build the whole thing up from scratch, board by board, nail by nail. Up from the foundation. At least they had that.

Upstairs he found the old liquor carton—NAPOLEON BRANDY. Carefully he packed his father's journals in the bottom, then a copy of his published volume on the radical movement, and finally his rough-draft manuscript. In that order. Seeing them there in a single box for the first time gave him a new perception. Were they all allegories for himself? Even the journals? An astonishing notion.

They did fit rather neatly into one carton. And into one head? All this time he had thought that rationality was his highest value, but if these were three aspects of himself, neither his writing nor his choice of reading had been conscious choices.

All that talk about good source material. He'd believed it. And maybe it was. But not the way he'd thought. Here he was, a rational man doing battle with his father at the crossroads, trying to kill him. And all the time trying to join him, trying to rejoin the age, enter the sepia print he held of that age. Surely he wasn't the only one playing games like that, but he'd played it harder, more dangerously.

The next thing was to get out of this tomb of a house. Strange how quiet it had become. Not just the absence of family, but the absence of voices. He could feel their presence, but they weren't talking. A great hush. He hadn't realized until now how many different voices there had been in the past months. A regular chorus, dinning in his ears. Min's kind of voices. Crazy Min. Crazy Kraft. Or at least he stood halfway between her and Tammy, a part of each.

He moved all his belongings downstairs and stacked them next to the front door—cartons, laundry bags, the old suitcase. Tammy would want to pack her own things, and the children . . .

Back up the stairs—his last trip—he looked into Ric's room. Had he any right to take all this away from the three of them? Had the government any right? For an instant the old rage returned, a great rushing squall, the sound of wind driving out all thoughts.

It passed. The children had never been enamored with the place the way he had been. For them, another spot would do just as well. Perhaps better. Something more accessible. In touch with the world. Smaller. In scale with the age in which they lived. They had no need for a goddamned realm.

A realm. An odd, faded word. Archaic flavor to it. On its way to obsolescence. He was drawn back to his study once more and to the dormer window, a moment of illicit sentimentality. The great, gray expanse of scrubland, the curve of the shore, the sea. Once the realm of the French, defended against raiders, against invaders. Later, the province of the British. Held for the glory of the crown.

Somehow he, the fourth Kraft Means, had ended up playing a version of the same game. Commandant. Commodore. King of the dung pile.

Looking upstream, he caught sight of movement. On the other side of the fording point. A pickup truck. And a car. A patrol car. A damned CMP patrol car. Well, what had he expected? They were going to make it hurt a little. That was a part of it.

He thumped down the stairs for the last time, put on his yellow foul-weather jacket and boots, headed out the front door, down through the McKnight cemetery. Someone should set those stones up, clean them, cut the brush. He had meant to. Other things had always seemed more important. Now it was up to the province. So be it.

He passed the barn. One step at a time. He kept his eyes directly in front of him, watching out for stones in the path. Each blade of the tall grass was studded with droplets, water glistening in what would soon be direct sunlight.

Halfway to the stream, he stopped. The truck, the car, four men leaning against fenders, chatting, perhaps. The redneck image tightened his stomach.

There, too, was his Jeep. The water had receded. It was only hub deep. Motor ruined, probably. One more problem. His own doing.

The fender-leaners had seen him now. Eyes turned his way. They were waiting for him. No call to arms. No bullhorns. Just waiting there. He wanted to call out to them: They could have the damn place. Take it all. But it was too far to shout. Everything would have to be played out in measured time.

As he approached the stream, a battered tow truck appeared. Pulled up beside the patrol car. Kraft recognized it—the only one this side of Liverpool. When the doors opened, a man and a woman got out of the cab. Good; Harry and Min hadn't deserted him completely, hadn't given him up for mad. Returned, no doubt, to give Tammy support, but perhaps with some lingering affection for him as well. He'd have to do some rebuilding there too. Then another woman. That would be Tammy. And from outside, back of the cab, a young girl in jeans. His princess. No, his daughter. Then the two boys. Everyone.

The children saw him now and all three waved. They would pass the lightest sentence. The most intuitive. He would like to think he had damaged them the least. And Tammy? She was looking in his direction, blank-faced like the Canadians. Then a reluctant half raise of the hand. It was not the gesture of a woman who has preferred charges. Nor all-forgiving. Conditional.

Face it. An act of will. Walk down the road to the stream. One step at a time. Cross it. Take what comes.

He didn't move. Almost against his will, he turned for one last look, one last deep and dangerous swallow of nostalgia.

Picture: Lawns rolling up from where he stood, terraced walkways of crushed white oyster shells edged in brick, tree roses trimmed round as plums, statues of Greek heroes, wrought-iron love seats, tables with striped umbrellas, a copper birdbath polished that very morning to catch the first rays of the sun. And there at the crest, the great sprawling summer home, French doors opening on grass patios; above that a multitude of dormers, the uppermost one his, a view from there so grand you could see the coast of France.

On the front lawn—good God—a man in white flannels, white shirt, white tennis sweater; and beside him a lean and splendid woman, white pleated skirt, midi-length, standing at his side. Actors, of course; too perfect to be other than actors on a set, stage crew hidden, the two of them magnificent and pathetic in the same instant, like the set itself, the whole show. He could feel the old pull, wanting to run on stage, join the performance in the last act; and, equally, to burn the place, raze it, free the stagehands. Had nothing changed?

But this time he raised his hand high, a salute, a warm and open-handed salute, neither grasping nor rejecting, and—wondrous—they raised theirs; they saw him for the first time, recognized him even after all these years, after all these words, and greeted him. A farewell across those spacious lawns, across those decades.

Then gone. In their place, a deserted, weathered hulk of a house, beyond repair, sunk in a tangle of bullbrier and chokecherry, ledges and tombstones.

He turned, suddenly hungry, deeply hungry, and lumbered in great, awkward, stumbling steps down the grassy road, across the stream, toward those who were waiting for him in the sunlit bank of the other side.